A Matter of I

By

Bill Breckon

Copyright © 2014 Bill Breckon

All rights reserved, including the right to reproduce this book, or portions thereof in any form. No part of this text may be reproduced, transmitted, downloaded, decompiled, reverse engineered, or stored, in any form or introduced into any information storage and retrieval system, in any form or by any means, whether electronic or mechanical without the express written permission of the author.

This is a work of fiction. The persons and events in this book may have representations in history, but this work is entirely the author's creation and should not be construed as historical fact.

ISBN: 978-1-291-70558-4

PublishNation. London
www.publishnation.co.uk

Acknowledgements

Many people have helped me in the research and writing of this book, not least my wife Lois, who has given unstinting help and perspicacious criticism, as well as tea, *vino rosso* and sympathy.

My thanks also to my friend and distinguished art historian Elizabeth Trenerry and to Dr Susan Russell, formerly Assistant Director of the British Institute in Rome, both of whom read the manuscript and made pertinent comments.

In Florence, my thanks are due to Patrizio Mannucci, Stefano Lapini and Paolo Ferrara, of the *Comune di Firenze's* administration at the *Palazzo Vecchio*, to Silvia Nanni of the *Venerabile Arciconfraternita della Misericordia di Firenze* and to Paola Laurella and her staff of the *Società Dantesca*, who showed me round the wonderful guildhall of the *Arte della Lana*, which is now the society's headquarters. (Thanks, too, to Jill Harrison from the Open University, whose paper on Being Florentine: 'A question of identity in the Arte della Lana, Florence', introduced me to the splendours of the wool guild's meeting place.)

I should also thank the city of Florence itself, whose art and architecture are always truly inspirational. I have, of course, read many books in the course of my research, but I have sometimes taken liberties with the timing of events, to enhance the dramatic content: this is a work of fiction, not a historical document. Any historical errors are, however, entirely mine.

The cover painting is by Tom Schaller,
celebrated American watercolourist and friend, who is also a
painting tutor at the present-day Watermill at Posara.
(www.watermill.net)

For Lois, forever.

Perspective (visual or 'natural'):
the way in which objects appear to the eye.

Perspective (graphical or 'artificial'):
the technique of representing the effects of visual perspective in drawings.

Perspective (cognitive):
'point of view', a context for opinions, beliefs and experiences.

Jacopo Alderici examines the stone block he has just added to the rim of the unfinished dome. Proud of his skills, he runs his hand over the dressed sandstone, feeling the smoothness of the finish. Above him the Spring sky is a luminous light blue and, although there is a faint breeze, Jacopo feels the heat, having drunk far too much Tuscan wine the previous night.

To admire his new row of masonry blocks as a whole, he steps back carefully, almost to the very edge of the wooden scaffolding, beyond which is a dizzying drop to the cathedral floor more than two hundred feet below.

He hears footsteps on the stairs that lead up darkly between the two overlapping shells of the dome and sees a figure emerge and edge towards him, a hand on the stonework for support. As the outline becomes clearer Jacopo gives a start of recognition.

"You!"

"Yes, me."

"What are *you* doing here?"

"I brought you this, you bastard."

Jacopo ducks instinctively as a small wooden box swings towards his head. It strikes his temple and he staggers back, arms flailing. He grabs the box, but loses his balance. For one moment, his eyes wide in terror, he is poised on the edge of the scaffolding. Then he falls, screaming, into the void.

Jacopo dies soon after he hits the floor, unaware that, like his body, the box has broken on impact and its contents are scattered over the unforgiving stones.

A few weeks earlier…

1

"Amazing," said Luigi, Cardinal Mazzini as he looked upwards, taking in the massive proportions of the dome of the cathedral of *Santa Maria del Fiore* in Florence. "Truly amazing."

After a further moment or two of contemplation the corpulent Cardinal, splendid in his blood-red cassock, cape and biretta, turned his gaze earthwards again. "I never cease to be impressed by the dome of the Pantheon in Rome, but this is even larger. Just how big is it?"

"The span," said Cosimo de' Medici proudly, "is seventy-two *braccia*." He held his arm straight out to indicate the Florentine measure of length, the *braccio*, based on the distance between a man's shoulder and his fingertips, "and already the rim of the cupola is some one hundred *braccia* above the ground. When it is finished it will be one hundred and forty-four *braccia* high."

"Extraordinary."

It's more than extraordinary, thought Luca Pasini: it's a work of genius. As a mere Assistant Building Supervisor, Luca shouldn't really have been there at all, of course, but he'd managed to wriggle his way into the party accompanying the Cardinal. He tried to make himself as inconspicuous as possible behind the wooden posts of the colossal ox-driven hoist that enabled masonry blocks, timber beams and baskets of bricks to be lifted high into the shell of the dome.

Luca, usually known as Luca da Posara from the village of his birth, was nineteen years old and he'd been in Florence for just over twelve months. He was inordinately proud of being involved in the construction of the biggest dome the world had ever seen and he'd soon grasped the intricacies of masonry, bricklaying and carpentry.

"You're worth your weight in gold florins," his rotund uncle Battista d'Antonio, one of the Superintendents of the dome building project, had quipped one evening at supper, "not that there's much weight on you. You could do with fattening up."

There was no sign, however, of gold florins or even silver *lire* for that matter: his post still had not been officially approved by the *Opera del Duomo*, the body in charge of the cathedral works, and Luca was dependent on his uncle for his food and lodgings. Despite the precariousness of his position and his finances, however, Luca could think of nowhere else in the world that he'd rather be. The very air seemed alive with fresh ideas: it was as if a door had been opened into a new world – and here he was, a young man from a country village, among the first exhilarated explorers.

An odour of ox-dung, and a fainter smell of the animals themselves, drifted towards him as he stood beside the hoist and looked over to the group of ecclesiastical and civic dignitaries that had coalesced around the Cardinal. Representing the Church were a chubby Bishop in a purple cassock with amaranth piping and a trio of Chaplains of Honour in black with purple facings, while most of the civic luminaries were wearing their 'uniforms' of crimson long-sleeved *cioppe*, overgowns made with the highest-quality woollen fabric. These gowns identified them as members of the ruling classes, but while their *cioppe* were of a similar colour, the men's doublets, many woven in silk, were startlingly varied and vibrant – a creamy yellow, an apple-green and a dazzling white among them.

Luca realized that there was a definite language of clothes: these men wanted to be identified as part of the ruling elite, but they also wanted to express their individuality and their wealth. Among them, only Cosimo de' Medici, banker and merchant and perhaps the richest of them all, appeared to have no need to make a sartorial statement. His woollen doublet and hose matched the colour of his *cioppa*, as did his brimless cap, from which his large ears protruded.

Outside, on this cloudless morning of Wednesday the twentieth of April, in the Year of our Lord one thousand, four hundred and twenty-five, the sun's warmth caressed the city with a mother's embrace. But here in the cavern of the cathedral it was cooler and the browny-grey air, pierced occasionally by spears of pale yellow sunlight, seemed somehow denser, trapped in the enclosed space.

"Your Eminence will have noticed," Cosimo de' Medici continued, supporting the Cardinal's elbow as they both looked upwards again, "that the cupola is being constructed without any wooden centring to hold the shell in position until the vault is completed."

"How very courageous," said the Cardinal, "but how can this be done? Surely the weight of all that brick and stone will bring it down?"

A whiny voice replied: "An excellent question, your Eminence." It came from Giovanni Ferrante, Notary to the *Opera del Duomo*, a tall man with a pinched face and a turned-down mouth. As thin as the Cardinal was fat, Ferrante was enveloped in a black scholar's gown that had seen better days. Thrusting forward his pointed beard like a dagger, he said: "Unfortunately the only man in Florence who can answer that question is not here. I suspect that he, too, shares the doubts expressed so clearly by Your Eminence." He added vehemently: "He can't face us. He doesn't know how he's going to build the dome. And he just can't face us."

He was talking, of course, about Filippo Brunelleschi, architect and engineer, the genius behind the construction of the cupola. Brunelleschi was Luca's hero and he felt like hitting Ferrante for talking about him like that. But Luca also had to admit that, along with almost everyone in Florence, he too was concerned about whether the dome could be finished successfully. As its height and weight increased, wouldn't it come crashing to the ground and with it, the city's pride?

"What nonsense." Cosimo de' Medici said to Ferrante. "Of course Brunelleschi knows how to build the dome." Turning to the Cardinal: "As I explained to you earlier Luigi, er, Your Eminence, he is indisposed, a fever ..."

"Huh," Giovanni Ferrante retorted, "but how can we be sure this fever of his is genuine? It won't be the first time he's pretended to be sick at a crucial point in the dome's construction."

"Gentlemen, gentlemen," said the Cardinal. "Men must always have doubts in all their endeavours; only God can be certain of the outcome. Have faith that the dome will be completed to reflect His glory."

During this exchange Luca noticed Battista d'Antonio, slipping away. His uncle found these official visits irksome: they interfered with the smooth running of the construction work. While the masons and bricklayers had been given the morning off, with pay, in honour of the Cardinal's visit, all the menial day-labourers were now going to have to be signed-on for the afternoon work period. They wouldn't be happy to have lost half-a-day's wages, even at the meagre rate they were paid.

The Cardinal extended his hands skywards and warming to his theme continued: "This vast space evokes the dome of heaven itself. Here we can acknowledge how insignificant we are compared with our Creator and the universe He has made."

We could acknowledge Man's creative genius, too, Luca said to himself.

But the Cardinal had other matters on his mind: "Talking of the vault of heaven," he said, looking round his audience, "I am increasingly concerned about these new ideas, emanating from north of the Alps, that our Earth is not the centre of our universe, but rather is itself in motion around the sun. This is contrary to the teachings of the church and to the explanations of Ptolemy and others, whose celestial spheres show us just how the planets and the stars move about us. The sun moves around the earth, not the other way round."

"Perhaps it's all matter of perspective," said Cosimo, "from where, as it were, one stands to observe things. From the Earth, the sun appears to move. From the sun, maybe the Earth would seem to do so."

"Hazardous waters, Cosimo," retorted the cleric, "beware your ship of rational reasoning does not flounder in a sea of heresy! Only God views the world and only the Church can tell Man what God sees. "

The group seemed to reflect for a moment or two on the Cardinal's words and it was Giovanni Ferrante who broke the silence. "Speaking of perspective," he said, "would Your Eminence like to try Filippo Brunelleschi's famous experiment?"

"Indeed I would," said the Cardinal. "Enough of these theological matters for today. We're not in a seminary." Stepping round a pile of steaming ox dung as delicately as a maiden at a dancing class, he led his party down the nave.

2

Perspective! Another wonderful innovation brought to the world by Luca's hero, Filippo Brunelleschi. He'd invented the rules of graphical perspective, precise techniques for the accurate depiction of depth in painting and sculpture, a dozen or so years earlier. Or perhaps he'd rediscovered them in old documents: he kept that to himself. When he'd shown Luca the famous experiment a year or so ago, he'd certainly implied he'd made the discoveries on his own.

Whatever the truth, Brunelleschi's revelations had inspired artists everywhere. Paolo Uccello, for instance, was so obsessed with perspective that it was affecting his married life. His wife said that he stayed up all night in his studio making intricate drawings and when she called for him to come to bed, he would cry out: "Oh what a sweet thing this perspective is!"

Luca's friend, the sculptor Donatello, was also enamoured with the new methods and had proudly shown him a marble panel in low relief celebrating Christ's birth. The floor of the stable was a chequerboard carved in careful perspective. Not exactly historically accurate, it had to be said, but it was much admired for the aesthetic correctness of its mathematics. Luca looked around for his friend, who had also been in the party, but he was nowhere to be seen. Presumably he'd escaped, too, to continue chipping away at his sculpture of the prophet Habbakuk, his current obsession.

To demonstrate the accuracy of his new drawing system, Brunelleschi had made a painting of the Florence baptistry for his celebrated experiment. It was staged on the steps outside the West door, where the Cardinal and his party were now heading. Luca tagged on to the back of the group as it moved slowly past the sturdy pillars of the nave and the pointed arches supporting the lime-washed vaults. He couldn't stop counting the paces to himself as he walked: "One, two, three … ninety-two, ninety-three…"

Just before the party reached the great West Door the Cardinal stopped in one of the shafts of sunlight thrown from the high round windows, leaving his entourage in the shade. I'm sure he did that on purpose, thought Luca, edging in behind a pillar as the prelate's pectoral cross, hanging from a red and gold cord around his neck, glinted in the brightness. The Church can always be relied on to put on a show.

The notary Giovanni Ferrante signalled to a servant, who brought forward a wooden panel, covered in a tawny woollen cloth. Pulling this back, Ferrante revealed a painting of the baptistry, with all its angles, vanishing points and foreshortenings drawn according to the rules that Filippo Brunelleschi had formulated. But it was the sky that first caught your attention: it wasn't painted at all, just a thin plate of burnished silver fitted around the outline of the building. This silver plate now reflected the rubicund face of the Cardinal who, after examining the picture, led his procession outside.

Emerging through the monumental West portal, Luca squinted in the sudden glare and, shading his eyes, looked out across the piazza towards the baptistry. The sun encouraged colours to bloom: here, a façade as yellow as a blackbird's beak; there, a stall's rosy awning and directly opposite, the glowing panels of the baptistry's gilded bronze doors.

Half-a-dozen men-at-arms had cleared a space below the steps, but beyond them the piazza was crowded with people going about their daily tasks: among them a woman laden with vegetables from the market and a man selling cooking pots whose wares were festooned about his body like an eccentric suit of armour, which gave a dull clank every time he moved. Boys ran in and out of people's legs, engrossed in their own world, and a file of pack mules slowly crossed the square, stooped under bales of wool wrapped in hemp sacking, their muleteer cursing as the crowd impeded their progress.

There were a couple of flimsy stalls, the one with the rosy awning selling cheap hose and woollen jerkins, the other amulets and potions to ward off illness and evil spirits, its owner loudly proclaiming their benefits above the general hubbub.

Fussing about the Cardinal, Giovanni Ferrante made sure that the prelate was positioned in precisely the right spot on the steps and then handed him Filippo's painting, with its reverse side towards him. Giovanni pointed out the 'sighting hole' bored through the centre of the wooden panel. It was as big as a ducat on the back surface of the panel, but receded conically to the size of a lentil on the painting side. The Cardinal bent his head towards the back of the panel and looked through the sighting hole towards the baptistry.

Giovanni then brought out a hand mirror, which he held in front of the panel, so that it reflected the painting of the baptistry and of the sky from the burnished silver inlay. "It will be necessary for Your Eminence to hold this mirror himself," he explained, "in order to adjust it accurately."

As Giovanni held the picture the Cardinal again looked through the sighting hole and slowly altered the angle of the mirror so that the painting was reflected back to him. Then, instructed by Giovanni, he moved the mirror out of the way so he could see the baptistry directly through the sighting hole.

"Remarkable," said the Cardinal, moving the mirror in and out of position a few times before lowering his arm. "A true convergence of the real and the artificial."

Giovanni Ferrante said: "Of course, the presence of people in the piazza somewhat distracts you from appreciating how precisely the shape of the baptistry follows the lines in Brunelleschi's painting. Allow me to clear the square for a moment so that you can see this better." And before the Cardinal could say anything, Giovanni waved again to his servant who, with a handful of men seemingly employed by him for this purpose, ran down the steps, through the men-at-arms, and began moving people from the piazza. It was empty within a couple of minutes of stalls, boys, mules and all.

The Cardinal bent to the sighting hole once more. "Yes, I see what you mean, *Ser* Giovanni. It is very hard to distinguish between the real scene and the painted one..." Still peering through the painting, he added: "But what is that shapeless mound lying by the corner of the baptistry? Is it real or not?" He stood back from the painting and looked out over the empty piazza. "Ah, I see that it is real. But what is it?"

Luca, younger and sprightlier than most of the Cardinal's retinue, leapt down the steps and ran across the square. As he reached the mound he saw it was a canvas sheet, of the sort masons or sculptors use. Pulling back a corner, he uncovered a human head. The face was unrecognizable. It had been beaten into a pulp – eyes, nose and mouth no more than a bloodied mess.

For a moment Luca crouched there frozen, his hand compulsively gripping the edge of the sheet. His brain could not take in the information coming from his eyes. This had been a man, yet the sight before him resembled some animal that had been fought over by feral dogs, a mass of splintered bone, torn flesh and congealed blood.

There was a sound like rushing water in his ears and the bloodied head, the canvas sheet, his hand – all seemed suddenly to recede and spin around.

Luca fainted.

3

Luca found himself lying in Donatello's arms. The sculptor was kneeling with Luca's head in his lap, stroking his hair. "Luca, my dear Luca, are you all right?"

When he opened his eyes everything had a dreamlike quality. The Cardinal was a scarlet-sailed merchant ship crossing the piazza, his minions bustling about him like pilot boats. Uncle Battista was staring down at him, his face puffed out like the Winds in old maps and as red as the Cardinal's biretta.

Luca savoured the intimacy of Donatello's embrace, but his feeling of security rapidly changed to consternation as he remembered what had happened. His eyes darted towards the corpse: mercifully, the battered, bloody head had been re-covered by a corner of the canvas sheet, although much of the rest of the body, as immobile as a painted saint, was now exposed.

Luca saw every tiny detail with an extraordinary clarity: the man's grey gown, dusty from the piazza; his dark-blue tunic, fur-trimmed; his belt with dagger and bulky leather pouch; his sturdy light-brown boots, muddied as if from a journey. His one visible hand, square-fingered, was scarred and had chipped nails.

The dignitaries fell quiet as they gathered around the corpse and it was some moments before the Cardinal spoke. "God rest this sinner's soul," he said, making the sign of the cross. "Does anyone know who he is?"

Cosimo shook his head and asked his servant to remove the canvas once more from the dead man's face. Luca looked away, but heard the onlookers gasp and then Cosimo smoothly taking command, his voice soft, but authoritative. To one man he said: "You, run to the *Misericordia* and get someone here with a stretcher cart." To another: "You, summon up the Podestà." And to a third: "Cover up that face, for pity's sake. No-one, not even his mother, will ever recognise him."

"Which," said the Cardinal, "makes it very difficult to know who he is – let alone how he got here."

"Perhaps the contents of his purse will give us a clue to his identity," said Giovanni Ferrante and Luca, opening his eyes again, saw the notary bending over the body and undoing the clasp of the leather pouch. A dozen coins rolled out on to the flagstones of the piazza, a few florins and a couple of Venetian ducats among them.

"Obviously the motive wasn't robbery," said the Cardinal. "Is there anything else?"

"There's this, your Eminence," said Giovanni, bringing out a rectangular packet wrapped in oiled paper, secured with a purple ribbon tied in a bow. Pulling the ribbon apart Giovanni exposed a sheaf of papers, perhaps twenty buff-coloured octavo sheets. He read out the title page: *"A Humble Petition to the Wardens of the Opera del Duomo concerning the dome of Florence cathedral."*

Giovanni looked up, his eyes blazing, then glanced down at the papers again. "It is signed *Bartolomeo da Siracusa, Mathematician.*"

"A Sicilian," said the Cardinal. "They've caused nothing but trouble for decades. What's he doing here?"

Giovanni leafed through the sheets, which Luca, lying in Donatello's arms, couldn't see very clearly, but which seemed to contain handwriting in black ink, interspersed with diagrams. Ferrante scanned the pages. "It appears, Your Eminence, that this Bartolomeo has – or rather had – a serious complaint about Filippo Brunelleschi and his methods for constructing the dome. Not to put too fine a point on it, he accuses Brunelleschi of stealing the secrets of the method of construction." Then, looking at Donatello, he said: "He also accuses Brunelleschi and Donatello here of geomancy and practising the Black Arts."

"Let me see that," said Cosimo de' Medici, snatching the packet. "You seem to have an exceptional ability to read and assimilate these writings very swiftly."

As Cosimo took the sheets, Donatello gently raised Luca to his feet. Standing just beside the banker, he couldn't resist looking at the papers. But the tight-knit writing was not easy to read and the diagrams, at first sight at least, were impossible to interpret. One phrase, however, was written in a bigger hand and was more easily legible: *"... the aforementioned Filippo Brunelleschi stole the secrets of the construction of domes from an engineer in Rome, who then died in suspicious circumstances ..."*

"What's to be done about this," Giovanni said loudly. "Allegations of fraud, murder and heaven knows what else. It will have to be investigated."

He was interrupted by the arrival of a wheeled handcart, pulled by two men in red monkish habits, their faces covered by tall conical hoods, with apertures for the eyes and nose. When he saw them Luca felt his legs go weak again and he needed all of Donatello's support.

He knew that they were members of the *Misericordia*, Brothers of Mercy, a pious confraternity set up to carry out acts of charity, and that they wore hoods so that their good works would be anonymous. They were a common enough sight in the city's streets. Their mission was to visit the sick and bury the dead and they also ran an ambulance service and even had their own hospital.

But it still brought a chill to his heart to see them, for Luca recollected a similar band of Brothers in Fivizzano, the market town in Lunigiana, the border area way to the North-west of Florence, where he was born and brought up. When he was five years old his parents took him on Good Friday to stand in the square and watch the ceremony which marked the death of the Saviour. A statue of the dead Christ, with painted blood flowing from the wounds in His hands, feet and side, was brought from the church on a black-draped catafalque and taken in solemn procession around the streets. It was followed by the priest and two altar boys, with most of the population of the town walking behind, holding candles. What was etched on Luca's memory, however, was the image of the black-robed Brothers who accompanied the procession.

The two men at the front were alarming enough, carrying flickering torches which illuminated their conical hoods and glittering eyes behind the slits. Others, who walked beside the statue of Christ, also carried torches. But there were some who held short knotted ropes with which, from time to time, they lashed their own backs.

The procession had moved quietly through the main piazza, the only sound being the shuffling of feet, the repetitive swish of a rope and a stifled grunt of pain. Luca had screamed when he saw the flagellant Brothers and continued sobbing so uncontrollably that his mother had taken him home to the village of Posara, a walk of a mile or so down the moonlit pathways in the valley of the River Rosaro.

He had never forgotten that evening and the fears it had engendered were not buried very deeply in his mind, so that the sight of these hooded Florentine Brothers, even though they were dressed in red rather than black, revived his childhood memories. He felt his head reeling and was grateful for Donatello's muscular arm around his waist.

But he found himself unable to look away, staring with fascinated horror as the Brothers bundled the body on to the ambulance cart and covered it with an off-white linen shroud, leaving the bloodied canvas sheet behind on the flagstones of the piazza. "God's wounds," said one of them as they struggled with the body. "He's heavier than he looks."

Cosimo had a whispered conversation with them before they left, then turned to Luca's uncle. "Battista, wait for the Podestà's men and tell them what happened, if you please. They'll want to examine this canvas sheet, so watch it doesn't disappear. We'll leave you the men-at-arms to keep the crowds at bay."

Giovanni Ferrante reached out a hand to take the Sicilian's packet back from Cosimo: "If you would kindly give me those papers, I will ensure they are delivered to the Consuls of the Wool Guild. As you know, they're meeting tomorrow afternoon to review the work of the *Opera del Duomo* and I will be reporting to them. They'll certainly be most interested in these documents."

But Cosimo pulled the packet away from him: "No, no, they will be quite safe with me. I am a Consul myself and I'll report to the guild tomorrow."

"And I shall examine them, too," said the Cardinal. "I don't like the sound of this geomancy and Black Arts." He looked at Donatello: "Have a care not to go beyond the city walls until these matters have been properly examined – by both church and state."

Giovanni Ferrante smiled as he heard these words. Cosimo hurriedly interposed, telling Donatello: "Take that young man somewhere where he can sit down. He looks as if he is going to pass out again."

Donatello put his arm around Luca's shoulders and together they walked away from the sunlit piazza into a street shaded by the imposing bulk of the cathedral.

4

"Speak, Pumpkin Head, damn you, speak," muttered Donatello, motionless and intense.

They were in the sculptor's workshop, only a few minutes' walk from the baptistry square. But Luca was aware that Donatello wasn't talking to him as he sat on a stool, still feeling a little weak, but to another figure which dominated the room: the Old Testament prophet Habbakuk, a bald-headed, stubble-chinned, open-mouthed, middle-aged man.

Donatello had been working on this extraordinary full-length marble sculpture for more than two years now and it was still unfinished. The head was carved with crude strokes, left intentionally rough; even the prophet's robes had a dishevelled look and you sensed that the man was skin and bone beneath them.

The rest of the workshop was cluttered with a dozen trestle tables, some holding pieces of sculpture on which apprentices were working: on one, a capital in the Corinthian order, on another the folds of an angel's wings and on a third a tiny round-cheeked cherub emerging from his marble block. Scraps of paper, with sketches in charcoal and blood-red sanguine chalk, hung from iron nails on the wall beams.

Wooden trestle tables held a profusion of sculptors' tools: mallets, hammers and dull grey chisels, some pointed, some rounded like a giant's fingernails, some flat-faced, some with multiple teeth. The apprentices' workplaces were on the whole untidy, but on Donatello's own table beside Habbakuk his mallets, hammers and chisels, rasps and files were neatly laid out in order of size. Donatello had a reputation for scruffiness and, unlike the aspiring members of the ruling families, seemed indifferent about what he wore. But when it came to the tools of his trade, he liked to keep everything properly in its place.

The four apprentices, all good-looking boys in their early teens, had stopped work when Luca and Donatello came in and the sculptor had dismissed them, telling them to take their mid-morning meal. One had grabbed a few coins from the canvas satchel hanging from a hook on a ceiling beam and they'd left, smirking, as Donatello sat Luca down and gave him a goblet of light-red Tuscan wine. But solicitous as Donatello had been, he'd almost immediately been distracted by Habbakuk and he'd stood in front of the statue, imploring it to speak.

His statue is more alive than that poor man in the square, Luca reflected, his recent memories again resurfacing. Such a brutal attack – and for what? He said: "Something peculiar's going on. I can't quite put my finger on it..." He shivered once more. "For example..."

His words were interrupted as Donatello, dragging his gaze from Habbakuk and, kneeling before Luca, held his head tenderly in his hands and kissed him fully on the lips.

Luca responded willingly, almost eagerly, then pulled back, briefly holding Donatello's hands before letting go. Their eyes met before Luca cast his own downwards. When he and Donatello had become lovers, a few weeks after he'd arrived, he'd found it intoxicating, thrillingly forbidden. And, at the same time he'd felt safe, as safe as he'd been when a child in his mother's embrace. He reached towards Donatello again, then drew back. A recurring image of himself with a wife and children came into his mind. That's what his mother wanted – and that seemed right and safe, too. Donatello could never give him that. And yet, at nineteen, he'd still not been to bed with a woman. No wonder his mind was a confused mass of sensations.

The sculptor's promiscuity didn't help either. There was always some new lover, one of his apprentices more often than not. Donatello was now in his late thirties, but he still seemed to see himself as an ardent teenager, finding angelic boys – and many not so angelic – irresistible. Was it the principle of love between men that Lucca objected to, or that Donatello wasn't his exclusive lover?

Donatello raised himself upright again: "Ah, my dear boy, I see you are having second thoughts."

"Can we talk about it some other time?" said Luca. He just couldn't get the image of that man's head out of his mind. Who would batter his face so viciously? He said out loud; "They must have hit it time after time, with a blunt object, like a..." Luca looked around the workshop to where Donatello's sculpting tools lay on the trestle table "...like a sculptor's mallet".

Donatello stepped back. "By God's teeth, Luca, you're not suggesting that I..."

"No, no, of course not," Luca interrupted quickly, though he had noticed that one of Donatello's mallets was missing from its place. There had always been four, arranged by size in a neat row. Now there were only three.

Suddenly all his thoughts about the morning's events in the piazza came pouring out, as if someone had opened a sluice in a millstream. The man couldn't have been killed in the baptistry square that morning. A hundred people would have seen it happen. The murder must have been carried out elsewhere and the body later moved to the piazza and covered with the canvas sheet. But how could they hide it? Under the trestle of that market stall selling potions and amulets? But why wasn't it discovered when the square was being cleared?

More questions rose unbidden to the surface of Luca's mind, like *pisellini* bubbling in a pot of boiling water. What was uncle Battista doing in the piazza? Wasn't he supposed to have been organizing the afternoon's work? And why did he seem so flushed? For that matter how come Donatello was also there? He'd disappeared earlier, before the Cardinal's party had reached the top of the steps.

Luca looked up at his friend, who was now pouring himself a goblet of wine from a glazed earthenware jug. "As a matter of interest, where did you get to this morning? I thought you'd come back here to work on Pumpkin Head. But you were in the piazza so quickly you couldn't have."

"Oh well, um, I've seen Filippo's painting a dozen times before." Donatello looked embarrassed: "When a man needs a piss, he has to go. I was back in a few minutes and just as I came out on to the front steps, I saw you fluttering to the ground, like a bird struck by a stone from a boy's sling..."

"Hardly surprising, given the sight I'd just seen." Luca shuddered, then looked up again at Donatello. "But what about those accusations of geomancy and the Black Arts that Giovanni Ferrante found in the papers the Sicilian was carrying?" Luca presumed Black Arts meant conjuring up the devil, but what on earth was geomancy?

"Ferrante! I really dislike that man. He's as skinny as a stiletto and as deadly."

"Yes, but what is geomancy – and why should you and Filippo be accused of it?"

"Well, it's more than twenty years ago now." Donatello paused. "Let's see, 1402, it must have been. I was fifteen or sixteen at the time, still Filippo's apprentice. He took me to Rome after he'd lost out to Lorenzo Ghiberti in the competition for the bronze panels on the baptistry doors."

"Brunelleschi left in a sulk, some say."

"Giovanni Ferrante was the loudest saying so, but it's true that Filippo was disappointed and angry, though some of Lorenzo's doors, you must admit, are rather wonderful."

"Could that be because you had a big hand in making them?" Luca smiled up at his friend.

"Well, yes, but give Lorenzo his due, his designs and his production techniques were better than Brunelleschi's." Donatello smiled back: "But don't let Filippo know I told you that."

"Geomancy," Luca prompted. "What is it and why were you two accused of it?"

"Well, my little squirrel, didn't they teach you anything in that rural backwater of yours? Geomancy is a method of divination. You use handfuls of soil, or sand, or rocks and you toss them about. You're supposed to be able to foretell the future by the patterns they make."

"D'you think you can?"

"I've no idea. Geomancy didn't interest us. Filippo wanted to find out all about the ancient buildings. We spent our days like sparrows in the ruins, rooting about, digging up the remains of columns and pediments and heaven knows what else, sketching and measuring them. And of course, as his apprentice, I had to help with the digging."

"And you threw handfuls – well, spadefuls – of dirt about and the Romans believed you were geomancers."

"Half of them did. The other half thought we were treasure-hunters."

Luca laughed. "Why didn't you tell them what you were doing?"

"Well, you know Filippo, his lips were tightly sealed. He just wrote everything down in code in his notebooks, which didn't help matters. And when he started shinning up the Roman Pantheon our fate was sealed."

"But you could have convinced them otherwise."

"What? The Romans change their minds? It'd be easier to persuade a fallen leaf to go back to the tree."

Donatello looked thoughtful. "But no-one's talked about those accusations for years and no-one took them very seriously at the time. Why should they surface again now?"

"And why should anyone accuse Brunelleschi of stealing his ideas for the dome?"

"Well," Donatello replied, "There is no denying that he's irascible, pugnacious ..."

Luca interrupted: "... secretive, stubborn..."

Donatello chuckled: "... cunning, manipulative..." He paused: "But the truest friend a man could ever have."

"And the greatest genius," said Luca, adding quickly "apart from yourself, of course."

"No, no, I am just a worker in the vineyard."

Luca glanced again at Habbakuk, a sculpture the like of which neither he nor anyone else had even seen before. "I wouldn't be too sure of that," he said.

"Well," said Donatello following his gaze, "I swear by the faith I have in old Pumpkin Head here that Filippo would never steal anything from anyone. So it must be a plot, to discredit him."

He looked at Luca. "I see you've a little more colour in your cheeks. If you feel well enough, we should go to Filippo's house straightaway and decide what to do next."

Luca nodded and Donatello pulled him gently to his feet.

5

After the discovery of the body Giovanni Ferrante lingered in the piazza in front of the baptistry. He wanted to murmur insinuations about Brunelleschi and Cosimo de' Medici into as many receptive ears as he could: "One's a madman, the other's like Caesar, getting too big for his boots."

The Podestà arrived and started chatting amicably with one or two of the dignitaries as if at some social event. He was a foreigner: the Florentines didn't trust their fellow citizens to administer impartial justice. Giovanni considered the man to be a buffoon who owed his position more to his influential friends than to any intrinsic forensic talent, but he greeted the Podestà with deference: "Your Honour, how excellent that you are here. What an appalling affair! Have you seen that sculptor's canvas sheet, covered in blood? And that unfortunate man, his face battered, as if with a hammer... A pity the body was removed."

"In due course I shall have one of my men examine it," said the Podestà, a little brusquely.

"These grave allegations against Brunelleschi and Donatello need to be investigated immediately. As Notary to the *Opera*, I ..."

The Podestà interrupted him: "I hear Cosimo has taken the papers. That, too, is a pity."

"Your Honour might demand the documents."

"Hmm. One hesitates to demand anything of a Medici these days. I shall consult with my colleagues."

"There is surely a *prima facie* case... "

"*Festina lente*, Notary." Make haste slowly, as the motto has it. The Podestà paused. "Mind you, there's no harm in questioning Brunelleschi and Donatello. Let's see what they have to say about this incident. I'll put it in hand straight away."

"As always Your Honour is wise."

Well, at least the insufferable Brunelleschi would be under investigation. And even the Podestà and his constables could work out the connection between Donatello and the canvas sheet.

But now Giovanni Ferrante had a further task, to mobilize public opinion against the conceited architect and, by association, against Cosimo, his high-and-mighty protector. Then the authorities would have to act against them.

After paying exaggerated respects to the Podestà, Giovanni set off across the piazza. No more than five minutes later his thin shadow darkened a doorway in a street just to the north, the entrance to the workshop of Lorenzo Ghiberti, sculptor and bronzemaker. As he slipped inside Giovanni saw Lorenzo sitting at a table, drawing. Moving silently behind him, Giovanni looked over his shoulder at a splendid charcoal sketch of a nude Eve, plucked by God from the sleeping Adam's chest, while a group of angels, peering over a cloud watched the scene.

"Magnificent, *Maestro*," Giovanni murmured and Lorenzo looked up, startled. His concern turned to a smile as Giovanni continued: "So vibrant, so lifelike, so natural."

"It's for one of the panels in my new baptistry doors," Lorenzo said. "My most valuable commission so far."

Here he goes again, thought Giovanni: within any conversation it isn't long before he informs his listeners just how many florins he's received for his current commission, or how the Duke of this or the Bishop of that had praised his work. But he said: "And how perspicacious of the Cloth Guild to entrust you with the work without bothering with another competition." Echoing the words he had already heard half-a-dozen times from the lips of the artist himself, Giovanni added: "You were undeniably the only man for the job."

Lorenzo's smile broadened and he gave the notary a slight bow from his sitting position.

Giovanni put an intimate hand on his shoulder: "Only a few moments ago I was again admiring your first set of doors. How wonderful the reliefs look when the morning sun catches them." Lorenzo preened even more.

Giovanni glanced round at the large room where half a dozen assistants were working on Ghiberti's current projects. On a trestle table a bronze casting was being 'chased', hammering and polishing revealing its shining details. In a far corner fierce light from a huge furnace silhouetted the bodies of two workmen and sent out long shadows as dark and sharp as a blade of obsidian.

The radiance highlighted Lorenzo's round cheeks and shone on his bald pate, surrounded by a fringe of hair like a monk's tonsure. He looks like any old greengrocer, Giovanni mused, but thanks to those confounded doors, his enduring fame is assured.

Nonetheless, Ghiberti still seemed insecure and needed constantly to sing his own praises – and to put down his arch-rival Filippo Brunelleschi at every opportunity.

That suited Ferrante's purposes very well and he had found Lorenzo an avid listener a few days earlier, when he'd told him about the imminent arrival of a Sicilian mathematician and his sensational information regarding Brunelleschi's theft of the methods for constructing the dome.

Giovanni had told him to expect the man that very day. They'd listen to his story and then help to broadcast his allegations, like seed into the fertile ground of Florentine politics. Bartolomeo's death would unsettle Lorenzo, making him an uncertain ally in the plot.

As if reading his mind Lorenzo looked up: "Is he here then, our Sicilian friend? What does he look like? Does he have the documents?"

But Giovanni put a finger to his lips and, with a brief movement of his head, indicated that Lorenzo should follow him to a far corner of the workshop. Standing in the shadows he began to relate the morning's events.

"Murdered?" Lorenzo cried out, "What do you mean, murdered? You promised he'd be here. And Brunelleschi would be disgraced."

Giovanni again shushed him, looking about the room. The workmen and the apprentices seemed intent on their tasks and no-one was paying any attention to them. Giovanni indicated two stools, close together on the angle of a bench. They sat and he put a shielding arm around Lorenzo's shoulder and in a low voice told him about the discovery of the body.

"It's clear he was killed to silence him," Lorenzo whined, "and now we'll never hear his allegations. Brunelleschi will carry on, his reputation unsullied. Damn the man."

"Courage, Lorenzo. All is not lost. The murdered man was carrying papers. I found them in his pouch. He alleges Brunelleschi stole his ideas from a man in Rome …"

"I knew it."

"…who died in mysterious circumstances…"

"The villain!"

"And there's more. They also accuse Brunelleschi – and Donatello – of involvement in geomancy and practising satanic rituals. Cardinal Mazzini was very interested in that, I can assure you."

"Evidence at last. Let me see those papers."

Giovanni watched the light in Lorenzo's eyes die as he explained how Cosimo had taken the papers from him and refused to give them up. Lorenzo complained: "He's going to get away with it again!"

"Not if we're clever. I made sure the Medici's enemies got to know about the Sicilian's denunciations. They'll pounce on Cosimo if he tries to hide anything. Our job is to make sure everyone hears the allegations, so the Podestà will have to take action against Brunelleschi."

"What did he say when you found the papers?" Lorenzo asked.

"He wasn't there."

"What?"

"He wasn't there. Said he was ill."

"Not again! That damned man's so devious. Another of his 'diplomatic' illnesses, I suppose."

Neither man spoke, but Giovanni had no doubt that, like himself, Lorenzo was contemplating his humiliation at Brunelleschi's hands a year or so ago. It concerned the construction of the dome, a more prestigious artistic commission than even the baptistry doors. The wardens of the *Opera* had been worrying about it for decades, but the problem was that, although the dome had always been part of the cathedral's original design, no-one had the faintest idea how it was going to be built. Lorenzo Ghiberti had put forward his own proposals and six years ago had even submitted a wood and brick scale model of the dome but, despite Giovanni's support as Notary to the *Opera del Duomo*, all his ideas had been rejected.

On the other hand Brunelleschi arrogantly told the *Opera* that only he knew how to build the dome, even how to put it up without centring. He, too, produced a model, which impressed the Wardens, but he was cantankerous and evasive when questioned, and he steadfastly refused to tell anyone how he was going to do it.

Nonetheless in 1420, despite Giovanni Ferrante's objections, the Wardens appointed Brunelleschi as *Provveditore della cupola*, Superintendent of the Dome. The only positive thing to come out of it was that they'd installed Lorenzo Ghiberti as fellow Superintendent – and Giovanni had enjoyed watching Filippo's furious face when he was told the news that he was not going to be in sole control of the cupola's construction. Almost as an afterthought, the Wardens had also appointed Battista d'Antonio, *capomaestro* of the masons, as a third Superintendent.

Lorenzo, basking in the prestige of official recognition, seemed content to let the other two get on with it. As he'd pointed out to Giovanni, he and Brunelleschi were employed as 'consultants', while Battista was in day-to-day charge of the actual construction process. If Brunelleschi wanted to spend more time fussing about the dome himself, that was up to him.

But, Ferrante remembered, Brunelleschi couldn't leave well alone, could he?

6

A couple of years after Brunelleschi, Ghiberti and Battista d'Antonio had all been appointed *Provveditori* the time came to build a wooden 'chain' circling the dome, to help strengthen the structure. Filippo had again produced a scale model, which the Wardens of the *Opera* approved, but there'd been many delays in preparing the twenty-four giant chestnut beams needed for the ring, three for each of the octagonal dome's panels: on more than one occasion Giovanni Ferrante had been dispatched to find out what was taking the carpenters so long. Eventually, however, the beams had all been stacked in the cathedral square ready for the work to start.

But then Filippo Brunelleschi had been 'taken ill'. Or so he said. He'd been confined to his bed for several days, his housekeeper suggesting that he was 'at death's door'. A delegation of the dome's masons and bricklayers had gone to his house and persuaded him to return to meet his fellow Superintendents and the Wardens of the *Opera*.

Filippo had arrived at the cathedral with his head bandaged and a bulging woollen pad strapped ostentatiously to his side. With doddery steps he'd crossed the square, examined the chestnut beams and pronounced them perfect for the job. "I'm far too sick to work," he'd told everyone, "but it seems to me there are two pressing tasks: the fixing of the wooden chain and the design of scaffolding inside the dome, to allow the men to work safely. I don't have the strength to do both, but to allow us to get on, why don't we divide the work?" Brunelleschi had turned to Lorenzo Ghiberti: "Which will you do, *Provveditore*? Build the chain or design the scaffolding?"

Giovanni had watched as Lorenzo squirmed: he had no choice but to opt for one task or the other without losing face. As he told Giovanni later, he may have known little about how to construct the chain, but he understood even less about scaffolding: How on earth would it surround the inside of the dome if there was no centring? He said he'd make the wooden chain, for which, at least, there was Brunelleschi's model to work on. After Lorenzo had made his reluctant choice, Filippo had shrugged and shuffled back to bed.

So Lorenzo had found himself in sole charge of fixing the wooden beams of the chain together. Filippo's model turned out to be useless: the details were incomprehensible to the uninitiated. There was a similar, but much smaller, chain in the dome of the baptistry and it was on this that Lorenzo based his efforts.

But as soon as the first two lengths were joined together, Filippo had made a spectacular recovery, visiting the site, almost skipping up the steps to the cupola to inspect the beams. Giovanni had looked on as Brunelleschi shook his head and sucked his teeth: "These fastenings are worthless. They'll never contain the stresses of the dome." The chain, Filippo had explained, required complex fastenings, oak plates held in place with iron bolts. Then the beams were to be wrapped in iron bands, to prevent the bolts splitting them. He'd looked with contempt at Lorenzo: "These fixings are a total disaster. They'll have to be replaced."

They were – and that caused more delays and involved considerable expense. Lorenzo was disgraced. Filippo Brunelleschi was now effectively in sole charge, although Lorenzo still retained his title of *Provveditore*.

'The affair of the wooden chain', as it came to be known, left Lorenzo keen for revenge. He was always complaining to Giovanni about 'that damned man' and even last year's triumph with the baptistry doors couldn't wash away the public embarrassment he'd suffered. So when, a couple of weeks earlier, Giovanni had whispered in his ear about a Sicilian scholar, and about evidence that would destroy Brunelleschi's reputation, he'd found in Lorenzo an eager collaborator. Now he needed to reassure the bronze-maker that, despite Bartolomeo's untimely death, the game was still afoot.

"You're right, *Maestro*, he said to Lorenzo, "He was obviously killed to silence him. The question is, who would want him dead?"

Giovanni waited as Lorenzo's thoughts were mirrored in his face. "You don't think Brunelleschi murdered him do you?" he said, wide-eyed.

Giovanni leaned even closer. "Perhaps. Or maybe..."

Now it was Lorenzo's turn to look around the room to see if they were being observed or overheard. "Or maybe…?"

"Or maybe Brunelleschi and Donatello had him waylaid. Perhaps they questioned him about his allegations and …"

"And?"

"Perhaps they argued, then Donatello killed him, in a rage. He's perfectly capable of it. You remember that German in Pistoia all those years ago? Donatello beat him about the head with a stick, just about killed him."

"Oh, yes," said Lorenzo, "that was when Filippo took him on as his apprentice."

"And talking of apprentices, do you remember how Donatello set off for Ferrara a few years ago, screaming blue murder and threatening to kill one of his own apprentices who'd run away?"

"A lover's tiff, no doubt."

"But it shows just how fiery a temper Donatello has, especially when someone he cares for is involved – and he's devoted to Brunelleschi."

"Do you think they…"

"Well, Brunelleschi calls Donatello his *strettissimo amico*. How close is close?"

"Neither of them has ever married …" Lorenzo shook his head: "But we've little evidence that they ever shared a bed – and none at all that they kidnapped or murdered that unfortunate man."

"Rumours don't need evidence, said Giovanni, rising to his feet. "Come on, we've work to do. I'll go to the Santa Croce quarter, you to Santa Maria Novella. Let's give wings to our words. Ghiberti will triumph over Brunelleschi after all."

"Amen to that," said Lorenzo, following Giovanni out of the workshop.

7

Florence was preparing for its noontime break and the streets were crowded as Luca and Donatello set out from the sculptor's workplace. A gaggle of clerks pushed by, fingers ink-stained, escaping from their gloomy counting house and heading for the solace of the tavern. Artisans were laying down their tools and shopkeepers were putting up their shutters. Clumps of men and women gathered in the square, talking no doubt about that morning's gruesome murder. Was it Luca's imagination or did they whisper conspiratorially when they saw him? "That's the boy who found the body!" "What a shock. I'm glad it wasn't me!"

Luca refused to walk through the baptistry square. Just thinking about it brought back memories of his horrible experience, so they made a detour through narrow streets overshadowed by tall houses. They could hear the clatter of cooking pots and Luca's keen nose picked up the aroma of onions and hot olive oil drifting from an open window. They met one of Donatello's apprentices, black-haired and dark-eyed, who looked sulky at seeing Donatello still in Luca's company. The sculptor gave him a reassuring squeeze on the arm and explained that they were headed for Filippo Brunelleschi's 'on a matter of business'.

Rounding the corner of Brunelleschi's street they heard raised voices, and saw a group of three or four men crowded in front of the architect's door. Brunelleschi, guarding his portico, was waving his arm and shouting loudly at them. As Luca and Donatello approached, his words became clear. "... so, just piss off. I'm trying to work. If you want the blessed dome of your sainted cathedral finished, leave me alone to get on with it."

"Sir," said one of the men, smaller in stature, but clearly the leader of the others, "a murder has been committed and the dead man has accused you of a number of crimes."

"A dead man's accused me! How can this be? Florentine genius now knows no bounds! We can now make the dead speak!"

"There were documents on his body," the man answered patiently, "which accused you of murder and other crimes. The Podestà has instructed me to examine the case." He looked round and saw Donatello. "Ah, and you, too. I was coming to look for you."

He addressed Brunelleschi and Donatello in a formal style, drawing himself up to his full height, little as he was, and consulting a paper he held in his hand: "Filippo di *Ser* Brunellesco and Donati di Niccolò di Betto Bardi, I must inform you that you are being officially investigated in the case of Bartolomeo da Siracusa, deceased."

"Never heard of him," said Brunelleschi.

"Nonetheless, I must ask you to answer my questions, specifically about your whereabouts this morning and last night."

"Go away, little man. I've no time for this nonsense."

"If you won't answer our questions now I must ask you to present yourself at the *Bargello* at four o'clock this afternoon to assist us with our continuing enquiries into this fatality. You, too, Donatello. In the meantime, neither of you must leave the city."

"Leave the city! By the blessed Virgin, I'm too busy to ..." Brunelleschi began, but Donatello put a gentle restraining hand on his arm.

"Come, *Provveditore*," he said, "let's do as this gentleman asks. It is the law and as responsible citizens, we must uphold the law."

Luca looked at his friend with amazement: it was not every day that one heard the passionate Donatello coolly upholding the principles of the law. Brunelleschi seemed surprised, too, but nonetheless he allowed Donatello to take his arm and steer him into the house.

"Until four, then," said the Podestà's diminutive representative, turning and walking away self-importantly, his men falling in behind him. Luca followed Brunelleschi and Donatello inside.

"Where's Rosa?" Donatello asked as they entered the cool of Brunelleschi's sitting room.

"She's in Fiesole," Brunelleschi replied. "Her mother's not well and she's been away for a couple of days. That's why I had to answer the door to the Podestà's men myself. Otherwise I'd have got her to shoo them away."

In contrast to the cluttered study where Luca normally met Filippo, the sitting room was elegantly, if sparsely, furnished. There were three armchairs in polished walnut with dark-brown cushions and, along one wall, a cedarwood chest with a crucifix above it. By one of the chairs was a low table, perhaps two feet square, with an intricate parquetry top in coloured woods. The design, in perfect perspective, incorporated a set square, a ruler and a pair of dividers, all wrapped up in a fluttering golden ribbon and floating over a sky-blue background.

They sat in the armchairs, Donatello next to Brunelleschi, taking his hand in his own as he outlined the morning's events. The architect was a smallish man, but he radiated a nervous energy which somehow made him seem much bigger. He's made a very rapid recovery from his life-threatening fever, thought Luca. It was true that his eyes were red-rimmed, that what remained of his wavy hair was ruffled and that his aquiline nose was beakier than ever, but as Brunelleschi sat there in his creased maroon day-gown he seemed as healthy as any other man in his late forties and a lot more vigorous. So Giovanni Ferrante had probably been right when he alleged the architect had been faking his sickness.

Brunelleschi all but confirmed this when he said to Donatello: "Look, I'd no time for the Cardinal's visit this morning and I've even less to respond to these ridiculous allegations." He removed his hand from the sculptor's and patted him on the arm. "Thank you, my dear friend. I'm grateful, as ever, for your concern, but right now we're in the middle of a technical crisis and I've been up half the night trying to solve it. I've got to get these dratted bricks sorted out."

Unlike Filippo's illness, the engineering problems were all too real. In recent weeks, often accompanied by Luca, Brunelleschi had spent more and more time in the shell of the dome itself, examining every clay brick before it was laid, rejecting many that were malformed or cracked, and fretting anxiously over the mixing of the special mortar he'd invented. Now he picked up a scrap of parchment covered in calculations and diagrams from the table. "Look at this, Luca," he said, "I've done the figures a dozen times. As we build higher, I think we are going to need some more bricks of a slightly different shape." He thrust the parchment into Luca's hands.

"Filippo," Donatello remonstrated. "I know the dome's important, but I don't think you have been listening to a word I have been saying. We ignore these allegations at our peril. There are plenty of people around here who would like to do us down. If you're arrested, what's going to happen to your precious dome then? We need to prepare our defence."

Brunelleschi, still obviously preoccupied with his calculations, shook his head, as if to clear it and concentrate on what Donatello was saying. "Well, how about telling the truth? I've never heard of, let alone met, this man, er, what was his name? Bartolomeo from somewhere? I didn't murder him. I didn't steal my ideas. And as for this geomancy you talk of, you or I wouldn't know the significance of a pile of earth – unless we tripped over it."

"Be serious, Filippo ..."

"I am serious. This will all blow over before suppertime. The complaints are meaningless and there's not one shred of evidence against us ..."

"There was a very dead body in the piazza," said Luca softly, "and somebody killed him and put him there."

All Brunelleschi cared about was the dome and Donatello seemed more concerned with politics and plots than with the death of that unfortunate man. And – Luca felt cold at the idea – the killer could well be someone he knew. Walking around, planning some fresh evil.

"One thing puzzles me," said Brunelleschi. "You say the body was discovered less than a couple of hours ago. So how did the Podestà's men get here so quickly? Given the normal speed of our bureaucracy I wouldn't have expected them before the middle of next week."

Donatello made an exasperated gesture: "That's just what I'm trying to tell you Filippo. I'm concerned for your safety. There's dirty work afoot. I'm sure it's all a plot, to do you down. And I reckon Giovanni Ferrante is at the centre of it."

"That skinny gargoyle!"

"He'd do anything to get the better of you. What I don't understand is why he hates you so much. You were at school together, weren't you?"

"Yes and he was a pain in the arse then, too!" Filippo pondered for a moment: "I suppose it's simply envy. When we were boys we both wanted to be famous artists. But Giovanni's father insisted he should follow him into the legal profession. My Dad was also a lawyer, but he encouraged me, even had me apprenticed to a goldsmith. Plenty of money there, he said."

"That's true," said Donatello, "But you'd think Ferrante would've got over it after forty years."

Well, I wouldn't, Luca said to himself, not with the way Brunelleschi treats him. He couldn't stand the crabby notary either, but he sometimes began to feel sorry for him when Filippo turned on the scorn. One time, Ferrante had suggested that the dome was going to be gloomy inside and that it needed bigger windows and Filippo had barked: "Numbskull! Are you wholly ignorant of engineering principles? Larger windows would critically weaken the structure, as any half-wit should know." And he never addressed him by his proper legal title, '*Ser* Giovanni'. It was always '*Messer* Giovanni the idiot' here and '*Messer* Giovanni the dimwit' there.

"Whether Ferrante's jealous or not," said Donatello, "the allegations in those papers could send us to jail or into exile ..." He shuddered theatrically, "... or even condemn us to death."

"Don't be so melodramatic Donatello. They are obviously untrue..."

"But can we prove it?"

Brunelleschi leaned forward and put his hand on Donatello's knee. It seemed, at last, that he was willing to take his friends' concerns more seriously: "You're right. Even I can feel the cold touch of unjust suspicion. So what d'you suggest we do?"

"Bad decisions are taken on empty stomachs," said Donatello, "And I'm ravenous. Come on, let's go to the tavern on the corner and we'll talk as we eat."

They stood up, but just as they were moving towards the hall, there was a frantic rapping on the front door. When Filippo opened it, they found Luca's sister Maria on the step, hot, flustered and out of breath. For a moment she seemed unable to speak. Luca, as ever, was overwhelmed by her beauty and her vulnerability. "Maria, Maria! What on earth is wrong?"

Her words came out in a sudden rush: "Oh Luca," she cried, "I've found you at last. Have you seen Jacopo? He's been missing for three days and I am frightened something dreadful has happened to him." And she fell, sobbing, into her brother's arms.

8

In Luca's opinion, his sister's marriage had begun badly and become progressively worse. It had all started with a natural disaster, of course, the earthquake of March 1423 which caused extensive damage to the family's watermill in the wilds of rural Lunigiana and which brought Jacopo Alderici into their lives.

In his mind's eye, Luca could see Jacopo on the day he'd arrived, a strutting, sure-of-himself man in his early twenties, well built and handsome. He'd surveyed the damaged watermill, but seemed more interested in sixteen-year-old Maria, who was trying to revive the vegetable garden, than in the intricacies of rebuilding.

But Jacopo was a skilled *scalpellatore* and *muratore* – a stonemason and a 'wall-builder' in both stone and brick – and he came recommended by Don Giuseppe, the village priest, who had used him recently to repair the apse of the parish church. He was also inundated with requests for his work following the earthquake, so Luca reasoned that if his father Francesco noticed the looks that passed between Maria and the cocky mason, he chose to ignore them. Perhaps he reckoned that Maria's beauty was a way to attract Jacopo to Posara and keep him there while the mill, and the family's livelihood, was restored.

Luca certainly saw Maria perpetually glancing under her long eyelashes as she pretended to tend to the poor cabbages, whose precise lines of planting had been broken by the tremors like soldiers scattered by grapeshot. Why did she have to behave like a common flirt? She was his beautiful, virginal sister and he wanted her to stay that way for ever.

That day, however, there were more pressing matters and, unusually, Luca was at the forefront of family affairs. Up until now all the decisions about the running of the mill had been taken by his father – and most of the work was done by his two elder brothers, Matteo and Marco, strapping fellows who thought nothing of heaving a *quintale* sack of grain on to their shoulders and pouring it into the pine hoppers that fed the millstones. Luca, more slender and delicate, helped where he could, opening and closing the sluices that controlled the millstream waters, for instance. But he often found himself daydreaming, fascinated by the way the water in some places scoured the millstream's stony bottom, while in others it deposited a fine sandy silt, washed by the river from the mountains. He made sketches of its eddies and currents, lost in another world, until an angry shout about the sluices brought him back with a jolt.

The workings of the mill machinery intrigued Luca, too, and he drew the millstream waters, divided in four, rushing down oaken channels to the spoon-like paddles of the mill's horizontal waterwheels. He even made models of all the machinery: the driving wheels, the silvery-grey millstones themselves and the simple, but ingenious, methods for raising and lowering them and for turning them over for cleaning and re-dressing.

With his mother's connivance, Luca had also become the altar boy at the church and Don Giuseppe had taught him to read and write and introduced him to the rudiments of mathematics. His father, however, saw small merit in such activities: "All this reading grinds no corn," he said. Luca's brothers teased him continuously. "What a girlie, more like his baby sister than a real man."

One evening after the earthquake Luca went to his father with several sheets of paper covered in diagrams and sketches. "Not now, Luca," Francesco growled, "I've enough on my plate without looking at more of your pretty drawings."

"No, father," Luca had persevered, "This is how we can restore our fortunes and make the mill much more efficient." That captured his father's interest and in the next hour or so Luca explained how the millstream could run more powerfully, how the millstones could grind more efficiently and how the mill could make more money by installing water-driven machinery to crush olives and squeeze out their oil. His father was impressed, especially when Luca showed him the improvements could be made at little extra cost.

So when Jacopo had arrived that Spring day in 1423 it was Luca, with his father's blessing, who was to brief the mason on how they wanted the mill rebuilt. And to give Jacopo his due, he soon became engrossed in Luca's proposals and even, for a moment or two at least, less focused on Maria's charms. He looked carefully at Luca's plans and calculations and had plenty of sensible suggestions: "I like that, but would it bear the weight? How about if we made a thin brick arch there?" Luca was impressed despite himself.

The restoration work progressed rapidly through April and May, but the more Luca got to know the mason the less he liked him. It wasn't just his arrogance and his lewd jokes, or how he appropriated Luca's ideas as his own, or how he often teased him for his lack of physical strength. No, to be honest, it was the way Jacopo looked at his sister. Every time she passed – and she seemed to pass much more often than was strictly necessary – he would leer at her. And she would encourage him, with a swift glance and a shy smile. Matteo and Marco noticed, too, but just laughed: "Falling for the charms of our little sister, eh? Mind you don't get ensnared!"

And then one day, just after noon, when it was too hot to work, Luca was lying by the small stone bridge that marked the beginning of the millstream, watching iridescent turquoise dragonflies dancing in the sun, when he heard a grunting noise coming from the copse beyond the *canaletto* that brought the river's waters to the millstream. Was it one of the badgers, who had a sett in the sandy soil at the edge of the trees? They'd hardly be out in daylight. Or a wild boar? But they, too, wouldn't be rootling about in the heat of the noonday sun. He heard the grunt again, and with it a regular gasping noise, as if an animal was in pain.

Silently Luca made his way across the *canaletto* and into the thicket. He moved silently towards a little grassy clearing at its centre and there, peering through the branches, he saw Jacopo's naked buttocks, covered in a thin sheen of sweat, thrusting up and down. And beneath him, Maria, her green skirt hitched high, her white legs splayed wide, gasping not in pain but with pleasure. Luca fled, his mind in turmoil.

For days he was morose and uncommunicative, but refused to tell anyone what was wrong, even his mother Annunziata. But it turned out that she, too, had had her suspicions that, despite her repeated entreaties, Maria and Jacopo had become lovers. Their mother confronted Maria, who'd confessed, protesting her love for Jacopo and his for her. Annunziata told her husband Francesco, who told his eldest son Matteo who, with his brother Marco, had an intimidating word or two with the stonemason.

The upshot was that within a month the pair were married, Don Giuseppe officiating in the tiny parish church. While Jacopo may have been a reluctant groom, his bride was delighted, besotted with her new husband and unable to see his faults. "Oh, Luca," she told him, her lovely face glowing, "I'm so happy. The man of my dreams..."

The couple went to live in Fivizzano, the nearby town where Jacopo's family had a house in the main piazza, and with their departure it seemed to Luca that a light had gone out. He'd seen her every day of her life, from the tiny swaddled bundle in their mother's arms, to the carefree companion of his childhood days, exploring the countryside and the river together, holding hands as they helped each other across the rocks and bathing naked in the swimming holes. He'd watched as her beauty blossomed, her pale face with its dark brown eyes framed by a bonnet of lustrous black hair.

When Maria reached fourteen, however, there was a subtle change. Her mother found more tasks for her in the kitchen and in the garden and Maria herself grew more self-aware. There was a quiet seriousness about her, as if she'd discovered a basket full of secrets. Nonetheless, she still found time occasionally to lie by the millstream with Luca as the evening sun cast long shadows over the grass and to listen as he told her of his dreams and ambitions.

After her marriage he saw Maria every week at the Tuesday market in Fivizzano and while she still professed her love for Jacopo, he began to think her enthusiasm was a little forced and his questions about her health and happiness were answered with a wary smile.

There was work for him to do at the mill, making adjustments to his designs so that the machinery ran smoothly and, when Autumn came, ensuring that the new olive press worked well. This was soon successful, with neighbours from many miles around bringing their basketsful of olives for pressing, in return for a share of the oil.

But despondency clung to Luca like a wet coat. He often took long lonely early morning walks along the misty millstream, missing his sister, longing for someone to talk to. He seemed to be of another species from his father and brothers, and even his beloved mother, caring and concerned as she was, was unable to break his mood.

Unbeknown to Luca, however, she'd been in touch with her brother Battista d'Antonio, Superintendent of Works at the cathedral of Santa Maria del Fiore in Florence, asking him to find a job for Luca there. Battista replied that he was looking for an assistant: "I'll take the lad, Annunziata," he wrote. "If he's half a clever as you say he is, we'll have the dome built in no time."

As soon as Luca heard the news his mood lightened. Here was a future he'd dreamed of. Instead of being stuck in a rural backwater, he'd be in Florence, centre of the artistic and intellectual world. The February parting from his mother was tearful, but he left the mill, his father and his brothers, with scarcely a backward glance.

Within a few months, however, Maria and Jacopo joined Luca in the city. Jacopo was apparently jealous of his brother-in-law's success (Luca had written to Don Giuseppe, who'd passed on all the news to his mother, who'd proudly told Maria). So the mason made the four-day journey on foot to Florence, seeking out Battista and asking for a job. It so happened that one of the eight master masons working on the cupola had just been killed in a tavern brawl and Battista needed a replacement urgently. He tried out Jacopo for a week and, impressed by his skills, gave him the job. Maria joined him soon afterwards and they took lodgings in Borgo la Croce, at the Eastern end of the city. And Luca's worries about his sister began all over again.

9

Maria plucked at Luca's sleeve as she told her story, seated at the kitchen table with her brother and Brunelleschi. The men had abandoned their plan to go to the tavern and Donatello was searching the pantry looking for food.

"He didn't come home on Monday night," Maria said, her face as pale as a pearl, "but I wasn't too concerned. He's working so hard on the dome that he needs some relaxation in the evenings with his mates. You'll understand that *Provveditore*," she said, appealing to Brunelleschi, who merely grunted. Maria went on hastily: "And sometimes he stays over with a friend and goes straight on to work."

She looked into each man's face in turn, seeking approval for her explanation. Brunelleschi grunted again, but said nothing. Taking Maria's hand in his own, Luca smiled reassuringly. But he knew that Jacopo had more likely than not been out on another drinking spree, locked in the tavern after curfew, unable and unwilling to go home.

In recent weeks Jacopo's behaviour at work had become increasingly tiresome. He was always talking behind his hand to the other workers, no doubt criticising Brunelleschi as the architect obsessively examined every brick and fretted over the mixing of the mortar. He grumbled about his wages and seemed to be inciting the others to do the same. And he was drinking too much.

In order to progress the work more efficiently, Brunelleschi had installed a kitchen in the dome itself, so the workers didn't have to leave for their mid-day meal – and he ordered that the wine served with it was well watered down, so the men would be sober in the afternoon. Jacopo had dismissed this as "women's drink", but he still took more than his share. And in the evenings he invariably took more wine, unwatered, in one of the many taverns in the city.

"When he didn't come home last night, either, I really began to worry," Maria continued, near to tears again. "He doesn't like me checking up on him, but by noon I was so frantic that I just had to go to the cathedral. And there's no sign of him." She pulled on her brother's sleeve once more: "Oh Luca! Where's he gone? Is he all right?"

Luca didn't know what to say and it was Donatello, coming out of the pantry with half a loaf of bread and small piece of pecorino cheese, who answered. "Don't worry, Maria. I am sure all will be well. It's been a difficult day for all of us, what with the Cardinal's visit and that awful murder in the piazza."

Maria's hand went to her mouth. "Oh yes, I'm so sorry. I'm so full of my own concerns. Uncle Battista told me about it. He was too busy to talk much and he said I should go home and wait. Then I met one of Donatello's apprentices and he said you were coming here..."

"I think going home is the best advice you've had all day," Brunelleschi said brusquely. "I am sure your husband will turn up soon. He'd better. I need every skilled mason I can lay my hands on." He paused. "Although, these days Jacopo is more trouble ..."

Luca interrupted before Brunelleschi could say anything more. "You're quite right *Provveditore*. Sensible advice."

He stood up and took his sister's hand to pull her up from her seat. "Come on, I'll go home with you. We'll walk via the cathedral and see whether Jacopo's signed in for work this afternoon."

It was Brunelleschi's turn to interrupt. "Oh no you won't. I need you here and I need you now. I want to go through these calculations once again and then I want you take the designs for the new bricks to Battista and get him to work making the moulds. Donatello, you take this young lady home and make sure she's all right."

Donatello, who was still holding the bread and the cheese, look dismayed. "Can't we eat first? I'm so hungry..."

Brunelleschi silenced him with a glare. "Go, go now. Luca, come with me and we'll double-check those calculations."

With a dismissive wave of his hand he urged Donatello to leave and the sculptor, after a moment's hesitation and a longing look, put the bread and cheese on the table, took Maria's arm and led her to the front door. "Don't forget we have to be at the *Bargello* at four," he shouted over his shoulder as they left.

Luca followed Brunelleschi into his sitting room and they began to go through the calculations. To tell the truth, Luca struggled to make sense of them, but the architect explained the figures line by line. Then he brought out a detailed drawing of a vertical section of the dome. "We're here," he said, jabbing his finger at the diagram where the sides of the cupola were just beginning to slope inwards, "and the critical moment's going to come in a couple of months when we'll reach an angle of thirty degrees from the vertical. From then on friction alone won't keep the bricks and masonry in place before the mortar sets."

Looking at the sketch, Luca once again marvelled at the revolutionary concept of Brunelleschi's design: there were two shells to the dome, one inside the other, a thick inner one connected to a thinner outer one.

But why didn't the internal shell, unsupported by centring, fall to the ground? One of the answers lay in the bricks, millions of them. Luca was amazed not only by their numbers, but also by their diversity: as well as rectangular ones, there were triangular bricks and ones with flanges and with dovetails, and they came in a variety of sizes. Brunelleschi had designed the wooden moulds for them all and there were so many varying sizes and shapes that at one point he ran out of parchment and he'd sent Luca out to buy old books so he could draw on their torn-out pages.

The architect had also paid careful attention to the quality of the finished bricks, rejecting many that were malformed or cracked. The content and consistency of the mortar was also a concern: it was vital that it cured as rapidly as possible, holding the bricks firmly in place.

But Luca learned that the real key to keeping the unsupported dome from collapsing was in the clever way that the bricks were to be laid. As they rose and inclined inwards the shell not only had horizontal rings of brickwork, but also incorporated spiralling bands of upright ones, creating a zigzag or herring-bone pattern, spreading some of the weight sideways and downwards rather than inwards and helping to hold the bricks in place until the mortar cured. Nonetheless the work progressed very slowly, because the *muratori* had to wait until the mortar in each course set before they could move up to the next,

Brunelleschi brought out three or four sheets with bold outlines of bricks on them, their measurements written in a neat hand and the angles precisely defined. "I've modified some of the flanged bricks for the upper part of the dome," he told Luca. "I want Battista to start making the moulds today. The clay'll have to cure for a month, so the sooner we get the brickworks busy the better.

"I'd go myself, but it wouldn't look well to turn up this afternoon after having missed the Cardinal's visit this morning. So you're going to have to take these to him. I want to keep the work moving forward."

He gazed at Luca fiercely: "Speaking of which, we've got to sort out that blasted brother-in-law of yours. He's nothing but a mischief-maker, stirring up the others. Have a word with him. If he doesn't change his ways I'll have to take action."

Luca nodded, but he doubted that anything he said would have any influence whatsoever on Jacopo. Taking the papers, he paid a respectful farewell to Brunelleschi and set off once more for the cathedral.

As he walked he realised that, at the back of his mind, something had been worrying him about the corpse of the Sicilian scholar he'd discovered this morning. It wasn't just the sickening, bloody, featureless head, though God knew that was troubling enough. No, it was the man's hand, revealed when the canvas sheet had been pulled to one side. It wasn't quite right. But Luca couldn't quite put his finger on it: the idea was as elusive as the smell of a primrose.

10

Seated at his dining table Niccolò Peruzzi, fat as butter, was dissecting an apple with his dagger. Like many plump men, his movements were delicate and precise. He stabbed a slice and was careful not to let the blade's sharp edges touch his thick bluish-red lips as they pulled it into his mouth. Giovanni Ferrante, standing before him, shuddered inwardly. Niccolò was only in his twenties, but close up he positively exuded malice.

A serving girl, her *camicia* low-cut, poured Niccolò a glass of wine from a silver jug. As she leaned forward her well-shaped breasts were clearly visible. Giovanni couldn't keep his eyes off them. As the girl straightened she gave him a knowing look, then laughed. Niccolò laughed too. "You like *la bella Elisabetta*?" he said, fondling her rump. "Maybe I'll loan her to you for a night if our project is successful." He smacked the girl on her bottom. "Leave us. I have business with Notary Ferrante." The girl pulled a face and flounced out of the room, closing the door none-too-quietly behind her.

"So, *Ser* Giovanni, the game's afoot. My cousin Rinaldo was present for the Cardinal's visit, so I know about the discovery of the body. But what of the documents you so cleverly found on the corpse? Have they had the desired effect?"

"Yes, My Lord..." Giovanni began, but Niccolò interrupted him with an expansive gesture.

"No need for the 'My Lord' *Ser* Giovanni. We are all citizens of a republic after all. A simple 'Sir' will suffice. 'Though I must say I do like the sound of 'My lord'. Maybe we should change our form of government again so it better reflects the natural order of things."

It's easy to say that, thought Giovanni, when you are born to wealth and influence. No-one could help but be impressed by the great hall in Niccolò's rambling family house. A fireplace in silvery *pietra serena* dominated one wall. Across its header two chubby *putti* held a roundel containing the Peruzzi coat of arms. On the wall at right angles to the fireplace, designed as a pair with it, was a stone wall fountain, also bearing the family arms, with shelves containing small sculptures as well as ewers, basins and bowls.

The room itself, filled with a diffused light from high windows covered with waxed paper, would have been quite austere had it not been for colourful paintings, mainly portraits, and splendid textile hangings. The russet-coloured terracotta tiles of the floor had been polished with beeswax to a glowing shine.

Giovanni began again: "Yes... Sir. After the body was discovered by Battista's brat of a nephew, I found the papers and I read out the allegations in front of the civic dignitaries and the Cardinal."

"Very good. And was there a satisfactory reaction?"

"Oh yes. Many of them already want to believe the worst about Brunelleschi. And Cosimo de' Medici looked most put out, I can assure you."

"It was unfortunate that he hung on to the papers." Niccolò pointed the dagger towards Giovanni. "That was a little careless of you, Giovanni. An error, one may say. And I don't expect errors from those in my service."

Giovanni stuttered. "Yes, but I..."

"It concerns me that the papers are in the hands of those cunning Medici bastards rather than with the Podestà, who is much more impressionable and malleable."

"But he snatched them from me and wouldn't give them back!"

"It was foolish of you to let them go in the first place." The dagger again waggled in Giovanni's direction and Niccolò's smile was like Winter sunshine. "Make sure nothing like that happens again."

"But all is well, My Lor ... er, Sir." Giovanni's words spilled out in a rush: "Everyone in the piazza heard the allegations and, with Lorenzo Ghiberti, I've made sure they're spreading throughout the city. And I pointed out to the Podestà that the body had been covered with a sculptor's canvas sheet and that the head wounds looked as if they'd been made with a sculptor's hammer. Even he realised that Donatello must be a prime suspect."

"That's all very well, Giovanni, but I'm still not happy that Medici has those papers." The dagger-waving subsided and Niccolò cut himself another slice of apple.

"And I met with the Podestà's man on the way here," Giovanni continued. "He's summoned Donatello and Brunelleschi to appear before him at four. They'll be arrested by half past, mark my words."

"That may be so, but is it enough?"

Niccolò played for a moment or two with the dagger, balancing its point on the table. "Now we must convince the Medici that someone is waging serious war against them and that they can no longer do as they please in this city. Time to escalate our campaign, I think."

He took some wine with a loud slurp and, after drying his lips with a large white *fazzoletto*, got up ponderously from the table. He moved to one of the shelves in the wall fountain and, unlocking a brass-bound box on one of the shelves, removed a glass phial, sealed with deep red wax. Niccolò held the phial up between a pudgy thumb and forefinger and Giovanni could see it held a brilliant white powder.

"*La cantanella,*" said Niccolò. "Pleasant to the taste, I'm told, but deadly. When that precious pair get arrested, I want you to ensure that this gets into their food."

Giovanni began to protest: "Murder Brunelleschi! I couldn't! I hate him, but I couldn't kill him. The cathedral ... the dome ..."

"Then give the poison to his friend the sculptor. Which one of them takes the fatal dose is of no consequence to me."

"No, no! I just can't do it. I've gone along with your schemes so far, but this is too much. You'll have to find someone else."

"Sit down *Ser* Giovanni," said Niccolò, his words a serpent's hiss. Returning to his own seat, he indicated a chair at the table to his right. Intimidated, Giovanni sat and Niccolò placed the phial between them. He smiled again, but while the smile reached his fat red cheeks, his eyes, with brown irises flecked with black, were cold. He picked up the dagger again, testing its point with his thumb.

"And how is your father, *Ser* Giovanni? Still gambling I fear."

Damn the man! And damn my father too, thought Giovanni. In his old age his father had taken to gaming in a big way. He'd wager on just about anything, but backgammon was his major addiction and most evenings he could be seen in one tavern or another huddled over a board. He lost, of course, and Giovanni had to bail him out on several occasions. But still his losses mounted and soon they were hundreds of florins. Then one day Niccolò Peruzzi had summoned Giovanni to this very room. He'd bought his father's debt.

"No problem at all, *Ser* Giovanni. One knows how distressing it would be for a man in your position to have his father thrown into *Le Stinche*." There was no hurry to pay the money back, Niccolò had said, but no doubt the distinguished notary would be able to help him out from time to time.

And that was how it had all begun: a titbit of information about the proceedings of the *Opera del Duomo* here, a spreading of a malicious rumour there, all trivial enough. Giovanni hadn't wanted to become involved in the plot involving the Sicilian mathematician, but as well as reminding him of his father's indebtedness, Niccolò had pointed out the precariousness of Giovanni's own position: "I don't think the Wardens of the *Opera* would take too kindly to their Notary revealing confidential information about their undertakings. It would be a pity if such activities became public. Of course there's no reason why they should do so... Now about this enterprise of ours..."

I was trapped, Giovanni told himself, trapped by this awful man, who seems to enjoy the suffering of others and for whom killing seems to be of little consequence. And now, to cap it all, he wants me to be a murderer. He tried again to dissuade Niccolò from his course of action. "Surely it will serve our purpose if Brunelleschi is indicted for fraud and sacked as *Provveditore della cupola*. The scandal will undermine and weaken his patrons, the Medici."

"Indicted, yes. Found guilty? Well maybe. Living men can strive to prove their innocence and influential friends can sway judges. But they can't save a corpse. No, this is the way we must proceed."

He pushed the phial towards Giovanni Ferrante, who reluctantly picked it up.

"Ah, *Ser* Giovanni. I was sure an intelligent man such as you would see reason. When the Peruzzi are in power I shall see you are well rewarded. For now, off you go. You have much to do." As Giovanni rose to his feet, Niccolò again picked up the dagger and pointed it at the trembling lawyer.

11

Luca summoned up the courage to walk back though the baptistry square. At this time of day, in the heat of the early afternoon, there were few people about and there was little or nothing to show of the grisly discovery that he had made a few hours earlier. The canvas sheet had disappeared and, although he did not look too diligently, Luca could see no sign of blood on the pavement. In fact it was almost as if the whole incident had never occurred. Only the man re-erecting the rosy awning over the stall selling hose and woollen jerkins served as a reminder that there had been any interruption to the normal day. The other stall, which had been selling amulets and potions, had disappeared

Luca walked over to the baptistry doors to give a surreptitious rub to the head of his name saint, St Luke, who was depicted on one of Lorenzo Ghiberti's bronze panels. The saint sat with his legs crossed elegantly, reading a book propped up on a lectern. There was a scroll on his knee and, somewhat incongruously, a bull lay quietly behind the desk. This was the saint's symbol and opinion was divided on whether it was a bull or an ox. It didn't seem to matter to most people, but Luca presumed it would have been of importance to the bull.

In the cathedral one of the workers told him that Battista was at the top of the dome checking on the progress of the work, so Luca started to climb the murky interior spiral stairs to the top of the octagonal tambour, counting the steps to himself as he did so. Then there was a long straight stretch between the two shells of the dome, which eventually ("...two hundred and seventy-two, two hundred and seventy-three...") brought him out into the sunlight.

There was a bustle of activity here at the topmost part of the works, with men milling around on the wooden scaffolding. In the section immediately in front of Luca two *muratori* were busy sorting bricks, wearing aprons smeared with lime mortar; a man in a brown doublet and red hose carried sand in a wooden bucket on his left shoulder; another had a sack of soda ash perched on a strip of linen wrapped around his head like a Saracen's turban; a third, carrying a plank of wood, cautiously mounted a ladder between two scaffolding platforms.

Edging around the staging, Luca found his uncle examining the final courses of brickwork. He looked up at his nephew's approach. "Ah, Luca. Are you all right? Such a shock this morning. Just what we don't need at the moment."

Before Luca could reply, however, Battista continued: "Look at this." He pointed to the rows of bricks laid in a herringbone pattern. "The mortar's cured perfectly. I must say I hadn't the faintest idea what it was all about when Filippo showed me the drawings. But look how these zig-zag bricks shift so much of the weight on to the vertical rib of the dome. Clever stuff, eh? I'd never have worked that out."

"Thank you for your concern, Uncle," said Luca, somewhat ironically, for it was clear that Battista's real anxiety lay with his beloved dome rather than the immediate well-being of his nephew.

"Is Filippo on his way?" Battista continued. "He'll want to inspect this course of brickwork."

"But you know he's ill."

"Oh yes, a fever isn't it?" Battista gave a heavy wink. "I think he might make a quick recovery now the Cardinal's visit is over."

"Yes," Luca smiled back. "I think you're right, Uncle. But he considered it diplomatic not to be seen in the cathedral, at least for a few more hours. He gave me these. He wants you to make the moulds for a new set of bricks." Luca moved across the planking to hand the designs to Battista.

"Have a care, nephew," Battista warned. "You don't want to go too near the edge. It's safe enough, but a bit bouncy – and it's a long way down."

It was when his uncle reached for the drawings that Luca realised what had been troubling him about the corpse's hand. The revelation – and its implications – made him feel quite dizzy and he swayed slightly, the planking creaking under his feet.

"Steady, lad, steady now," said Battista, grabbing Luca's elbow with one hand and taking the drawings with the other.

"I am all right," said Luca, looking at his uncle's roughened hand, his fingers pitted with scars from the mason's trade, the fingernails chipped and dirty. He pulled his gaze to Battista's face. "I'm fine, truly."

"Come on. This is no place today for a wobbly lad like you. Let's go down and I'll look at these in the offices of the *Opera*. Then you can tell me what they're all about."

And he led Luca away, preceding him all the way down the dim and dusty steps, so that were Luca to have fallen he would have landed on his uncle's bulk rather than the hard stone. He does care for me after all, Luca thought fleetingly, but another idea dominated his mind, so much so that he soon lost count of the steps. The corpse, Bartolomeo da Siracusa: was he really the man they thought he was? And if he wasn't, who was he? He needed to look at the body again to be sure of his suspicions.

But first there was the dome, the blessed dome, the obsession, it seemed, of everyone around him. His uncle led him into the workshops of the *Opera del duomo*. The doorkeeper, who had been dozing after his midday meal, woke with a start and greeted his boss respectfully: "Good afternoon *Provveditore*," he said, standing and giving an exaggerated military-style salute. Battista ignored him, marched into a workroom and spread out Brunelleschi's diagrams on a trestle table.

"So he wants me to make moulds for all these bricks? And I suppose he wants them by yesterday?"

Luca smiled again: "He did imply that would be very satisfactory."

"Well, it looks straightforward enough to me. I'll get the barrel-maker on to it right away and send the moulds to the brickworks this evening. I'd be pleased if you went out there tomorrow and checked with the foreman when they might be ready."

"They're to go above the next stone ring," said Luca. "When's that going to be finished?"

"I've no idea, but we're ready to start putting it in position. The masons have been hard at it, shaping the blocks." Battista looked at Luca: "Well, seven of the eight of them have. I've seen neither hide nor hair of your precious brother-in-law for two days." He leaned forward conspiratorially: "Luca, we've got to sort out Jacopo. It's a matter of family pride: he's making life very embarrassing for us. He's your sister's husband and it was me who gave him the job. I could murder him for the way he's carrying on."

"I'll have a word," said Luca, echoing his reply to Brunelleschi's earlier request, "but I don't know if it will have any effect." But his mind really wasn't on Jacopo's behaviour. He now realised what he had to do – and he wasn't looking forward to it. Despite all his fears, he had to have another look at that corpse, now watched over by the Brothers of Mercy in their nearby mortuary chapel. "Uncle, I must go," he said. "I have another errand. Excuse me." Before Battista could utter one more word, he was out of the offices of the *Opera* and back into the hot cathedral piazza.

12

Within the walls of the city nothing was very far from anything else. It was possible, for instance, to walk from the Franciscan church of Santa Croce in the East to the Dominican basilica of Santa Maria Novella in the West in less than half an hour. So Luca reached the doors of the mortuary chapel of the *Misericordia* in only a few minutes. It was just as well that the journey wasn't any longer, for at every step his fears heightened and his resolve weakened. What business of his was it that a stranger had been brutally killed? None whatsoever! Death was everywhere in *quattrocento* Florence, where the plague was a regular occurrence, and where violent death, what with wars and family feuds, was commonplace. In such cases the wise man kept well out of the way.

Nevertheless the fact that he had uncovered Bartolomeo's corpse did give Luca a feeling of responsibility for the man, however illogical that might be. Something was driving him to find out the truth about the Sicilian's death and his determination to do so was reinforced by the apparent indifference of his friends and colleagues, all engrossed with their own concerns.

The chapel was set within the street itself, with Gothic arches on its façade and a flight of four well worn stone steps leading up to two tall recessed copper doors, green with age, each with a series of skull-and-crossbones designs raised from the surface. One of the doors was ajar and standing for a moment at the bottom of the steps, Luca could see into the chapel. The sunlight lit up a section of the elaborate off-white plasterwork and dark wood panelling. Plaster skeletons lounged indolently in the frieze, grinning from their toothless skulls, while on the oaken panels their wooden counterparts brooded, stiff and unmoving. On the stuccoed walls above the altar there were more skull-and-crossbones motifs and a plaster scroll with the words *Quoniam tamquam faenum velociter arescent*, which Luca with his rudimentary Latin took to mean something about grass swiftly withering.

In the centre of the chapel was an open coffin on a trestle, with four large pillar candles in floor-length holders at each corner. And in the coffin, the body of Bartolomeo da Siracusa lay at peace at last. Two hooded Brothers in red vestments sat in a shadowy side chapel. Taking in a deep breath and pushing back his shoulders, Luca climbed the steps and entered. He stood for a moment just inside the door and one of the Brothers, alerted no doubt by the temporary blocking of the sunshine, stood up and walked towards him. Luca felt his heart fluttering in his chest like a small bird held in the palm of the hand.

"Good afternoon, citizen," the Brother said quietly through the gash in his crimson hood. Two brown eyes regarded Luca curiously through the upper slits. "What brings you to this house of mourning?"

"Er, I came to pay my respects to the departed," said Luca, in a voice he scarcely recognised as his own.

"We didn't realise he knew anyone in Florence. We expected him to lie here for two days unmourned, except by members of the Brotherhood."

"It was I who found him," Luca stammered, "and somehow, I felt a responsibility for him."

"The responsibility lies with those who killed him, not with you!"

"Yes, yes, of course. Nonetheless, could I...?" Luca raised his eyes towards the corpse, noting with relief that, while the body was laid out in the clothes in which it had been found, the head was discretely covered by a cloth.

"Of course..." With a sweep of his arm, the Brother indicated the coffin and went back to join his companion.

Luca knelt near the centre of the coffin, crossed himself and once again contemplated the corpse of the Sicilian mathematician in his grey gown, dark-blue fur-trimmed tunic and yellow hose. He was able to examine these clothes more thoroughly than he had earlier in the day and now he noticed that, although they were well made, they seemed somehow ill-fitting. The stockings were slightly wrinkled around the man's thighs and his light-brown boots were loose around his calves. The well built body and muscular legs were also vaguely familiar. But he needed to see the hands...

Bartolomeo was lying on his back, with his arms folded on his chest, but over them was laid a linen band, extending to the sides of the coffin, with a gold embroidered cross at its centre. Luca began murmuring the prayers he remembered from his days as an altar boy. The Brothers looked up as he did so, but soon looked away again and continued whispering to each other.

Still praying, Luca tried surreptitiously to lift the linen band, but it was tucked in tightly between Bartolomeo's gown and the side of the coffin. He gave it a tug, but nothing happened. Another tug; the linen moved, but as it did so one of the brothers glanced his way and Luca hastily re-clasped his hands and continued his prayers with renewed fervour: "*De profundis clamavi ad te, Domine. Domine, exaudi vocem meam ...* Out of the depths I cry to Thee, Lord. Lord, hear my voice ..."

After a moment or two he tried tugging on the linen band again and this time it pulled free. He gave a quick glance at the Brothers. No, they weren't looking. He lifted the cloth a little higher – and there were the hands.

Yes he was right! These weren't the hands of a scholarly mathematician, pink and smooth, perhaps with a hint of ink on the forefinger. No, these were gnarled and pitted, not as much as Uncle Battista's it was true, but still bearing the telltale marks of physical work in stone. A building labourer perhaps – or a mason. And yes, there was a rim of stone dust under the chipped nails.

Luca found he was shivering again and it had little to do with the clammy dampness of the chapel. The hands were familiar to him. They ought to have been. He'd worked with them every day for two months as Jacopo, now his brother-in-law, had helped them to restore the watermill. Reeling with the implications of his discovery, Luca made to rise from his knees, but suddenly the chapel door swung shut with a bang. The candles flickered, spilling wax down their sides, and he felt a strong arm on his shoulder. "One moment, brother. May we have a word?"

13

Cosimo and the Cardinal hadn't remained long in the baptistry piazza after the discovery of the disfigured corpse. Luigi Mazzini's retinue had returned to the *palazzo* specially set aside for his visit, but the prelate and the banker had walked on together to the old Medici house near the church of *San Tommaso*, home to both Cosimo and his father, Giovanni di Bicci de' Medici, founder of the bank and the family's fortune.

Cosimo felt the house was a bit of a ramshackle affair and was contemplating commissioning a new *palazzo* which would more accurately reflect the Medici wealth and standing in the city. Nothing too flamboyant, of course: he was ever mindful of his father's advice not to make an ostentatious show of their wealth. The old man strove strenuously to avoid the limelight and when, for example, his name was put forward to participate in the Florentine government he usually chose to pay a fine to escape having to serve.

No, Cosimo's father's passion was his business and a dozen or so years ago he'd succeeded in becoming the Church's banker, as well as managing the financial affairs of Popes and Cardinals and securing lucrative tax-gathering contracts. Now the Medici bank was a multi-national business, with branches throughout Italy and beyond, earning a tidy fortune through trading in Bills of Exchange.

Giovanni had also created a network of supporters for the Medici cause: churchmen, politicians, kinsmen and business partners loyal to the family in their feuds with the other oligarchs of the city. Part of that scheme had been to procure for his sister's son, Luigi Mazzini, a Cardinal's red *galero*, the tasselled hat that proclaimed him a Prince of the Church.

Cosimo himself had been in charge of the bank since his father's retirement five years ago and now profits were running at well over ten thousand florins every year. At least, that was the figure bandied about the *Orsanmichele*, the church of the Florence guilds, around which the bankers had set up shop. Cosimo knew the exact figure, but never commented. Nonetheless he couldn't help feeling a glow of satisfaction at the fortune he and his father had accumulated. He reckoned they were worth well in excess of one hundred and fifty thousand florins, at a time when an unskilled labourer earned around thirty florins a year, an apprentice in the bank, twenty – and you could buy a slave girl outright for fifty florins. Even Croesus would have been hard pressed to be so well off. Time for a new house.

Keen to study in detail the sensational allegations in the dead man's papers Cosimo and his cousin hurried to an anteroom where Cosimo undid the purple ribbon around the oiled-paper packet and took out the twenty or so buff-coloured octavo sheets. Having read the first page of Bartolomeo da Siracusa's *'Humble Petition to the Wardens of the Opera del Duomo concerning the construction of the dome of Florence cathedral'* he handed it to the Cardinal and he did the same with each subsequent sheet.

The writing was neat and easy-to-read and the denunciations clear. The principal allegation leapt out from the page: "... *the aforementioned Filippo Brunelleschi stole the secrets of the construction of domes from an engineer in Rome, who then died in suspicious circumstances ...*"

The Roman engineer in question was named in the manuscript as Tommaso Bignone and there were dates when he and Brunelleschi were supposed to have met. The Sicilian mathematician said that Bignone had been regularly consulted by Filippo and had helped him with many of the calculations. Then one morning Bignone had been found dead, after Brunelleschi and Donatello had visited him the previous night. Following that insinuation there followed many pages of diagrams of domes and stones and bricks, with neat annotations and mathematical formulae.

When the Cardinal had finished the last page he looked up and asked his cousin: "Well, what does all that mean?"

"Just as that slimy notary Ferrante told us: accusations of theft and suggestions of murder. But it's all such a long time ago, more than twenty years, and it's all hearsay."

"Yes and the allegations of geomancy and the Black Arts don't add up to a bag of beans, either." The Cardinal pointed to the diagrams and mathematical formulae. "But this technical stuff is a mystery to me."

"Me too, Luigi. We'll have to get someone who understands it to tell us what it all means. I'll get Battista d'Antonio along: it's probably best not to involve Brunelleschi himself at this stage, since the allegations concern him."

"Can you trust Battista?"

"Oh yes, he's a good fellow, loyal to the core. No genius like Brunelleschi, but an excellent master mason. He should know what all these drawings mean."

"Well, let's have him in. We need to get to the bottom of this. Meanwhile, I don't know about you, but I'm in need of some sustenance."

"Of course," said Cosimo, "My kitchen has already anticipated your needs. We'll take our dinner in half-an-hour and I'll ask Battista to come at four o'clock."

14

Despite the clammy chill of the mortuary chapel, the hooded Brother's grip on his shoulder seared like flame. Luca looked at Bartolomeo's body lying in front of him. Had they noticed his fumblings with the linen band that had covered the corpse's hands? What was the punishment for desecration of a corpse? Flagellation? He tried to get up and, surprisingly, the Brother moved his hand and, putting it under Luca's elbow, helped him to his feet.

"Come with me, my dear young man," the Brother said softly.

My dear young man? That didn't sound like a prelude to flagellation!

"My friend and I would like a word, if you'd be so kind," the Brother continued, leading Luca into the vaulted side chapel where his colleague sat on the semi-circular stone bench that ringed it. There was a table at the centre, covered with a hempen cloth, and on it the remains of a loaf of bread, a jug of wine and a bowl of preserved cherries swimming in a murky liquid. Two dull-red terracotta plates with breadcrumbs and cherry stones and two glazed pottery beakers, still half-filled with red wine, were also on the table. A lone candle in a brass stick provided scant illumination.

"It is traditional to take a last meal with the departed," said the seated Brother, indicating that Luca should join him. Luca did so, sitting opposite on the curved bench and having to shuffle along as the other Brother squeezed in beside him. Luca felt his alarm returning. Now he was truly trapped.

"Usually the relatives would be here, of course, but this poor sinner has none, or at least no-one nearby who knows of his death. So we eat in their place. Now that you are here, perhaps you would join us." He reached into a niche and brought out another plate and a beaker, setting them before Luca and pouring him some wine.

"Please break bread with us – and try some of these cherries in grappa. They are from my brother-in-law's *orto* and my sister preserved them last Summer."

Luca was totally confused. One moment he was fearful of goodness knows what punishment for his sins, the next he was being asked to partake of a formal meal, just as if he was visiting his maiden aunt. And then there was the terrible realisation about the identity of the corpse. He was sure it was Jacopo. He had to get to Maria's house and talk to her.

"I must go," he stammered. "An urgent appointment ...

"We shan't detain you long, but please eat, drink and pay your respects to the deceased."

Luca had no choice but to take a sip of the wine and break off a piece of bread.

"We were most affected by your piety," said the Brother who had brought Luca to the table. "You don't know the deceased at all, yet you came to pray for his soul."

"Such fervent prayers – and so many of them!" said the other Brother. "So we were wondering if you would like to join our confraternity."

Luca would have laughed out loud had he not been in so solemn a place. He was trying to stifle childhood fears of hooded Brothers and they were asking him to join them! As if to reinforce the absurdity of the situation, one Brother said: "You haven't tried any of my sister's cherries. Please do, they're delicious."

"Thank you, thank you, but I must go," said Luca, grabbing one by its damp stalk. He shuffled along the stone bench, pushing against the Brother, who was forced to move and to stand up. Luca eased past him: "I'll think about your proposal. I know where you are."

Then he was at the portal, lifting the latch, dropping the cherry in the process, and pulling the heavy copper door slowly towards him. He stepped out into the glorious sunlight and walked rapidly down the street, taking in lungfuls of the city air and letting the sun warm his bones.

But his feeling of elation did not last long as he hurried towards Maria's apartment. How was he going to tell her the dead body was her husband?

On their arrival in Florence Jacopo had rented two rooms on the third floor of a tenement block (the landlord called it a *palazzo*) in Borgo La Croce, a street running from the church of Sant'Ambrogio to the Porta la Croce, one of the gates in the East of the city. It took Luca fifteen minutes' walking to reach the street door beside a carpenter's shop, push it open and walk into the dreary hall-space, smelling of boiled cabbage, cats' piss and God-knows-what besides.

Sighing, Luca began to climb the stone stairs. The walls, half-heartedly whitewashed several years ago, were scuffed with dirty marks and the iron handrail was loose in its fittings. There were ten steps up to the half- landing, a turn, then a dozen more steps to a larger landing with a scuffed door to an apartment. As he turned into a narrow corridor with windows on to a dingy internal courtyard, Luca tried to stop counting. A voice inside his head told him it would be bad luck if he were not to do so, but he was conscious that this perpetual counting was becoming an obsession. Turning to mount more steps, he deliberately lost count. As he climbed Luca could hear voices raised in argument, but they were too far away and muffled to make out who they might be or what they were saying.

He reached the top-landing, as shabby as the others below, and there was the door of Jacopo and Maria's rooms, its stained surface faded and patchy. The only bright spot was a well polished brass plaque with the legend 'Alderici. Master Mason.' in bold letters, though whoever clambered up here to read it was anybody's guess.

Luca knocked on the door. After a minute or so when there was no response, he knocked again. He heard a shuffling noise before a crack appeared and one of Maria's brown eyes peered out. Recognising her brother, she opened the door wider. While earlier in the day she had been pale, now she was flushed and her hair was dishevelled. She was wearing nothing but a crumpled shift: she was barefooted and stockingless. With a somewhat unenthusiastic gesture she waved Luca in.

What a mess! Tidiness had never been Maria's strong point and he'd always been appalled by the state of the rooms whenever he'd come to visit. Their only advantage as far as he could see was the inspiring view from the farther room, the bedroom, of the cathedral dome rising above the city. It was particularly special in the evening, when the setting sun threw into sharp relief the half-finished cupola, and the imposing tower of the *Palazzo della Signoria*, over to its left, twin symbols of spiritual and secular power in the city.

If anything the living room was more unkempt than ever: there were clothes on the floor and a chair had toppled over and lay on its side in the centre of the room. Luca picked it up and placed it under the table, then took both his sister's hands in his.

"Maria," he said. "I've some important news to tell you. Jacopo's..."

Luca tried desperately to find the right words. "Jacopo's ..."

"Jacopo's what?" said a throaty voice behind him.

Turning, Luca saw his brother-in-law, loosely wrapped in a sheet, leaning on the jamb of the bedroom door.

15

Luca was dumbfounded. He'd convinced himself that the dead body of 'Bartolomeo da Siracusa' was actually that of his brother-in-law, Jacopo Alderici. But here, leaning on the door jamb of his bedroom, was the all-too-living proof that he was wrong – and his brother-in-law asked again, a little more harshly this time: "Jacopo's what?"

There was no doubt that Jacopo was still handsome. His skin was dark and his work as a mason had made him well muscled. There was, however, a puffiness about his face and the whites of his eyes were dull. But Jacopo leaned arrogantly in the doorway, as sure of himself as ever and impatient for Luca's reply. Luca dropped Maria's hands. What could he say? He had half a mind to tell Jacopo about his discoveries and their implications, but the mason's truculent attitude held him back. "Er, I just came to ... to tell her you were still missing, but I see you are safely returned," Luca said in a rush of words.

"How very solicitous of you, brother-in-law. Not that it's any of your business..."

"But nice to know he cares," Maria interposed.

"Yes, yes, he's always cared for you, I'll give you that," said Jacopo. Addressing Luca directly he added: "As you see, I'm safe in the bosom of my family. And a very nice bosom it is, too." He held out his hand for Maria and she went to him. He pulled her towards him and kissed the top of her head.

"Will you be coming in for work this afternoon, then?" enquired Luca, a little timorously. "Uncle Battista tells me there is much to do, especially cutting the stone for the next restraining ring."

"You and your precious dome! If only they paid us masons and the bricklayers what we're worth, we might get along faster."

"But you're paid the official rate – and *Messer* Filippo ensures you're well looked after."

"We're still overworked and underpaid and I intend to keep reminding your precious *Messer* Filippo Brunelleschi of that. If he doesn't start paying us more he'll soon have a strike on his hands. The others are already muttering."

Thanks to you provoking them, Luca thought, but he said: "Well, all of them have signed on for the afternoon. Will you be there? What shall I tell Uncle Battista?"

Jacopo made a mock bow: "Please convey my apologies to your uncle. Tell him I am indisposed, as Brunelleschi was this morning, or, better still, tell him I had another, more pressing engagement." He pulled Maria still closer and kissed her long and hard on the lips. The sheet around his waist slipped a little. Maria, tight in Jacopo's embrace, waved her arm behind her back in a gesture suggesting Luca should go. He was glad to do so.

He tumbled down the steps of the tenement block (...fifty-eight, fifty-nine, sixty..., no, stop counting!), through the dimly lit hall and once again out into the sunshine, just as the bell of the parish church of Sant'Ambrogio struck four sonorous 'dongs': four o'clock! Surely it can't be, thought Luca, what's happened to the day? And I haven't had a thing to eat since the morning collation, except a bite of bread and a sip of wine. I need some food and I need to think. Even if that corpse isn't Jacopo, it's somebody. So, who is he and why would anyone want to kill him?

Luca walked briskly along Borgo La Croce to the Piazza Sant'Ambrogio and just beyond it turned down an alleyway and entered a tavern where he had been taken by Jacopo on a couple of occasions.

The thin light from high leaded windows was augmented by the glow from a huge brick fireplace at the back of the room, with a spit above it and several pots and cauldrons around its base. The rough stones of the tavern walls were exposed and along one of them there was a bar with a row of brown barrels behind it and, on shelves beside them, a phalanx of green *caraffe* and light-brown stoneware pitchers, in which wine would be served. A balustraded wooden gallery ran round three sides of the room, supported on square oak posts.

The dozen or so tables were rustic and sturdy, as were the circular stools around them. At one table a man in a green doublet sat with his head in his hands contemplating the pitcher of wine in front of him. At another, three men were playing cards, slapping them down on the table with occasional cries of delight or dismay.

Luca chose a table by the door and he'd no sooner sat down than a young man of about his age, wearing a beige shirt and a long green apron, came over to take his order. "What'll it be then?"

Luca looked up at the open face, freckled and smiling, and with a shock of brownish hair. "What's the dish of the day?

"The dish of the day is beans. That is," the waiter said, putting on a more formal voice, "fresh fava beans cooked in meat broth with parsley and mint."

"Sounds good."

"Only it's finished. You're a bit late for the dish of the day. All gone."

"Oh, what do you have?

"Let's see," said the young man looking over to the fire. "I do believe we've some *carbonata* left."

"I'll have that, then."

"Good choice! One *carbonata* it is. Red wine?"

"Yes, please."

"On its way." The waiter hurried off and was back in a couple of minutes with a plate of bread, a pitcher of wine and a glazed stoneware beaker, before going over to the one of the iron cauldrons by the fire and ladling out a generous portion of *carbonata*, a stew made with salted beef.

"There you go," he said, putting the plate in front of Luca. "*Buon appetito!*" He hurried off towards the card players, one of whom was waving a pitcher, indicating they needed a refill.

Luca attacked his meal ravenously. The stew was excellent, a hint of cinnamon enlivening the sauce, and he soon finished it off, wiping round his plate with a hunk of bread and quenching his thirst with the cool red wine, which was also unexpectedly good. Refilling his goblet, Luca tried to put the events of the day into some sort of order. As so often when he was thinking, he tried unsuccessfully to flatten the unruly tuft of his hair.

One: the body he'd found was not that of a scholar or intellectual but rather that of a man who worked with his hands and undoubtedly involved in the building trade. *Two:* the ill-fitting clothes were not his and had presumably been put on the corpse after his death, a grisly and challenging task. *Ergo:* 'Bartolomeo da Siracusa' was not the man he was supposed to be. In fact 'Bartolomeo' hadn't existed at all. Somebody had invented him.

Three: that being so, the documents found on his body were as false as 'Bartolomeo' himself. *Four:* the allegations against Brunelleschi and Donatello were as false as the documents. *Ergo:* Donatello was right: it was all a plot. But to what end – and by whom? He had a hunch that the slippery notary Giovanni Ferrante was involved in some way, but he couldn't have acted alone.

"More wine?" It was the waiter, interrupting Luca's thoughts.

"No, thanks."

"How was the *carbonata*?"

Luca pointed at his empty plate, wiped clean. "As you see, very tasty. Perhaps a bit salty."

The waiter tapped the side of his nose. "Makes you drink all the more. Good for wine sales."

Luca was about to reply when a door opened from one of the rooms in the gallery above and a woman walked along the balcony and began descending the stairs. Luca stared and the waiter stopped clearing the table, Luca's empty plate in mid-air. The card players fell silent and even the lone man lifted his head from contemplation of the pitcher.

She was tall and her long blonde hair tumbled in waves, half hiding her face, with its rosy cheeks and a small pointed chin. It was clear that she was well aware of the impression she'd made on all the men in the room as she descended, her shoulders held back, a slight smile on her lips. She stopped at the bottom of the stairs and looked round the room with her light-blue eyes. Luca would have been captivated by these alone had his own eyes not been pulled inexorably downward.

The woman was wearing a full-length dress in carmine pink with long-sleeves. Low-cut, it was surmounted by a bodice in black velvet, tight-laced at the front with black cord though brass eyelets. Her firm breasts, two golden pomegranates, were constrained and upthrust, demanding attention, and it was with some difficulty that Luca dragged his eyes again to the woman's face. She turned and walked slowly to the far end of the room, every man watching her rounded buttocks under the pink dress as she bent to pour herself some wine from a barrel into a *caraffa* and settled herself at a far table.

For a second or two, although it felt longer, the figures in the room seemed frozen in time, like a fresco on a chapel wall, though the subject matter was far less pious. The only movement was the woman sipping her wine. Then, almost simultaneously, all the men breathed out and the room became animated again. Luca tried again to smooth down his hair. The waiter picked up his empty beaker and placed it on the plate. One of the card players dealt another hand and the lone man returned to his quiet contemplation of the pitcher in front of him. The door in the gallery above opened again and a man, his black cloak about his face, came rapidly down the stairs and out of the front door.

Still staring at the woman, Luca asked the waiter: "Who is that? Is she the owner?"

The waiter laughed: "God save you, no." He lent down towards Luca's ear. "That's *La Bionda*. Best whore in the whole of this parish, and beyond I dare say. Cost you half-a-week's wages, but worth every *soldo*."

16

Luca told the waiter that he'd changed his mind and, yes, he would have another beaker of wine after all. He looked surreptitiously across the room at *La Bionda*, watching her as she teased the waiter on his way to get Luca's drink and then flirting with one of the card players who'd moved over to her table. The man's back obscured much of his view, but Luca could still see the glorious tumble of blonde hair and the sensuous mound of her breast straining in the bodice, illuminated by the flickering firelight. His wine arrived and he continued his furtive glances as he sipped it. Minutes passed.

"Will that be all, Squire?" The waiter's voice interrupted his reverie. Good Lord, what was he doing sitting there? He'd vital information about the plot to destroy Brunelleschi and Donatello and who knows what else besides, and here he was daydreaming in a tavern. He asked what he owed and was paying, using most of the few coins he had in his purse, coins that had come from the cornucopia of Donatello's generous satchel, when the waiter asked: "Did you hear about that horrible murder in the baptistry square this morning? Battered to death he was. They reckon that Donatello did it, with one of his sculpting hammers. And that Brunelleschi's involved, too."

Luca hurried out into the street as old Sant' Ambrogio's bell tolled five. He needed to tell someone about his discoveries. But who? Filippo Brunelleschi and Donatello had been summoned to the *Bargello*. He could go there and voice his suspicions, but somehow he felt that his revelations would only muddy the waters. And if there was a plot, it was one instigated by powerful enemies, so it would be better to enlist influential friends before going anywhere near the authorities. He'd tell his uncle Battista, who was well connected in the city. He'd know what to do next.

When he reached the workshops of the *Opera del Duomo*, however, the doorkeeper came running out to meet him. "Where've you been? The *Provveditore*'s been looking for you. He said that as soon as you showed up you were to get over to the Medici house as fast as you could. He's been summoned there and needs your help."

"Help with what?"

"He didn't say. He's not going to tell me anyway, is he? He just said 'Get that lad over there *rapidamente.*' He was in a right mood, I can tell you, what with his work being interrupted again and so much to do."

So Luca set off on yet another ten-minute walk, to the Medici house near the church of *San Tommaso*. He was expected and a servant took him up to the library, where he found Battista sitting at a desk near the window, with a jumble of papers all around him.

There were books everywhere in the room, some lying on chests, others stacked on shelves and in open cupboards. As well as elegantly bound modern volumes, there were dilapidated old books and ancient parchment scrolls wound around rollers, but Luca had no time to admire any of them, for his uncle growled: "Here you are at last. Pull up a chair and look at these. I've been puzzling over them for ages and they don't make any sense at all." Luca did as he was told and Battista held up some pages, which he recognised instantly as those Giovanni Ferrante had discovered on the body in the baptistry piazza.

"Before we start, Uncle," Luca said, "I have to tell you that there was something peculiar about that Sicilian."

"And I have to tell you there's something peculiar about these papers."

"Yes, that's because ..."

"Look, here we are. First diagram. Vertical section through a dome. All very well as far as it goes, but it doesn't go very far. Second diagram. Detail of the two dome shells. Not much better. It's as if somebody just went and looked at what we've built and made a drawing of it."

"Yes, uncle, that's probably because ..." But Battista was in no mood to listen. He handed Luca diagram after diagram.

"None of them tell us anything about how to make a dome without centring and there's nothing here about how to withstand all the forces on the dome as it gets heavier and begins to turn inwards. Except perhaps this..."

He handed Luca a sheet on which there was a diagram of a dozen bricks laid out in a herring-bone pattern. "When I saw this page I believed that we were on to something. Laying the bricks like this is a real innovation. But when I looked at it in detail I realised it didn't show us <u>why</u> they were laid in this particular way, how the forces got distributed so the weight didn't pull the whole lot to the ground. Again it just looked like someone's made a diagram of what we've built, but they've no idea why it was built like that. Look, there's arrows pointing this way and that, but it's just meaningless. I could no more build the dome from this than I could fly."

"Yes, uncle, that's what I've been trying to tell you. Bartolomeo da Siracusa is a fake and the documents are forgeries."

"What on earth are you talking about?"

So Luca had to explain that 'Bartolomeo da Siracusa' was not who he seemed to be and, that being the case, the papers, too, were fakes. Luca didn't see the point of telling Battista about his fears in the mortuary chapel, nor of his unfortunate error in identifying the body as Jacopo Alderici. This was too much detail, he felt.

It took Battista a moment or two to assimilate the information. "Fake, forgery ...," he muttered holding a sheet up to the light of the window as if it would reveal some hidden writing. "So, it's a plot. Definitely a plot. We must tell Cosimo de' Medici. He'll know what to do." He got up abruptly from the desk, opened the library door and shouted for a servant.

17

No more than two dozen *braccia* away Cosimo and the Cardinal were still sitting at the chestnut dining table in the great hall. Their meal was long finished, but there was a silver salver of preserved Apio apples on the table. Cosimo remembered that these had been Luigi's particular favourite when they had spent Summers together in their youth at the Medici villa in the *contado*, the Florentine hinterland. They'd watched the cook grate and sieve the apples, boil them with honey, then add sweet spices. The mixture was spread on a board, allowed to cool and harden, then cut into squares before being stored in a box with layers of bay leaves. Luigi had always been impatient, sneaking into the kitchen to steal a square or two (or three or four) and earning, on one occasion at least, a rap over the knuckles from the cook. Today's preserved apples had been cut into elegant diamond shapes, served on a bed of fresh bay leaves, and the Cardinal had lost none of his youthful enthusiasm for them.

Chewing contentedly, he cast his eyes over a marble *rilievo schiacciato* panel hanging on the wall. It depicted Diana and Actaeon, at the moment when the doomed huntsman sees the beautiful goddess and her female companions bathing naked in a stream. The 'flattened relief' technique used both finely engraved chiseled lines and subtle carving, so the creamy marble reacted to the light, producing a variety of textures and showing up the most delicate features of the sculpture.

"A magnificent work, so lustrous, so serene." said the Cardinal. "Donatello's, of course?"

"Yes, inspired by the discoveries on perspective made by Brunelleschi."

"Inspired by God, I hope you mean."

Cosimo considered that for a Cardinal his cousin was in danger of becoming far too religious. He'd always had a serious side, even when young, and he now seemed to be deeply involved with all this theology. He'd taken to making (dare one say it) pontifical remarks about all sort of issues, but especially about Humanism, Cosimo's particular passion.

Cosimo said. "Surely we can agree that the sculpture is truly beautiful – and that beauty represents inner virtue." He added hastily: "It's an essential part of our journey towards God."

"Well, that's as maybe. What concerns me is that you Humanists seem to believe, for example, that your cathedral's dome will rise or fall through Man's efforts alone and that God has no part in it."

Cosimo answered: "Of course we believe in God and his almighty power."

"May the Lord be praised for that! But you also believe in human autonomy?"

"In the capacity of humans to make independent decisions? Yes, we do."

The Cardinal looked his cousin in the eye: "But can't you see the difficulties that the concept of self-determination can make for the church's teaching that all things emanate from God."

"Yes, and our God-given creative and intellectual potential should be used to the full," said Cosimo. "The classical philosophers show us how we can make the world a better place through our own efforts."

"Those ancient Greeks and Romans you think so much of were all pagans," said the Cardinal, "unenlightened by the teachings of our Blessed Saviour, Jesus Christ."

Cosimo smiled: "Yes, Luigi, but it's perfectly logical to argue that they were inspired by God the Father. It's our duty to try to understand God's purpose – and to help bring it about."

"Dangerous territory, Cosimo. *Canst thou by searching find out God?* I think not!" Further discussion, however, was curtailed by the entry of a servant who came over to Cosimo and whispered in his ear.

"My apologies, Luigi," Cosimo said when the servant had finished speaking, "no doubt we'll continue this argument later, but that was word from Battista to say that he's examined the Sicilian's papers and needs to talk to us urgently."

"We'll go to him at once, of course." said the Cardinal, rising and taking another piece of preserved apple from the dish.

18

The aroma of frying chicken calmed Giovanni Ferrante's troubled mind. The portions spluttered in the hot pork fat as he turned them with a spoon. He found cooking very soothing, perhaps the only thing in his life that pleased him. The Lord knew he had enough to put up with, what with arrogant incompetents in the *Opera del Duomo* and in the city administration; a father who seemed intent on squandering all their money at the backgammon table; and a malicious madman who had him in his clutches and was, seemingly, never going to let him go.

In the past his wife had cooked for him and his father, who had lived with them, but when she died seven years ago he'd taken to preparing supper himself. His housekeeper Fidelia made the mid-day dinner. She was perfectly competent and more than willing "to leave something for you to heat up" for the evening. But one day he'd taken a fancy to cook a meal himself and he found he enjoyed the whole process, from selecting the best meats and vegetables in the market all the way to arranging the dish on a platter so that it was pleasing to look at as well as good to taste.

"It's the only time I see that sour face of yours relax," his father had said one Friday evening as he tucked into a plate of succulent fish, "and I must say you seem to know what you're doing . Truly delicious!"

Giovanni had acknowledged the compliment with a thin smile, and there was no denying his pride in preparing an especially delicious dish. Curiously enough, although he enjoyed tasting his creations as he was cooking them, he still had a tiny appetite and picked at his food while his father cleaned his plate.

Tonight's meal was particularly significant, since not only was his father going to eat it, but he was going to take some to Donatello too. At around five o'clock he'd called into the palazzo of the *Bargello* to see whether the sculptor and his crony Brunelleschi had obeyed the Podestà's summons. The architect hadn't turned up, but Donatello had and, after some further questioning by the Podestà's man, had been arrested on suspicion of Bartolomeo's murder. He was now confined in a cell on the first floor of the palazzo.

It was a relief to Giovanni to know that he would not have to poison Brunelleschi. He couldn't think why. After all, he'd hated the man for decades. But there was still Donatello to be dealt with and, after considering all his options in the face of Niccolò Peruzzi's ultimatum, he'd resolved on the only course of action he could see open to him. He'd bought a chicken and some pork fat *lardo* at the butcher's and some dried ground ginger at the spice merchants – and he'd run some crucial personal errands as well, to a bank, to a lawyer's office and to an inn near the *Porta al Prato*.

The chicken was ready now, a golden-brown all over, so he poured water and some sour grape juice over the four portions in the heavy-bottomed casserole and waited for it to come to the boil. He added a little of the ginger, some ground mace and cinnamon and a few golden-yellow threads of saffron, then covered the casserole and moved it to the cooler embers on the fire so that the dish would simmer gently.

As he walked across the large first-floor room, which was used for sitting as well as dining and cooking, he could see through the doorway of his father's bedroom where the old man was dozing. On a long, low chest beside the bed there was a backgammon board with a game in progress. He's been playing against himself, Giovanni thought; it's the only time he ever wins.

Moving to his desk by the window, he unlocked the drawer and took out some sheets of paper on which he began writing, slowly and painstakingly. The process involved the copying of the signature of one of the administrators of the Signoria and the use of wax seals and a short length of thick red ribbon. After half an hour or so, satisfied with his work, he sanded the final sheet to dry the ink, then blew it off. He put the papers in his satchel and burned everything else on the fire, including the contents of the desk drawer.

Returning to the casserole, he checked that the chicken was cooked, piercing a thigh with a knife, noting with satisfaction that the meat was tender and the juices ran clear. Now it was time to make the sauce, but he prepared only one portion, beating up an egg yolk and more sour grape juice in a saucepan, bring the mixture just to the boil over a low heat. He ladled out a chicken leg on to a fine cream-coloured ceramic plate, poured over the sauce, wiped the edges of the plate clean, nipped out a sprig of basil growing in a pot on the windowsill and placed it on top of the chicken.

His father was still sleeping, so he called through the bedroom door: "Supper, father. Time for supper."

"What?" said his father as he woke. "Double – and re-double!"

Giovanni sighed as he placed his father's plate on the table and poured some clear blonde *trebbiano* wine into two pewter goblets.

Yawning as he came into the room, the old man said: "What, just one plate? You not eating tonight?"

"I have an appointment. I'll eat later."

"You're always working. Want to get out more. You know what they say about all work and no play."

"Yes, father, so you've told me many times. But I'll take a glass of wine with you."

After they sat at the table they toasted each other: "*Salute*, Giovanni."

"Your health too, father."

"This smells rather good," said the old man, before tucking into the chicken. "and it tastes excellent," he said between mouthfuls. "Does it have a name?"

"*Gratonata di pollo*," his son replied. "I am glad you like it."

As he ate the old man talked about his plans for the evening: "I've also got an important meeting tonight – with that old rascal Bernardino and the backgammon table. Worked out a new strategy. Can't fail. Double and re-double, just at the right moment. That's the way to do it."

"I'm sure you're right!"

"What, no scolding? You generally go on at me like some wife-y nagging her husband to death."

"It's *my* new strategy, father," said Giovanni, allowing himself a tight smile. "My old one seemed as unsuccessful as yours at backgammon."

Giovanni's father had the grace to look abashed. "Well, yes, I must admit things haven't exactly gone to plan, but with this new technique ..."

"I wish you luck, father."

The old man finished the plate of chicken and, scraping back his chair, got up from the table. "I'll be off then."

Giovanni rose too and, in a sudden, awkward gesture, embraced his father, who looked very surprised.

"You all right, Giovanni? You're in a funny mood tonight."

"I'm well, father."

"Well, you take care of yourself. You could be sickening for something."

"And you take care too," said Giovanni as the old man left the room and walked to the stairs to collect his evening cloak.

After he heard the front door close he went to the fire and prepared a larger portion of sauce, pouring it over the remaining three pieces of chicken in the casserole. He put some cloths in the bottom of his wicker shopping basket, to ensure the base wouldn't burn, and placed the casserole in the basket, covering it with another cloth with light blue checks. Then, pausing only to collect his satchel and pull on a dark-brown hooded cloak, he descended the stairs with the basket.

As he left the house he noticed a thick-set, bull-necked man with a shaven head lingering on the corner of the street, whom he recognised as one of Niccolò's gang of thugs. The man had obviously been sent to check that the notary had carried out his instructions, but Giovanni was quite happy to be followed as he set off for the *Bargello*.

19

In the Medici house, Luca was overawed to be in the presence of not just one, but two illustrious personages. The Cardinal swept into the library, a field of scarlet silk, followed by Cosimo de' Medici, still in the simple crimson gown and matching brimless cap he had been wearing in the morning.

Battista d'Antonio was standing by the desk, clutching 'Bartolomeo's' papers, when the Cardinal entered. He dropped them untidily on the desktop, a couple of sheets drifting to the floor, and made an awkward bobbing movement, a vague parody of a woman's curtsey, before bending forward to kiss the gold papal ring on the Cardinal's extended hand. Luca followed suit, flustered, not quite knowing whether to grab the proffered hand or just kiss the air. He settled for the latter and the Cardinal smiled down on him.

"Bless you, my son," he murmured. "Shall we all sit? It's a hot day and we should rest our bodies while we exercise our minds." He chose the largest chair, in dark oak with a red leather cushion on it. It creaked as he sat and Luca noticed that Cosimo de' Medici gave a slight wince. I'll bet that's his favourite chair, he mused, where he sits when he's reading all these old books. But the banker smiled and took another, smaller chair next to the prelate.

"I'd rather stand, if it's all the same to your Eminence," said Battista, signalling with a gesture of his hand that Luca, who was just beginning to sit, should remain upright too. Battista picked up the papers from the desk, Luca retrieving the ones from the floor and putting them neatly on the table.

"At your command," Battista began, looking at Cosimo, "I have been examining these papers. And I must say they were a mystery to me. It's Luca here who solved the problem. He's my nephew, Luca Pasini, better known here as Luca da Posara, the village from where he comes."

"Posara?" said Cosimo, "Where on earth is that?

"It's near the town of Fivizzano, sir," said Luca nervously, "er, in the area of Lunigiana, north of Massa and the marble mountains of Carrara."

"Ah, yes. Border territory. One is never quite sure which power holds sway in that region. I suspect currently it's the Duke of Milan, or one of those dratted Malaspinas."

"Yes, sir," said Luca, who was ignorant of the politics of Northern Italy.

"The thing is," said Battista, waving the sheets, "they're all rubbish, forgeries. And the man who wrote them, or rather didn't, isn't who he says he is, or was, since he's dead."

"Slow down, my dear Battista," said Cosimo, "Try to take it step by step. You're confusing us."

"I think I'd better let my nephew explain, Sir."

And so, diffidently and hesitatingly at first, but with growing confidence, Luca again outlined his discoveries about the body and the forged documents.

"I see, said Cosimo thoughtfully, "and you're sure of all this?"

"Well, I'm as sure as I can be, Sir. The clothes aren't the corpse's and the hands aren't those of an intellectual, Sicilian or otherwise. Bartolomeo da Siracusa is the man who never was!"

"Hmm. In that case ..." But Cosimo could say no more as the Cardinal interrupted.

"You know what this reminds me of? The Tale of the Fat Woodworker. You'll remember it, Cosimo? Must have been the best part of twenty years ago, but how we all laughed. A tale worthy of Boccaccio himself."

Luca was bemused and it seemed the Cardinal could see the bewilderment in his face, for he spoke directly to him as he continued.

"It was all in the finest tradition of our Florentine *beffe*, and at the centre of the hoax was none other than Filippo Brunelleschi – and young Donatello was very much involved too, as I recollect. Brunelleschi believed he'd been insulted in some way, I never knew what, and went to enormous lengths to convince the man ..."

The Cardinal looked at Cosimo:"What was his name? He had a shop near San Giovanni, working in wood, a specialist in *intarsia*, making inlaid prayer tables, sacristry wardrobes and so on. We had one in our parish when I was a priest here. What was his name?"

"Manetto Ammannatini," said Cosimo, "but is this really relevant? It seems to me ..."

The Cardinal was not to be diverted from his story. Still addressing Luca he said: "Manetto, that's it. Manetto, the Fat Woodworker. The story made him famous. Now where was I? Brunelleschi and half a dozen cronies took the greatest of pains to convince Manetto that he wasn't Manetto at all, but rather some other man, called ..."

"Matteo," said Cosimo, "but ..."

"Yes, Matteo. For three days Manetto believed that he had somehow been transmogrified into a ne'er-do-well called Matteo. It was an elaborate plot, all conceived by Brunelleschi and acted out by him and his friends. They got Matteo's brothers involved, Donatello addressed Manetto as Matteo in the street, they even had him put in *Le Stinche*, briefly, for debt. For a day or more he truly believed he was Matteo. Poor man, he was very upset when he found out he wasn't, but the rest of us laughed for weeks – and Filippo Brunelleschi was admired all the more for his ingenuity and meticulous planning."

"Well, the rumour round the cathedral works is that Filippo was involved in this plot, too, and that Donatello killed the man in a rage," said Battista.

Luca was becoming increasingly impatient with the turn of the conversation. Surely if the Sicilian wasn't who we thought he was, and the papers were false, then the plot was concocted by someone else, to implicate Brunelleschi or Donatello and damage the Medici. But the older men seemed bound up in their reminiscences, even Cosimo, who said: "Ah, Donatello! He has a reputation for being friendly and courteous and it's true he has the sweetest disposition most of the time. But he can easily lose his temper, especially when artistic projects are under threat. I remember that Genovese merchant he made bronze heads for. Were you here at the time Luigi?"

"I don't think I was."

"There was a dispute about the price. They both came here for me to arbitrate. We met on the roof terrace and Donatello put the bronze head on the parapet. He said they'd agreed forty florins for it, but the merchant said it was so small that it was worth half that. He reckoned Donatello had worked on it for no more than a month. He'd pay twenty florins and that would give him more than half a florin a day.

"Donatello took this as a personal insult. He'd worked on it for many months, he said, and he'd specially made it small and light so it was easily portable. Then he shouted: 'But I've found a way to destroy it in a hundredth part of an hour' and he gave the head a sudden blow and knocked it down into the courtyard, where it broke into a dozen pieces.

"He told the man he should stick to arguing about the price of beans, not statues. If I hadn't been there, I think he would have hit him. So he'd be quite capable of murdering a man in a rage."

Luca's exasperation got the better of him. He blurted out: "Gentlemen, this is all beside the point. The men who killed Bartolomeo were not Brunelleschi and Donatello. It was done to destroy their reputations, delay the dome project and, by implication, to cause damage to the Medici's standing in the city."

Luca's uncle Battista looked very embarrassed by this outburst and even the Cardinal's benign smile seemed frozen, but Cosimo looked at Luca with quiet composure, nodding his head. "This young man's quite right. We've allowed ourselves to be carried away by our reminiscences. What we need now is logic, not story-telling. So, Luca da Posara, let us proceed logically. Take us through your conclusions once more."

Battista noticeably relaxed and the Cardinal's smile was warm once more, so Luca went through the main points again. "*One*, a person or persons unknown killed a man. This was a complicated plot, so quite a few people are likely to have been involved. *Two*, they dressed the corpse in someone else's clothes, to make him seem other than he was, and beat his head into a pulp so no-one would recognise him. *Three*, they planted false documents on the body to make everyone think he was a Sicilian mathematician with damning evidence against Brunelleschi.

"*Four*, they can't have murdered him in the square. It must have been done earlier, then the body hidden, probably under one of the stalls, to be 'discovered' this morning..."

"Why do you suppose they had to kill him?" Cosimo asked.

"I suppose the first idea might have been for him to make the allegations himself, but he would have had to have been a first-rate performer and I don't think his story would have stood up to cross-examination."

"Particularly if Brunelleschi got hold of him," said Cosimo. "So he could tell a better tale if he were dead."

"I think so."

"And of course, if Giovanni Ferrante had kept the papers and presented them to the Consuls of the Wool Guild tomorrow, and if you hadn't cast doubts on the identity of the body, we'd all have been taken in."

"Quite right," said the Cardinal, "and let's move on to points *Five* and *Six*. *Five*, whoever did this had power, money, nerve and determination. *Six*, the motive is undoubtedly political and the object is to disgrace Cosimo and the Medici. Our problem is that there are so many powerful families in Florence – ruthless and determined ones – that it could be anyone of them, the Strozzi, the Capponi, the Albizzi ... A man makes enemies as he rises to the top."

"True," said Cosimo," but that slippery notary Ferrante must have been involved. When he discovered those papers he knew far too much about the contents to have been reading them for the first time."

"Funny you should say that," said the Cardinal, "when I was looking through them myself I felt I was in the presence of a notary's hand. Something in the phraseology, I think, those over-formal sentences. Why don't we question him? I am sure we can find ways of making him talk."

"We will, but perhaps it might be better to do so at the Wool Guild meeting tomorrow. That way we'll disgrace him publicly and all Florence will know of his downfall in an hour."

"Well, yes, but you still won't know who his backers are."

"We will soon after we've arrested him for forgery."

"Well, I still think it might be better to question him now. The Inquisitor could help."

Their conversation was interrupted by a soft knock on the door and the entry of a servant who came to whisper in Cosimo's ear.

Cosimo stood, looking solemn: "Gentlemen, Donatello has been imprisoned on suspicion of murder and there's a warrant out for Brunelleschi's arrest."

20

Luca watched as Cosimo once again took control of the situation. At first glance the banker did not look particularly prepossessing, being of less than medium height, with a long nose, beetle brows, and those large protruding ears. But his brown eyes were clear, his voice was firm and he was again as decisive as he had been in the baptistry square that morning.

"Our first task is to get Brunelleschi out of harm's way," he said and, turning to the servant who'd brought the message, he told him: "Hurry to *Messer* Filippo's house and bring him here. He'll stay with us tonight. Take two other men with you and brook no argument. Bring him by force if you need to." He turned to the Cardinal: "Donatello's in the *Bargello* and I'm concerned about what might happen to him there overnight. We must ensure he's safe. With your permission, Luigi, I would like to use your Secretary Don Antonio for that task."

"Of course," replied the prelate, "I'll go and get him myself."

Battista, who was gathering up all 'Bartolomeo's' papers into a pile, said: "It didn't take long for those rumours to have their effect."

"The flames are being fanned, certainly. We must be careful not to be burned," the Cardinal said as he left.

He returned a few minutes later with Don Antonio, a tall, imposing man in his early twenties and Cosimo explained what had happened. He added: "It's disturbing they've locked Donatello up in the *Bargello* itself, instead of *Le Stinche*. I'm sure I'll be able to get him out tomorrow, but it's going to be impossible tonight. We need to look out for him, Don Antonio, and make sure no-one gets to him. Poison, the stiletto and the garrote are all too often the instruments of policy in our poor republic."

"He'll be well guarded, no doubt," said the priest.

"I will provide you with a letter which should get you into the palazzo, and I'm sure His Eminence will do the same." He added, giving a tight little laugh: "I'll also provide you with a pouch or two of florins which I am sure will open more doors."

Luca, alarmed at the potential threats to Donatello, asked: "May I go as well. He's my good friend and I'm also worried about his safety."

Cosimo seemed reluctant to let Luca go, but Don Antonio said: "Let him come with me. I'd be glad of some company and I'll see he's safe."

And so, half-an-hour later, Luca found himself walking down the *Via dei Leoni* carrying a basket containing cold chicken, a dozen preserved apricots and some red wine in a stout *caraffa* plugged temporarily with a cloth, a meal prepared for Donatello by the Medici kitchen. Neither man noticed the notary Giovanni Ferrante, brown-cloaked and hooded, scurrying down the street, but they did see a bull-necked man, who crossed their path as they approached the forbidding walls of the *Bargello*.

It proved surprisingly easy to get in. The captain of the guard was impressed by the letters from Cosimo de' Medici and, in particular, from the Cardinal, which had an impressive red seal attached to it, bearing the impression of his ecclesiastical coat of arms. The captain took them through a series of dim passageways and up a flight of stairs, arriving finally at a landing and an iron gate beyond which was an anteroom with two barred cells side by side at the rear. There was no natural light and two candles in dull brass holders on an untidy desk did little to enliven the gloom.

"I've got more visitors for you, Giulio," the captain called out.

"What, more? It's like market day in here." A gaunt misshapen man got up from the desk and brought a candle to the iron gate.

"What's all this then?" he asked, thrusting his pinched, foxy face forward. Luca could see the salt-and-pepper stubble on his chin and smell the man's rank body odour, coupled with a blast of garlic when he opened his mouth.

Another voice cried out from the gloom of one of the cells: "Who's that? Help get me out of here."

"Shut up you," said the jailer.

"It's all right Donatello. It's me, Luca. Help is at hand."

Unlike the captain of the guard, however, the jailer seemed less inclined to be influenced by the letters or by Don Antonio's powers of persuasion. It was only when the priest held up a leather pouch, and shook it so the coins within jingled, that the man, still grumbling, shuffled to the desk, picked up a metal ring with several keys on it and came back to unlock the gate, extracting the pouch from Don Antonio's hand with a swift, deft movement.

"Very well, but make it quick."

Luca rushed over to the cell where Donatello was held. "Are you all right? I was so worried about you."

Donatello thrust his arm though the bars, squeezing Luca's hand long and hard. "Thank God you are here. Have you come to get me out?"

"I don't think we'll be able to do that tonight. But we're here to see you come to no harm."

"Yes, it had struck me this is not the safest place to be."

"We'll get you out in the morning."

"The morning! I'll starve to death before then. I never got any dinner." He lowered his voice: "Some other well-wisher brought me food ten minutes ago, but that bastard of a jailer refuses to hand it over. I think he's going to eat it himself, despite being bribed to give it to me."

He pointed over to the desk, beside which sat a wicker basket covered with a blue check cloth. "Bring it over to me, would you. Seeing it sitting there is driving me mad."

"For goodness sake, don't touch that, whatever you do," said Luca in alarm. "It's probably poisoned! Here, I've got some proper food." He reached into his own basket and handed Donatello a leg of chicken. "And I've got some wine." He tried to push the *caraffa* through the bars, but the space between them was too narrow. Looking back towards the desk he saw that Don Antonio and the jailer were having an intense conversation. The priest towered over the small man and was talking animatedly, but the jailer still shook his head. Another pouch of coins, however, seemed to resolve the matter and in the end he nodded.

Don Antonio came over to the cell door and Luca introduced him to Donatello. The priest said: "I've managed to persuade that man to let me stay here through the night. He's going to lock me in the cell next to yours. I don't expect we'll sleep much, but we can have interesting discussions on art and its religious implications."

"Being locked in with a priest and talking about religion is not my idea of heaven," said Donatello, rather ungratefully, taking another bite of chicken. "But I suppose it's better than the alternative."

Don Antonio spoke to Luca: "He'll only allow one of us to stay and it'll have to be me, so you must go home. Donatello will be perfectly safe with me next door." The priest's face broke into a smile and he seemed so sure of himself and his abilities that Luca was convinced that all would be well. Don Antonio signalled to the jailer, who came over to unlock the gate of the second cell. Pausing only to pick up the basket containing the provisions brought from the Medici house and the *caraffa*, the priest entered the cell and was locked in.

"But the wine, "said Luca, "the *caraffa* won't go though the bars."

"Fear not," said the priest, removing two pewter goblets from the copious pocket of his cassock. "It always pays to think ahead."

"Come on you. Let's get you out of here," said the jailer. Luca gave his friend's hand another squeeze through the bars and, picking up the basket covered in the blue check cloth, moved to the outer gate, which the jailer had already unlocked and by which he was waiting impatiently.

21

Standing once more beside Niccolò Peruzzi's dining table, Giovanni Ferrante felt a sense of elation. Perhaps it was because earlier in the afternoon, after several hours of inner turmoil, he'd finally taken a decision on his course of action. After that, implementation seemed almost mechanical, each step following the other without any need to consider the consequences. It reminded him of fishing as a boy, watching his float gently moving downstream and having, from time to time, to reposition it, a task achieved without conscious thought, so that the minutes passed in an almost dreamlike sequence.

He took care to disguise his feelings from Niccolò. This man had hidden antennae alert to anything that might threaten him, as a fly seems always to be able to detect, and move away from, the hand descending to swat it.

"So, *Ser* Giovanni, the deed is done." Niccolò adjusted his bulk on the seat. "Pity Brunelleschi wasn't there as well, but Donatello's death will show those damned Medici that their enemies are not to be disregarded."

"Yes ... but I feel sick to my stomach. I should never have done it."

"But you did, *Ser* Giovanni, you did. Our potion will take a little time to act, but by the morning Donatello will be no more."

"May the saints preserve me! So terrible."

"Get yourself under control, man. It is done now and I'll make sure you're well rewarded."

"But what's going to happen to me?" asked Giovanni, thinking of his soul.

"Why, when we Peruzzi are in power, you'll be wealthy and well regarded in the city. And your father will no longer be in our debt," Niccolò replied, apparently seeing only temporal outcomes.

"I must get away for a few days, maybe a week or more, said Giovanni. "To calm myself and let the storm over Donatello's death blow over. The jailer knows me and who knows how long he'll keep quiet."

"There were no problems getting in?"

"Not with the aid of your silver. The jailer was most obliging. I saw him take the poisoned dish to Donatello's cell with my own eyes. How I wish I hadn't."

"This simple assignment seems thoroughly to have discomposed you, Giovanni." Niccolò pondered for a moment. "Very well, you may leave the city, <u>after</u> you have attended the Wool Guild meeting tomorrow afternoon. We need you there to ensure Bartolomeo's story is believed – and to get those documents into the hands of the Podestà."

Niccolò rose from his seat and turned to the shelves in the wall fountain behind him, selecting the brass-bound box and placing it on the table. He unlocked it and brought out a semicircular leather purse, which he pushed across to Giovanni before re-locking the box.

"As you say, it might be wisest for you to go away for a while. In that purse you'll find fifty florins. That should help to keep you safe from harm."

"Most generous, My Lord."

"Where will you go?"

"To Greve," the answer came out smoothly, as Giovanni had planned. "A cousin of my late wife's is sacristan in the church of *Santa Croce* there. It's only twenty miles away, and as it's on the *Via Francigena*, there are lots of pilgrims about and they're used to strange faces. And I'm not known in the town."

Giovanni realised he was beginning to gabble and was grateful when Niccolò, still standing, leaned over to take a tiny silver bell from the table and, having rung it, said: "Excuse me one moment. I have some urgent business. I shan't be more than a minute or two. Perhaps you'd care to be seated and count your florins while you are waiting." He opened a door beside the fireplace and went through it, pulling it behind him.

Feeling the rapid and erratic beating of his heart, Giovanni was glad to take a seat. He shook out the purse and began to count the coins. But he heard the murmur of voices and he noticed that the door though which Niccolò had just left was not completely shut. There was a gap, half the length of a man's thumb.

On the spur of the moment and with a silent speed that surprised him, Giovanni went to the door and put his eye to the crack. He saw Niccolò in the room beyond, talking with the bull-necked man with the shaven head. They spoke in an undertone and it was hard to hear what they were saying, but the words '*Santa Croce* in Greve' and 'tomorrow' stood out and, as the man turned to go, Niccolò's final words were crystal clear: "And bring me back my fifty florins."

Giovanni hardly had time to resume his seat before Niccolò returned, looking at him rather oddly, he felt. But the he merely said: "All correct, *Ser* Giovanni?"

"I am sure, Sir, but I had no need to count them. I trust you completely," Giovanni said, brushing the coins back into the purse.

"Then you should be on your way."

Standing, Giovanni wondered whether he ought to make some formal farewell, but Niccolò had picked up the brass-bound box and turned away from him to put it back on the shelf. Giovanni's knees felt like straw as he crossed the room and left by the far door. Gaining the street, he found that the sky had darkened and he felt a few drops of rain. He pulled his hooded cloak about him and began to walk in the direction of his house, noting that the bull-necked man was again following him.

22

At the same moment, no more than a dozen streets away, Luca was letting himself into his uncle Battista d'Antonio's house, where he lodged. The ground floor had formerly been a shop and was now used for storage: there were three dark-green *damigiane* of red wine, shelves with jars of pickled vegetables that Battista's wife, Martha, had made in the Autumn and, in an untidy corner, planks of wood, bricks, iron brackets, screws, nails and a variety of other objects, of which his uncle had said "I'll keep that. It's bound to come in useful sometime."

Luca climbed the worn internal stone stairs (don't count!), dark now although it was only just past eight o'clock, and emerged into the room on the first floor. His uncle was standing at the window, beaker in hand, looking out into the street, while his aunt stirred a chubby iron pot suspended on a chain hanging from a metal rod over the fireplace. She looked up as Luca came in, her rosy face illuminated by the flames: "Why, here he is at last! You poor boy, you must be exhausted. What a day you've had! Give him a beaker of wine, Battista, and I'll see to some supper. You'll be famished. Sit yourself down."

Luca put the basket in a corner beyond the fireplace and gratefully took a seat at the dining table as his uncle poured him a beaker of wine and topped up his own. Battista lit the three stubby white candles in brass holders and sat down opposite his nephew.

"Well, as the wife says, what a day!"

"Well, at least Donatello's safe. Don Antonio's sleeping with him."

"Given Donatello's reputation, you might've phrased that a bit better," said his uncle.

Luca blushed: "No, I didn't mean ... he's locked in the cell next to him."

"Only joking, lad." Battista took a gulp of wine. "But it *has* been a peculiar day, what with corpses who are someone else and papers that don't mean what they say. I'm glad you've sorted it all out. Perhaps I can get back to work on the dome tomorrow. I've done hardly anything all day."

"There's still a man brutally murdered," said Luca, rubbing a hand through his unruly brown hair, "and whoever did it ought to be brought to justice. Isn't that what your 'civic humanism', of which you Florentines are so proud, is all about."

"That's a bit above me," said his uncle. "All I know is that we've got to get this dome built. And when we do, that'll be the pride of Florence."

His aunt arrived with spoons and a basket of bread and then, one by one, brought over steaming bowls of lentils in a meaty broth. "Get that inside you. It'll do you the power of good."

Luca was surprised to find that he was very hungry and was soon sopping up the remains from the plate with a hunk of bread. "What we do know, even if we don't know his name," he said as he ate, "is that he worked in the building trade." He looked again at Battista's scarred hands. "He was a mason, or perhaps just a day-labourer. Have you noticed anyone missing recently?"

"Well, none of the masons, except that blessed brother-in-law of yours."

"Oh, he's turned up. Didn't I tell you? I saw him this afternoon."

"Has he by God. Well, I wish he'd get off his arse and come to work," said Battista, quickly adding to his wife, "Begging your pardon, my dear."

"What about the labourers? Anyone missing there?"

"Impossible to say. As you know, we just take 'em on each day on a casual basis. Line 'em up and pick 'em out. It's impossible to remember who's there and who's not from one day to another."

Luca suddenly felt very tired. He yawned and his aunt Martha said: "Look at the poor boy, he can hardly keep his eyes open." She picked up a candlestick. "Here you are, take this up with you and get to bed. What you need is a good night's sleep."

Luca was in no mood to argue, so after saying goodnight to them both he mounted the stairs (too tired now even to count them) to his bedroom in the roof of the house, two storeys above. He fell on to his straw-filled mattress, pulling a thin coverlet over him. He was asleep within half a minute of blowing out the candle.

The first part of his night was filled with dreams of headless corpses, hooded Brothers and plaster skeletons, brought to life, dancing and cackling. He also dreamed of blonde tresses and honey-coloured breasts bulging over a tight-laced bodice, which resulted in an embarrassing damp patch in the bed.

Luca forgot all about the basket lying beside the dying embers of the fire. When Battista and his wife had gone to bed, not long after Luca himself, the cat sauntered across the room. It pulled at the blue-check covering with its paw and, after a few attempts, succeeded in dislodging it.

After the excitements of his dreams Luca fell into a deeper sleep.

23

The light was fading as Giovanni Ferrante left the Peruzzi *palazzo* and he had to hurry to get home before the curfew, after which no-one was allowed out on the streets of the city. He saw, through the corner of his eye, that the bull-necked man was following him: Niccolò was leaving nothing to chance.

He let himself into the dusky house and, climbing to the first floor, lit two candles on his desk and took off his cloak. Sneaking a look out of the window, but taking care not to be seen himself, he glimpsed a movement in a shaded doorway and guessed that the bull-necked man was waiting to ensure he'd settled in for the night. He sat at his desk for a few moments, the only movement the rapid beating of his heart, then blew out one of the candles and, taking the other, walked past the window to ensure he was in full view. Carrying his cloak under his arm, he moved to his bedroom at the rear of the house and blew out the second candle, too. He sat on the bed, retrieved the money belt from underneath it, strapping it on under his gown. It felt a bit bulky, but what could you expect from more than five hundred coins. His cloak, which he now pulled on, would cover any suspicious bulges.

He lay on his bed in the half-dark – it was a clear night and there was some moonlight – going over his plans in his mind, anxious yet at the same time excited. The curfew sounded and there was no sign of his father returning. He was still out gambling with Bernardino, no doubt, and would sleep in the tavern before returning home in the morning. After an hour or so, where every minute seemed the longest in his life, Giovanni rose and slowly felt his way down the familiar stairs, along a ground-floor corridor and out into the back yard. The latch on the wicket squeaked as he lifted it and for a moment he stood frozen. But no-one seemed to have heard and he slipped out into the narrow passageway behind the houses, full of rubbish and smelling of shit and piss.

Pulling up the hood of his cloak, he walked swiftly, ignoring the scuttling rats, turning to left or right seemingly at random, and made his way erratically, but inexorably, towards the Western end of the city. The streets were deserted now and there was no sign of the bull-necked man. Brain could outsmart brawn anytime, as long as brawn wasn't too close at hand.

When Niccolò had first outlined the plot against Brunelleschi and Donatello a month or so earlier, it had seemed like one of those elaborate *beffe*, the practical jokes that the city had enjoyed for generations. Complicated, it was true, and requiring skill and nerve to carry it off. But this *beffa*, in which he, Giovanni Ferrante, was to play such a vital part, was as clever as anything Filippo Brunelleschi had achieved, on a par with the hoax played on the fat woodworker all those years ago. Brunelleschi wasn't the only one with cunning, ingenuity and the determination to carry through a complex enterprise, as he would learn to his cost. The pity was that the plot required no-one finding out that Bartolomeo da Siracusa was not who he said he was and that Giovanni's own role should remain forever hidden.

Niccolò had told him that he'd found a talented actor who would assume the part of the Sicilian mathematician and arrive in the city during the Cardinal's visit to expose Brunelleschi and Donatello. The man would make his denunciations, hand over the papers (to Ferrante himself as Notary to the *Opera del Duomo*) and then make a quick exit.

"It's the papers that matter, not the man, Giovanni," Niccolò had said, "and only you can produce documents of such quality as to appear wholly authentic. It needs someone with a talented mind and with well developed mathematical and engineering skills."

Well, of course, he had all that, despite what Filippo Brunelleschi might tell him, or those incompetents at the *Opera*, who had rejected so many of his own proposals for the dome. He'd show them. In fact, he'd been keen to get on with the work and had listened impatiently while Niccolò outlined the allegations of foul play and the Black Arts, which were to be added to those which accused Filippo of stealing his dome-building ideas.

It had been a long task forging those twenty sheets, with many false starts and mistakes, working late into the night with a candle at his desk. He'd needed to disguise his hand and to do so he'd found he had to write very slowly, making some letters unnaturally fill with ink and splodge and run. Gradually he'd mastered the technique and there were fewer and fewer spoiled sheets to hide from his father and burn on the cooking fire as the old man slept in the late afternoon.

He'd also taken to visiting the top of the dome, which he had seldom done in the past due to his fear of heights and his suspicions of the safety of Brunelleschi's scaffolding, despite the fact that Filippo had demonstrated its stability by placing heavy weights on it and by himself jumping vigorously up and down. Pretending an interest in the progress of the works, Giovanni had looked at the stone blocks and the bricks, paying particular attention to those laid in a herring-bone pattern, which seemed to be of some significance. As soon as he'd arrived home he'd made a quick sketch and later incorporated a careful drawing of a dozen or so of these bricks into 'Bartolomeo's' papers.

"These are truly excellent, *Ser* Giovanni, or should I call you *Maestro*?" Niccolò said when he'd shown him the final version. "You should be designing the dome yourself. Soon you may well be doing so."

But then the fat young man had stopped speaking for a moment and had smiled his oily smile. "There has, however, been a slight change of plan. The papers are to be found on the dead body of the mathematician from Siracusa!"

Giovanni had been confused and unnerved, but Niccolò had explained smoothly. "It will be better if the documents are found on a body rather than presented by our player. Less chance of anything going wrong, of our man fluffing his lines." Giovanni looked at him aghast as he continued: "We've, er, found a corpse. We'll dress him in appropriate clothes and the papers will be discovered on the body. The dead Bartolomeo will be even more persuasive than the live."

Giovanni had wanted to protest and to ask, for instance: Where had this corpse been, er, found? But he realised it would be fruitless: he was already too deeply implicated to pull out, so he'd listened as Niccolò outlined the new scheme. It soon became clear to Giovanni that he was now to be the leading actor in the deception.

And how well he'd played his role: he'd made sure the body was discovered in the Cardinal's presence, he'd pointed the magistrate in

Donatello's direction (was it rather too pointedly in retrospect?) and he'd set that inveterate gossip Lorenzo Ghiberti to work, spreading, only too happily, the damning rumours about the sculptor and Brunelleschi. There, he felt, it should have ended, rivals discredited, enemies confounded. The way the corpse's head had been battered in was a shock, but there was nothing he could do about it.

But then Niccolò had asked him to murder Brunelleschi. Most men have a moral line they will not cross and for Giovanni Ferrante, misanthropic and devious though he was, murder was on the far, forbidden side of that line. And murder of a genius like Brunelleschi, even if he was rude and overbearing and even if he seemed to succeed everywhere that Giovanni had failed, was not to be contemplated. That went for Donatello, too. His ability to produce objects of such beauty was a gift from God and not to be cut short by the scheming of an evil man.

Giovanni had had to pretend to acquiesce, of course, since his protests had been so callously dismissed, and the consequences of disobedience so clearly defined, but he'd then put in train an emergency plan of his own, on which he had been working for some time.

Silently Giovanni slid through the unlit streets. There was a small scare when the night patrol came by, out to enforce the curfew, but they were noisy and he'd heard them a fair way off, so he was able to scuttle into an alleyway and shelter in a doorway as they passed on the main street, the glow of their lanterns hardly penetrating the passageway. Soon he was on his way again and within a few minutes he was at the back door of an inn near the *Porta al Prato*.

He'd been there earlier that afternoon, with a valise of clothes and a florin for the landlord, with the promise of another when he arrived that night. The landlord was to leave the back door unbolted and Giovanni's heart beat rapidly when it failed to open on his first push. It was only stiff and yielded to a stronger push with his shoulder. He was quickly inside and leaning on the wall, finding himself trembling with relief.

24

Luca slept late the next morning and was only woken by the screeches of swifts above the roof. He sat up and ran a hand over his tousled hair, but the attempt to flatten it ended, as usual, in failure. Standing on the mattress, he pushed open the skylight and poked his slim body out.

The overnight rain had washed the city clean and the tiled rooftops gleamed as they dried in the sun. He watched the swifts, marvelling at the way they soared and turned, diving at enormous speeds, swooping down by the walls of the houses and sweeping up again, unceasing, black against the azure sky. By standing on tiptoe he could see the top of Giotto's bell tower, with its white, green and red patterned stone and, just to the right, the shell of the dome rising beside it, its size emphasising the enormity of the task still to be completed. A church bell rang and Luca counted the notes.

Eight o'clock! He <u>had</u> slept late. Dropping from the skylight, Luca dressed and hurried down the wooden stairs to the first floor (twenty-four, twenty-three, oh dammit!) not forgetting to collect the slop-pail kept on his landing. He found his aunt sweeping the floor with her besom and Luisa, the pretty young girl who helped about the house, emerging from the lower stairs carrying an empty bucket. It was one of her morning tasks to pour away the excrement into the cesspit at the back of the house and she was returning with his uncle and aunt's slop-pail. If she was resentful that she would have to do it again with Luca's, she didn't show it, but rather gave him a slow, sweet smile and took the bucket from him.

"You're looking much brighter this, morning, that's for sure," said his aunt, now brushing around the fireplace, moving towards the basket with the blue-check cover Luca had left there the night before. Except the basket was no longer covered: the cloth lay untidily beside it. Luca rushed over and looked into the low casserole resting in the basket. All that remained were a few chicken bones. The sides of the dish were as clean as the doorstep of a house-proud wife.

"Aunt Martha," Luca cried, "you haven't eaten this, have you?"

His aunt peered into the dish. "Lawks a mussy! Someone enjoyed that! Not me, though, nor Battista neither. He was out of the house this morning like a rocket on *San Giovanni*'s feast day. No time to eat, had to get to work."

She called to the girl who was just leaving with Luca's slop-pail. "Luisa, have you been at this food, you naughty girl?"

"'Not me," said the girl, coming over to look. "I didn't even know it was there." She shook the slop-pail to emphasise her denial. Luca wished she hadn't.

"Must've been the cat," said his aunt.

Luca was distressed, though he kept his feelings to himself: he disliked suffering, whether it was in humans or animals. Better a dead cat than a dead genius, he told himself, but if only I'd put the basket somewhere safe the night before. I was rather fond of the cat.

"I must get to work," said Luca. "Well past eight, I'm very late."

"Don't you worry your head about that," his aunt said. "Battista told me to let you lie in, after all yesterday's troubles. 'I'll expect the lad when I see him', that's what he said."

"Well, he'll be happier to see me sooner rather than later. There's a lot to do."

Luca reached the cathedral in a matter of minutes. Within the vast space beneath the dome all was noise and bustle, seemingly chaotic, but the discerning eye could detect patterns of ordered activity. Brunelleschi's immense hoist raised half a dozen wooden planks slowly upwards in a canvas sling, the horizontal circular exertions of the ox being translated into a linear vertical motion by the system of ropes and pulleys. As the load creaked upwards it disturbed nesting pigeons, which fluttered around ineffectually for a few moments before returning to their roosts, cooing in disgruntlement. Dusty and sweaty men carried more planks to the base of the hoist and stacked them ready to be lifted, carefully supervised by Battista.

"Oh, here you are," he said as Luca approached. "Good *afternoon* to you, Luca."

"Sorry, Uncle. I slept in."

"No matter, I told Martha to let you lie. But now you are here..." Battista explained that Brunelleschi hadn't been to check the latest course of brickwork because he was still confined at Cosimo de' Medici's house. "I went over to see him earlier. Hopping mad, he is. Spitting blood you might say, but Cosimo's keeping him there until the Wool Guild meeting this afternoon. Donatello's there, too, hardly in a better mood. Cosimo sprung him from jail this morning but he's not letting him out of his sight either."

"What's *Messer* Cosimo up to?"

"I've no idea, but it's still all round town that Filippo and Donatello did the killing. Oh, by the by, *Messer* Cosimo said to tell no-one what you know."

"I haven't had a chance, but I wasn't going to anyway."

"So we'll have to wait until late this afternoon to check that brickwork." Battista looked at the creaking hoist and upwards to the rim of the dome. "In the meantime I'm getting everything I can up top and distributed round the scaffolding platforms. But at the rate we're going we'll all be dead and gone before we finish that dome."

Luca smiled at his uncle's tortuous logic, but before he could respond they were approached by a pay clerk from the offices of the *Opera del Duomo* who said he wanted to speak to Luca. His uncle turned away to direct another party of men pulling a large dressed stone on wooden rollers.

The clerk, a short man with black curly hair and thick eyebrows, said: "Sorry to bother you, but I wondered if you'd seen Rocco Rossi?

"Who?"

"Rocco Rossi. One of the day-labourers. Only he never cashed his pay chit this week and I haven't seen him for days. Of course, I normally wouldn't bother but, um, he owes me money and I'm a bit tight for cash myself."

"I don't recall him. What's he look like?"

"Well, let's see, he's sort of dark, dark skin, dark hair, um, dark eyes."

"Could be anyone. Anything else?"

The clerk pondered for a moment or two. "Well, he's a muscular sort of bloke, does a lot of heavy work here, y'know. Oh, and his hands are pretty rough and scarred, he helps the masons a lot, doing rough cutting of the stone."

Luca's brain whirled. Oh no, not again. 'Bartolomeo da Siracusa' wasn't his brother-in-law Jacopo, so could he be this Rocco Rossi? He asked the man: "Could you recognise him if you didn't see his face?"

"What d'you mean?"

"I mean, is there anything else about him that would make you know it was him and no-one else?"

The clerk looked at Luca curiously, but after a moment, then said: "Well, it's funny you should mention it, but he does have a strange birthmark. He showed it to me once. It's like the shape of one of those swords the Moors use, a scimitar isn't it? Sort of fat and curved. Anyway he's got this big birthmark. Said it proved his family had fought in the Crusades."

Oh, no, Luca repeated to himself, now there's a way of positively identifying 'Bartolomeo'. But if anyone thinks I'm going back to that mortuary chapel, they've got another think coming. Once was more than enough. And what are the Brothers going to say after I rushed out like that yesterday? Luca told the man to wait and went over to his uncle to tell him what he'd just heard.

"You'll have to go and see," Battista said, "If it is this Rocco Rossi, Cosimo will need to know."

"Well I'm not going on my own."

"I've no time to go with you. The clerk'll be there."

"I can't do it!"

Just at that moment, however, Luca saw Don Antonio, the Cardinal's Secretary, walking towards them across the North transept. He looked as fit as ever and when he reached them they could see that he was well scrubbed and well shaved and his shiny cassock was clean and crease-free. No-one would have believed he had just spent a long night in the cells. Battista explained the situation and asked if the priest would accompany Luca to the mortuary chapel.

"I'd be delighted," Don Antonio said, his face breaking into a broad smile, making it appear that he could think of no better pastime than peering at a corpse in a dank chapel. "I have the morning to myself. The Cardinal suggested I should rest after the night's exertions, but there's really no need."

So, pausing only to collect the pay clerk who, when the situation was explained to him, seemed as reluctant as Luca to visit the chapel, they set off, Don Antonio striding out, the other two struggling to keep up.

25

Don Antonio sprang up the mortuary chapel steps, with Luca and the pay clerk following sluggishly behind. They disturbed two Brothers in the process of screwing down the lid on Bartolomeo's coffin.

"What's going on here?" said Don Antonio in an authoritative voice. Tall in his black biretta and well built beneath his cassock, he commanded respect and the Brothers were suitably impressed.

"We are preparing the coffin of this poor sinner for burial, Monsignore," said one of them, elevating Don Antonio's clerical status by a notch or two.

"But I thought he was to rest here for two days," Luca blurted out. "That's the normal period for a vigil, isn't it?"

One of the Brothers looked at him sharply. "Oh it's you. The boy who left so abruptly yesterday afternoon. Very rude."

"Particularly when we'd had such high hopes for you, asking you to join our confraternity," said the other Brother. "No hope of that now."

"And you were fiddling around with the corpse's clothing," said the first. "We've heard about people like you."

The situation seemed to be getting out of hand, but Don Antonio was not flustered: "This young man was perfectly justified in his actions. Your corpse has been misidentified."

"Well, you're not going to get very far with identifying him now."

"What do you mean?"

"Not only is his head battered to a pulp, but his body's all swelled up, fit to burst out of the coffin," said one Brother.

"And he's beginning to smell to high heaven," said the other, not without relish.

"I'm off," said the pay clerk, looking very pale under his curls and making a move towards the door.

"Just you stay here," said Luca, grabbing the man by the elbow, though in truth he too would have liked to have made a hasty exit.

"The boy's quite right," said the first Brother again. "Normally we'd hold vigil over the body for two days after death. But the thing is, this man didn't die yesterday, when he was brought in. He must have been dead a good few days before that."

"Now he's swelling – and stinking," said his companion, with some satisfaction in his voice.

"Nonetheless, you must open the coffin again," said Don Antonio.

"Not sure we can do that," said the first Brother, "what with earlier desecration of the body ..."

"I only moved the linen band over his hands," cried Luca.

"... and now exhumation," the Brother continued.

"By all the saints," said Don Antonio, "we're not digging him up. We just want to look at him."

"Yes, but ..."

Don Antonio drew himself up and addressed the Brothers. "I am Secretary to Luigi Mazzini, Cardinal Archbishop, Papal Legate and friend to the Holy Father himself. In his name, and in my own, I order you to remove the lid of that coffin."

It was an impressive performance, thought Luca, though he doubted how much ecclesiastical authority it carried. It worked on the Brothers, however, and with only a little more grumbling they began unscrewing the coffin lid.

The Brothers were right, of course, and as they slid the lid away there was a horrible stench of rotting flesh. Luca felt a cold sweat on his brow and he felt a slightly dizzy. The pay clerk was whiter than ever and he clutched at Luca for support. Luca sneaked a look at the corpse under the flickering light of the four pillar candles. It was grotesquely bloated and the clothes, now stretched over the distended body, were damp and darkly stained. Even Don Antonio seemed taken aback. "Let's get this over with," he said and he asked the trembling pay clerk. "Where's this birthmark?"

"On his ankle," said the man, determinedly not looking at the body.

"On his ankle! Then it's underneath his hose and his boot."

"You're not going to get them off, that's for sure," said one of the Brothers. Luca risked another look: the stained yellow stockings were now taut about the corpse's thighs and the light-brown boots, once loose, were tightly fitting. The Brother was right; no-one could pull them off, even if he felt up to the task.

"We'll have to cut it away," said Don Antonio. "Has anyone got a sharp knife?"

There was no reply and with a sigh Don Antonio reached into the pocket of his cassock and, after some rummaging, brought out a small knife in a leather sheath, which he pulled off. The double-sided blade was no more than the length of a man's finger, and perhaps half as thick at the hilt, tapering to a fine point. This is a very resourceful man indeed, thought Luca, as the priest handed him the sheath. I shouldn't like to argue with him. Don Antonio made an incision in the corpse's boot with the point of his knife.

"No, no, stop!" the pay clerk cried out.

"It has to be done. Look away if you must."

"No, no, you're cutting into the right boot. The birthmark's on his left ankle." The clerk's curiosity seemed to have overcome his revulsion and he'd obviously sneaked a glimpse as Don Antonio began to cut.

The three of them, Luca, the priest and the pay clerk, were standing beside the coffin with the body's right side facing them. There was nothing for it than to traipse all the way round to the other side, avoiding the pillar candles in their holders. If anything the stench of putrefaction here, farther away from the door, was worse, but Don Antonio put one hand on the man's left boot and with the other made a long cut with his knife, then a shorter one at right angles, and peeled back the leather. The knife was obviously extremely sharp.

"It's a bit higher than the ankle," said the pay clerk, again not looking at the body. "On the outside of the lower calf, you might say."

The priest extended the incision and peeled back more brown leather. The wet hose bulged out as he did so. Pressing on relentlessly, he made a long slit in the stocking itself and pulled it apart. Large blisters had formed in the decaying skin and there was an eerie greenness about it, but there, just where the pay clerk had described it, was a ruddy-purple mark. It looked like a Mussulman's scimitar, with a blade thin at the hilt, curved and widening towards its end.

"Is that it?" Don Antonio asked, but the clerk was again not looking. "Come on man, face up to it. The sooner started, the sooner done."

Luca thought he'd physically have to turn the clerk's head to face the corpse, but summoning up some courage, the man looked at the swollen, discoloured flesh and the deep purple mark on it.

"Yes, that's it. That's definitely it."

"Are you completely sure?" Don Antonio asked.

"Yes, yes, I'm sure," said the clerk, but his words were indistinct as he broke away from Luca and ran out of the chapel door. They could hear him retching on the steps.

Don Antonio brought a square of cloth out of his cassock pocket and wiped from the blade some dark unidentifiable liquid. Luca shuddered to think what it might be. The priest held out his hand for the sheath, covered the blade and wrapped the knife in the cloth, which he then thrust back into his cassock pocket.

"I think we are done here," he said, turning to the two brothers who had kept a discreet distance during the operation. "Thank you, gentlemen. The Cardinal shall hear of your co-operation in this matter."

"Will you not break bread and take wine with us, Monsignore? As a mark of respect for the departed?" one Brother asked.

"And we've some fine preserved cherries," said the other, glaring at Luca.

The priest, stronger-minded than Luca had been the day before, declined their invitation. Waving his arm in the direction of the coffin he said: "I think you'd better seal him up again. And the sooner you get him deep under the earth, the better."

26

"So," said Cosimo de' Medici, "Bartolomeo da Siracusa turned out to be one of the *uomini senza nome e famiglia*."

Yes, 'men without name and family', thought Luca, that's what the ruling classes in this supposedly egalitarian republic call the lower orders. But he has, or rather had, a name. It's Rocco Rossi and however undistinguished his life, he was a unique human being. As well as a name, he undoubtedly had a family too.

"He leaves a widow and two small children, Sir," said the pay clerk, seeming to read Luca's thoughts, "a boy three years old and an daughter of eighteen months."

"You know them well?"

"His wife, er, his widow is, er, was a friend of my own wife."

"I shall see that they are well provided for," said Cosimo. "And I have already made arrangements to pay for the funeral."

Money! Well, that would certainly provide material help for the grieving woman and her two tiny children, but it wouldn't bring Rocco back to life, nor soothe their grief. Luca again had the feeling that everyone involved in this episode had scant concern for justice, bound up as they were in their own concerns, thinking only of their own interests.

The pay clerk seemed to confirm this hypothesis: "Speaking of money, Sir, he borrowed four florins off me. I was wondering ..."

The clerk had made a speedy recovery after his ordeal in the mortuary chapel. Luca and Don Antonio had found him at the fountain at the end of the street, washing his face, his curls damp and lank, his face still pale, and they'd insisted he came with them to report on their findings to Cosimo de' Medici.

The banker had received them on the cloistered roof terrace, probably the very one from which Donatello had swept his bronze head to shatter on the paving stones below. After helping Luca tell the story of the morning's discoveries (with only modest reference to his own role), Don Antonio left to report to his master, the Cardinal.

The clerk had a much better colour now, perhaps excited at the prospect of getting his money back. "So if you could see your way to settling the debt, I'd be much obliged".

"Four florins, you say," said Cosimo, for whom such an amount must have been a trifle. "Hmm, I see no obligation on the bank, or indeed myself, to pay what another man owes."

The clerk looked crestfallen: was it Luca's imagination or did his curls, still damp on his forehead, sag a little?

"However, since you and your posthumous friend have, albeit unknowingly, performed a service for us today, I will settle your debt."

Cosimo led them through a door into the library, pulled the oak chair up to the desk and began writing a note. "Fifty florins for the widow and children, I think, and for you, four was it?"

"Yes, Sir, only..."

"Only what?"

"Only the debt is of such long-standing that I wondered if you could see yourself clear to providing a little interest on my capital."

"Interest," shouted Cosimo, "have you no concern for your immortal soul? Interest is usury and that's a mortal sin!" He gave the clerk a look as if he were a weevil that had just crawled out of an old dry biscuit and handed him the note. "Here, take this to my Treasurer and go before I change my mind. Interest indeed!"

The clerk backed towards the door and left hurriedly.

Cosimo's anger, however, was more assumed that real, for he smiled at Luca, then laughed out loud: "Interest indeed!" he repeated. "These Florentines will do anything for money!" He waved at Luca. "Take a seat young man; pull up a chair near me."

Luca did as he was asked, though he felt diffident at being seated in the presence of such a rich and powerful man.

"So, Luca da Posara, you, too, have performed a great service for me in the last two days. I am most grateful. How old are you?"

"Nineteen, sir."

"Nineteen eh?" Cosimo leaned back in his chair, still smiling. "Nineteen! When I was your age I was in Rome or travelling with the Pope. What fun Luigi and I had in those days." He sighed: "As one gets older the affairs of business and the affairs of state grow weightier."

Cosimo gave Luca a cool, shrewd look: "And how are you employed here in Florence, Luca da Posara? You work with Battista d'Antonio on the dome, I believe?"

"Yes, sir, he's my uncle. I am the Assistant Building Supervisor." It did not seem the right time or place to mention that he had not been paid for his services for more than a year, particularly after the behaviour of the pay clerk.

"I was very impressed by your perspicacity in realising that 'Bartolomeo da Siracusa' was not the man we all thought he was," Cosimo continued, "and in your courage in examining the corpse to prove your theory correct."

Once more Luca did not think it appropriate to reveal his initial error in identifying the body.

"And when I mentioned your name to Filippo Brunelleschi this morning," Cosimo continued, "he, too, sang your praises, at least when he wasn't cursing at being confined to the house."

It warmed Luca's heart to hear those words. (It needed warming after his experiences in the mortuary chapel.) It was pleasant to hear that he was appreciated, especially as the words came via so exalted a personage as Cosimo de' Medici. The banker, however, brought him back to earth, asking abruptly:

"Do you intend to be an Assistant Building Supervisor all your life?"

"No, sir. That is, I am very much enjoying what I am doing now and I'm proud to play my part in the creation of the dome."

"Spoken like a politician, though the sentiments are admirable. From time to time, however, I could use the skills of a brainy and courageous youth like you. I will keep in touch Master Luca da Posara and my thanks again."

Luca took this as a signal to leave and was beginning to stand when Cosimo added: "And I have an essential task for you right now. This afternoon at the Wool Guild meeting I intend to expose this plot against us. I'll show our enemies that we Medici are not to be taken lightly."

"I'm sure no-one would do that, Sir," said Luca, sitting again.

Cosimo smiled. "Even though my father has advised against such a conspicuous course of action, it's too good an opportunity to be missed. My Secretary is currently preparing notes for me and he'll need to check all the facts about the identity of the body with you."

"Yes sir, of course, but the dome, Brunelleschi, Battista ..."

"We've been working on the dome for the best part of five years, Master Luca, and I dare say it'll be many more before we're finished. A few hours will make no difference. Oh, and I may also need you at the Guild meeting. My Secretary will ensure that you are admitted."

"Yes, sir," said Luca, rising again.

"*Sedit qui timuit ne non succederet.*"

Luca must have looked at him blankly, for Cosimo added: "Horace, of course. In one of his letters, if I remember rightly." He translated for Luca's benefit: "He who feared he would not succeed sat still."

27

Luca had been talking with Cosimo de' Medici's Secretary in his office for ten minutes or so when the door flew open and Brunelleschi burst in. He glared at Luca: "They told me you were in here. What have you been doing all morning?" He glowered at the Secretary, a mild, stooped, gray-haired man in a scholar's gown, who hastily rose from his desk.

"I think we are done here, *Messer* Lucca," the Secretary said, making for the door as fast as his dignity allowed. "I have enough information to prepare a presentation for my master for the meeting this afternoon. I'll bid you good morning and meet you after dinner, to accompany you to the guildhall of the *Arte della Lana*."

At the door he turned to Brunelleschi: "And good day to you, *Provveditore*. I look forward to seeing you later, too." Brunelleschi merely growled, and the Secretary, as if he'd been surprised at his own courage, beat a hasty retreat.

"It's all your fault," Brunelleschi told Luca, "if you hadn't gone gadding about tripping over dead bodies and then unearthing some ghastly plot against us, I might have been able to get on with my work. Now I am held prisoner against my will and I won't get anywhere near the blasted dome until sometime this evening."

"I'm sorry, *Provveditore*," Luca began, "but one or two other things ..."

"No matter. What's Battista been doing?"

"He's tidying up the scaffolding and sorting out the blocks ready for the next stone ring."

"Thank God for one sensible man in the whole of Florence." He looked at Luca more closely. "You still look pale. Didn't you get a good night's sleep?" Brunelleschi's anger seemed to have evaporated as fast as rain on a hot pavement and Luca couldn't help smiling at the concern in his voice. As he persuaded Brunelleschi to take the seat just vacated by Cosimo de' Medici's Secretary, he remembered their first meeting more than a year ago.

He'd gone with his uncle to the architect's house a couple of days after he'd moved to the city and Rosa, the housekeeper, had shown them into the architect's cluttered study, where he sat at his desk. Luca saw a small man with a beaky nose and above that, shrewd dark eyes. The morning sun shone on a balding pate. Seeing Battista with a stranger Brunelleschi had hastily gathered together the papers on which he'd been working and covered them with the sleeve of his rumpled over-gown.

"Who's this?" he'd demanded. "What's he doing here?"

"Be calm, Pippo," Battista had soothed, employing the diminutive of Filippo used by his friends, "he's my nephew, Luca, entirely to be trusted." Brunelleschi had relaxed and even managed a half-smile.

"He's my sister's youngest son," Battista had told him, "and she's been pestering me to take him in and find him a job. So I thought I'd employ him as my assistant. He can work for both of us; act as a go-between as it were. That way I'll have more time to get on with making sure the builders are doing what they should be doing."

"Hmm," Brunelleschi had said, "we don't need another pair of eyes penetrating our secrets."

With much cajoling, however, Battista had persuaded him that Luca should work with them: "We'll try it for a week or so, but I can't promise anything…"

Brunelleschi gradually began to trust him and for his part Luca found a growing affection for the architect who, despite his propensity for irascibility and pugnacity, engaged in many small acts of kindness and consideration, worrying, for example, that he was wrapped up well against the cold Florentine Winter. Luca began to understand why so many artists, and patrons, not only admired Filippo, but liked him too…

Luca's recollections were abruptly interrupted by Brunelleschi's bark. "What are you smiling at? This is no smiling matter. Delays, nothing but delays. We'll never get that dome finished….."

There was a light tap on the door and Donatello came in. Unlike Don Antonio, he looked slightly dishevelled after his night in the cells. "Luca," he said, coming forward and embracing him. "My lovely Luca, let me look at you. Well, you're still pale. I'll bet you didn't sleep well last night."

Luca, who had been feeling rather healthy before all this talk of paleness by his friends, smiled wanly: "I slept well enough, thank you, better than you I'll be bound."

"Well, that Don Antonio was talking half the night. Interesting man, a bit frightening if you ask me. I'll tell you all about it later. We've got to go now: we've been summoned to dinner and it doesn't pay to keep a Medici waiting."

"It's brickwork I want to see, not food," Brunelleschi grumbled as the three of them left the room.

28

Halfway across the city, Niccolò Peruzzi had no appetite for his dinner either. Leaning his left elbow on the table, his face in his hand, he pushed a slice of roast lamb around the plate with his dagger. Even the charms of Elisabetta as she bent to pour his wine failed to lift his spirits. Where in Hades' name was Giovanni Ferrante? And why wasn't Donatello dead?

The bull-necked man, who was called Federico, had finally reported in the middle of the morning, red-eyed and looking fearful of his master's response. He'd told some meandering tale about how Ferrante had disappeared into thin air: he'd watched the house all night, so he said, after seeing Ferrante snuff out his bedtime candles.

"Saw the housekeeper go in early in the morning, but when no-one came out after a couple of hours, I went and knocked on the door. The housekeeper told me there was 'no-one at home'".

"Did you check?"

"Yes. Beds were cold. Then the old man turned up: he'd been out all night, gambling again. Said he hadn't seen Ferrante since the evening before."

"You oaf! He must have slipped out early in the morning while you dozed. Cretin! Get out and find him!"

Niccolò had been sure that that Ferrante would soon show up; after all, he had a strong hold over him – and his father. The skinny notary wouldn't dare risk exposure and anyway, he'd want his hour of triumph at the Wool Guild meeting. As the morning drew on, however, and there was no word of Ferrante's whereabouts, Niccolò had grown more worried and then, at noon, the news came that Donatello had been sprung from the *Bargello* cells and that he and Brunelleschi had, like Ferrante, disappeared from view. No wonder he'd lost his appetite.

29

The noise in the audience hall of the *Arte della Lana*, the Wool Guild, was overwhelming. There were perhaps eighty men in the room that afternoon and it seemed as if they were all talking at once.

Luca sat in the front row, next to his uncle, Battista d'Antonio, who looked as solid and red-faced as ever. Luca tried to be as inconspicuous as possible but at the same time he wanted to see everything, take in all that was going on. Looking round he realised that the men here represented most of the influential families in the city. Some of them, Luca knew, were allies of the Medici, through blood and marriage, or beholden to them because of money and patronage: a loan here, a favour there, a job in the bank for a nephew or help in obtaining a lucrative post in the city's administration. Others were from families who had become wealthy through wool and silk manufacture, through trade and banking, and they formed shifting alliances with each other and with the Medici, the flow of their affiliations blown by the winds of self-interest. A third group were implacable enemies of the Medici, perpetually seeking political and economic advantage, scheming, forging fresh cabals to oppose them. To be honest, Luca wasn't quite sure who was who and he wished that Donatello, who was well informed about such matters, had been there to advise him. He resolved to watch them all as Cosimo made his revelations, to see which of them looked the most discomfited and might, therefore, be involved in the plot.

The voice of Lorenzo Ghiberti here, like Luca's uncle, in his capacity as one of the three *Provveditore della cupola*, rose above the clamour. "Where's Brunelleschi? That's what I'd like to know. Stole the secrets of the dome and now he's done a runner. And Donatello – hadn't he had a hand in that man's murder? Now he's disappeared, too. It's about time the authorities took some decisive action against them and those who protect them." His whine was like the droning of a fly, continuous, insistent, prompting an urge to reach out and swat him. You'll soon be singing another tune, *Provveditore*, thought Luca, when Cosimo de' Medici reveals the true identity of the 'Bartolomeo da Siracusa.'.

He looked round the audience hall, which occupied most of the first floor of the *palazzo*, and which reflected the prestige of this, the most powerful guild in Florence. Cosimo de' Medici and the other Consuls were seated behind a long table on a raised dais at the head of the room, with two tall windows behind them, through which the sunlight streamed. The walls were covered with fine frescoes from the previous century: ahead a Madonna enthroned with angels; to Luca's left, four saints: he recognised Peter and Augustine, but he couldn't work out who the other two were; to his right, framed by a gilded arch and set against a beryl background, the Roman judge Brutus sat on a bench in his light-red toga, resisting the honeyed words of The Flatterer on one side and the money purse of The Corruptor on the other in an allegory of justice; in the ceiling vaults the Virtues of Prudence, Fortitude, Temperance and Justice vied with the four Evangelists, all in their own *tondi* with red-and-white patterned surrounds. The guild's emblem, *Agnus Dei*, the Lamb of God, with his banner bearing the cross, gleamed from the two bosses of the vaults.

The hubbub from the hall continued unabated as each man made his opinion known. There was, however, one conspicuous absence. Where was Giovanni Ferrante? As Notary to the *Opera del Duomo*, his presence was certainly required this afternoon as the Consuls of the Wool Guild reviewed the progress of work on the dome. But there was no sign of the sour-faced notary. No doubt he'll be here soon, thought Luca, although he was cutting it fine and he was usually to be found gossiping and scheming well before the start of any meeting.

The Prior of the Guild, an elderly man with white curly hair and a full beard, stood up, cleared his throat and called for attention. It took some time for everyone to stop talking; Ghiberti's voice was one of the last, still complaining about "that damned man", but eventually all were settled in their seats.

"Gentlemen, welcome ..." the Prior began.

"Speak up," said a voice from the back.

"Gentlemen," the Prior said again, raising his voice. "We meet in unusual circumstances. We are not used to seeing so many men present to listen to our deliberations about the dome. Such technical meetings do not usually command such interest.

"As you may have seen, our esteemed architect is not currently present." That brought murmurings from the audience, but the Prior continued above them, "but *Messer* Cosimo de' Medici has assured me that he will arrive shortly. In the meantime *Messer* Cosimo himself has an important statement he would like to make."

That gave rise to more mutterings, louder this time and more antagonistic. They continued as Cosimo rose to speak. He waited silently, gazing straight ahead, occasionally glancing down at his notes, until there was complete silence. Even then Cosimo said nothing, just looked around the room. He let the silence linger for another moment or two, then spoke, almost shouted:

"Gentlemen, we are all victims of a plot!"

There was an audible intake of breath and then uproar again. Cosimo waited once more for it to die down before continuing, emphasising each clause: "Yes, a plot to discredit our distinguished architect, even have him arrested for murder; a plot to disrupt, even stop, the work on our magnificent cathedral, the envy of the world; a plot to disgrace our beloved Florence, the flower of Italy, the most beautiful city in Europe."

Cosimo picked up 'Bartolomeo's' papers, replaced in the packet tied with the purple ribbon: "It's all here. Evidence of both fraud and forgery. The murdered man is not who we thought he was. He's an imposter, and the papers he carried are fakes. Lies, damned lies, all of them."

The room was in tumult again, men shouting, others arguing with their neighbours. Cosimo sat down and the Prior rose again, trying vainly to restore order.

"Gentlemen, gentlemen ..." After several minutes there was some semblance of calm and Cosimo rose again. Speaking quietly this time and using his Secretary's notes, he went through all the evidence page by page, reaching a climax with the words: "It's clear to me these papers were forged by the Notary to the *Opera*, Ser Giovanni Ferrante. I see that he is not here. I demand that he be arrested and interrogated forthwith."

There was a roar of approval from the Medici supporters, while the rival factions sat silent. Luca scanned their glum faces, but in none could he detect any hint that he'd already known 'Bartolomeo' was a fake.

The Prior rose once more, his white curly beard trembling. "Gentlemen, gentlemen ... No doubt the Podestà will act on the evidence produced by *Messer* Cosimo. But may I remind you of the purpose of this meeting. We are here to discuss the progress of the work on the dome. The Guild and the *Opera del Duomo* are rightly concerned over the safety of the structure and whether work can continue without a thorough review." He turned towards Cosimo de' Medici. "But, despite your assurances, there is no sign of Brunelleschi, who should be here to answer our questions."

Cosimo rose and said loudly to the whole room: "You want your architect, the genius who will make our city the talk of nations for centuries to come? Well, here he is!"

He lifted his arm high, waving his hand, and a servant opened a door to an anteroom towards the rear of the hall. Filippo Brunelleschi stepped out, followed by Donatello. Cosimo started clapping and others soon joined in, some enthusiastically, others reluctantly. Soon cheers echoed from the vaults. Brunelleschi, looking more than a little embarrassed, raised his arms for silence.

"Time enough for applause when the dome's complete," he said. "So, let's get this questioning over and done with, and then for pity's sake let me get on with my work." He walked to the front of the hall and took a seat facing the long table where the Prior, Cosimo and the other Consuls sat in a row. "Your servant, gentlemen," he said.

Luca was impressed by the architect's patience during the questioning from the Consuls of the Wool Guild, quite unlike his normal belligerent self. Perhaps Brunelleschi realised that if he answered politely and succinctly, no matter how naïve or ill-informed the question, he'd be able to get out of there and back to work more quickly.

There was a tense moment when an ancient Consul, some relic of the previous century, asked: "Might it not be possible to create apertures in the upper part of the dome to allow the ingress and egress of the birds of the air, to enjoy the vault of the cathedral as they do the celestial vault itself?" Donatello, who had come to sit next to Luca and Battista, could hardly contain a snort and although Battista glowered at the sculptor, Luca believed that his uncle, too, had had more than enough of the ingress of the birds of the air, notably the pigeon.

Brunelleschi, however, had merely given a tight smile and nodded a few times, as if pondering the merits of such a suggestion: "Thank you, sir; we'll certainly take your comments into consideration."

After an hour and a half it was all over, but still Brunelleschi hadn't been able to get away: the Prior shook him vigorously by the hand and then Cosimo de' Medici started talking to him and Luca was well aware that when a Medici talks to you, you don't move away, whoever you are. Uncle Battista was, however, able to escape straightway and Luca followed with Donatello soon after.

30

It was a perfect April afternoon, with a light cooling breeze, as they began their walk from the palazzo of the Wool Guild. After a few paces they reached the *Orsanmichele*, the church of all the guilds, and Luca insisted on stopping for a moment in front of the niche that contained Donatello's St George, the marble statue that had established his friend's reputation as the foremost sculptor in Italy.

Patron saint of the Guild of Armourers and Swordmakers, George was caught poised for action, his brow furrowed, his muscles taut. He was balancing his shield on its point, but you could see that he was ready to pick it up in an instant.

"You like him, Luca?" Donatello asked, taking his hand and squeezing it.

"Of course I do." Luca replied, "I feel that if I looked away for a moment he'd be off to rescue princesses and slay dragons." But he took his hand away from the sculptor's and heard Donatello sigh.

"Still unsure?"

"Give me time, Donatello. Yes, I'm still confused."

They moved on. Somewhere a clock struck six.

"Pies, hot pies...." On a corner a man stood with a tray suspended in front of his round stomach by leather shoulder straps. "Fresh meat pies. Pies, hot pies ..."

"I could do with one of those," said Donatello. "I'm ravenous."

"How can you be? You had an enormous dinner at the Medici house."

"That was hours ago." Donatello bought a pie and bit into it eagerly.

"So tell me more about Don Antonio," said Luca as they continued walking. "You said earlier that he was an interesting man, but a bit frightening. I agree, there's more to him than meets the eye."

"Not my type, those muscular Christians," said his friend, "although I was glad enough to have his company in the cells. Scary place. God knows what goes on there."

"A resourceful sort of a man," said Luca, remembering the pewter goblets that fitted though the bars. He told Donatello about the priest cutting away the corpse's boot and hose, "with a knife like a lancet, which he obviously knew how to use."

"A bit of a religious fanatic, too, if you ask me," said Donatello unclearly, his mouth half-full of pie. "Went on about 'divine inspiration', about how everything, even my talent, came directly from God."

"Well, I suppose that's true enough."

"Of course, it is. He also went on about Humanism, saying it was mundermng he hmmhh f he hurch."

"What?"

Donatello finished his mouthful and repeated: "He said that Humanism was undermining the authority of the church." He swallowed and added: "I got the impression that Don Antonio, given half the chance, would take practical steps to prove the Humanists wrong."

"What on earth do you mean?"

"Maybe a shock, like a gruesome accident in the dome, would bring us to our senses and nearer to God."

"But surely he wouldn't do anything to damage the dome ..."

"I'm not saying he would. But I wouldn't be surprised if he did."

Luca was silent as they took their final steps into the baptistry square, but then he said: "Look, we must talk about this some more, but *Messer* Filippo will be back soon and he'll having us all running around like mad, making up for lost time."

"And Pumpkin Head is waiting for me. Come tomorrow when you can."

Donatello and Luca embraced, quite formally, not with their previous intimacy and, with another theatrical sigh the sculptor set off in the direction of his workshop. Luca stood alone by the baptistry doors, watching the departing figure. Then, with a sigh himself, he gave the bronze head of St Luke another rub for luck, before walking briskly towards the West door, skirting round the spot where he'd found the body (was it only a day and a half ago?), into the cathedral and down the long cavern of the nave.

When he reached the Crossing, Luca found Battista again fussing around the hoist, checking some stone blocks waiting their turn to be lifted skyward. A few minutes later Filippo Brunelleschi himself came bustling up. "Thank the Lord that's over. It beats me how idiots like that get to ask me questions about engineering principles. And as for the 'ingress and egress of the birds of the air,' words fail me."

"Be calm Pippo," soothed Battista. "You did well, and you're here now."

Brunelleschi looked upwards in mock bewilderment: "What's that vast thing up there? Why it's a dome. I'd quite forgotten what it looked like!"

"Now, now, Pippo, don't get yourself worked up."

"Quite right, Battista. Practical as ever. Right, let's get up there and inspect that brickwork, instead of standing here gossiping. And get that hoist working. All that material won't get up there on its own, you know."

"I see you're back to your normal self, *Provveditore*," said Battista, placing a hand on Brunelleschi's shoulder and steering him towards the stairway to the dome. Luca followed them, trying not to count the steps as they ascended the dark stairs.

Brunelleschi examined the latest course of brickwork, looking at each section in minute detail, even scratching off a bit of mortar with a knife and rubbing it between his fingers. Luca and his uncle watched apprehensively, but relaxed when the architect shouted over the noise of the hoist and of joiners hammering wooden planks above them: "You're quite right, Battista. It's been well laid – and adding that soda ash certainly makes the mortar stiffen quickly." He put his hand on one of the herring-bone sections: "And doesn't this work brilliantly?"

The noise precluded lengthy discussions, so they soon descended again and when they again reached the transept Brunelleschi said: "You can go now, Luca. As Battista told you, we'd like you to go the brickworks tomorrow morning early. Find out when they'll get those new-shaped bricks to us. We need to plan ahead."

Given an unexpected hour or so to himself, Luca decided to visit the tavern where he had had his dinner the day before. The contrast was extraordinary: the place was packed with men talking loudly, arguing, laughing, knocking back their wine and, some of them at least, eyeing him up suspiciously. There were women there, too, with painted faces and low-cut bodices, drinking as much as the men and, if anything, talking even more loudly.

Luca was glad he hadn't very much money on him as he squeezed his way towards the bar at the rear of the room, holding tightly to his purse. He ordered a drink and paid, making sure several times that his purse was properly closed. He took his stoneware pitcher and beaker and fought his way out from the bar. At first there had been nowhere to sit and he'd had to stand awkwardly near the fire, holding the pitcher in one hand and the beaker, from which he took nervous gulps of wine from time to time, in the other. Then a couple who had been embracing vigorously got up from a bench nearby and headed towards the door, so Luca was able to slip in and commandeer a corner of the table. He placed the pitcher in front of him and, like that man the previous afternoon, examined it morosely. For some reason he felt dispirited, downcast.

He should have felt the opposite, of course: his role in uncovering the plot against Brunelleschi and Donatello had been noticed approvingly by both Church and State, personified by the Cardinal and Cosimo de' Medici, which would do his future career in Florence no harm at all. But he had a sense of isolation, of loneliness, despite the affection of his friends and the respect of his colleagues.

Coming to the tavern had been a mistake, it felt loud and threatening, an alien world. From time to time Luca looked around the crowded room and stole glances at the balustraded balcony, but there was no sign of *La Bionda*, nor of the friendly waiter who'd served him yesterday. He sat there for a few more minutes, occasionally taking a gulp of wine but then, not bothering to finish the pitcher, he rose abruptly and made for the door. Another glance at the gallery showed all the doors shut and no signs of life.

Outside it was beginning to get dark: the curfew bell would be ringing soon. Luca felt chilly, although the evening was still warm, and he pulled the hood of his cloak closer around his face. As he reached Battista's house, he was cheered somewhat by the welcoming sight of candles burning in the upstairs window. He let himself in by the street door and as he did so, the house cat crept in with him. When he stood at the foot of the stairs it rubbed itself against his legs, arching its back and purring loudly.

31

Next morning, as Luca walked back from the brickworks, he was still thinking about cats, baskets and poisoned chicken dishes which apparently weren't poisonous. With each step he took, a phrase kept going through his head, insistent, like the refrain of some popular ballad. "The cat is alive, so the chicken is fine; the cat is alive, so the chicken is fine..." He ran his fingers through his hair as he pondered yesterday's events, trying to make it tidier.

Since the cat was undoubtedly still alive, the chicken couldn't have been poisoned. Nonetheless, somebody had left the dish with the jailer in the *Bargello* and had probably bribed him to give it to the sculptor. But who and to what end, if it was unadulterated? Some anonymous well-wisher simply supplying Donatello with a much-needed meal? That was hardly likely. Luca tried to think of the most outlandish reasons: maybe somebody was trying to convince somebody else that the dish was poisoned, even when it wasn't. No, that didn't make sense either, did it? Whoever it was would soon be found out when Donatello didn't die.

And what possible connection was there between the non-murder of Donatello and the mutilated body of 'Bartolomeo da Siracusa', the man who never was? The scrawny notary Giovanni Ferrante was certainly implicated in the production of the bogus Sicilian's forged papers. Was he also involved with the attempted poisoning (or not?) as well? And why hadn't he turned up at the Wool Guild meeting yesterday: had he been murdered, too? Luca's brain couldn't make sense of it all. Still, 'the cat is alive, so the chicken is fine', his brain told him at every stride. And his hair was as unruly as ever.

Luca had enjoyed visiting the brickworks, a walk of a couple of hours or so from the city, feeling the intense heat of the kiln with some twenty thousand bricks baking away and watching the brickmakers kneading the clay with their bare feet, as if they were treading grapes after the *vendemmia*. The foreman confirmed that it would be best to let Brunelleschi's new bricks season in the sun for a month or so before firing them. And then there'd be another couple of weeks after the firing before they were cool enough to transport. A longish wait, but that was the only way of ensuring a quality good enough to satisfy the architect.

It wasn't the cleanest of occupations, this brickmaking: there was a choking dust everywhere, creeping into the folds of your clothing – the joke on the construction sites of Florence was that the kiln-workers were the only men who washed their hands *before* going to the piss-pot, not that many of the others did so afterwards – and Luca felt grimy himself as he strode towards the city.

The road rose over a rounded hill and there, laid out in perfect perspective, as if some artist had been rigorously applying Brunelleschi's rules, lay the city of Florence. On this late April morning it seemed to Luca like a jewel, an elaborate medallion perhaps, crafted by some titanic master goldsmith. Girdled by the city walls, its towers, domes and spires reached towards the sun. He could see the shadowy yellow-ochre crenellations of Arnolfo's tower, tall above *Palazzo della Signoria*, and nearby, Giotto's elegant square *campanile*, with the enormous bulk of *Santa Maria del Fiore* lying beside it. Above it, the emerging shell of the dome itself was like the rim of a volcano glimpsed in a woodcut illustration. The terracotta tiles of the roofs of the city's *palazzi* glowed and even the Arno sparkled under its four bridges. Luca took in the sight for a few moments, cat and chicken quite banished from his mind, before setting off again with a warmer heart and a renewed spring in his step. Last night's despondent mood seemed to have disappeared with the enchantment of the day.

32

Bells were striking the noon hours when he entered the offices of the *Opera del Duomo*, where he found his uncle Battista and Filippo Brunelleschi talking to Cosimo de' Medici's Secretary.

"Ah, here's the lad," said Battista and the Secretary, already stooped with age, gave a creaky bow, which Luca awkwardly returned.

"My compliments, *Messer* Luca. We meet again. My master has requested that you attend him as soon as possible. I was just leaving a message with these gentlemen, but now you've returned we can walk there together."

"Not before he's reported to me about those bricks," said Brunelleschi. Luca told the architect that he could expect delivery of the new-shaped bricks in six or seven weeks.

"That should be just about right," Brunelleschi said: "we should have the second stone chain in position by then." He paused, nodding towards the Secretary: "It seems Cosimo has a job for you, though we've been sworn to secrecy. Not the ideal time to lose you from my point of view, but there it is."

"I am sure the task for my master will not take up all this young man's time," said the Secretary.

"Well, Battista's going to need him more than ever in the next couple of months," the architect said."

"It's all in hand, Pippo," said Battista. "Don't worry. Look, you're just supposed to be the supervisor, I'm the builder. I know what I'm doing and you've plenty of other work to do."

Luca knew that was true enough. Brunelleschi was involved in many other architectural projects, not least the *Ospedale degli Innocenti*, the Foundlings Hospital, for which he'd produced some wonderfully simple but elegant designs, and he was also overseeing alterations, additions and improvements to the Medici church of *San Lorenzo*.

"Yes, and don't think I don't trust you Battista, but soon we're going to need Luca as our messenger more than ever. I'm going to be somewhat tied up in the next few weeks."

Battista looked at Brunelleschi rather strangely, then said: "But if *Messer* Cosimo has need of him, we should not stand in the way."

"Of course," said the architect, looking at Luca, "but make sure you're here when we need you, too."

So Luca found himself walking again, this time through city streets busy as the dinner-hour approached, the swifts still screaming and swooping between the rooftops. The elderly man walked slowly, using a silver-topped ebony stick to help him along, but it wasn't many minutes before they reached the Medici house and went straight up to the library. Cosimo, sitting in the red-cushioned chair, was reading an ancient scroll. He looked up as Luca came in: "*Ho bios brakhys, hê de tekhnê makrê.*"

"I'm sorry, Sir?" Every time he met Cosimo face-to-face he seemed to be spouting some dead language. He recognised this one as Greek, but what it meant he had no idea. His incomprehension obviously showed on his face.

Cosimo laughed: "Forgive me Luca da Posara, but these ancient documents are my passion." He held up the scroll. "Hippocrates. Greek physician. Talks a lot more sense about medicine than many of the blood-letters who practice in this city today – and about life, too, come to that. You're probably more familiar with the Latin translation, *Ars longa ...?*"

"...*vita brevis*. Art is long, life is short."

"Bravo. Hippocrates was talking about the art of medicine of course, but his aphorism applies equally to all the arts: painting, sculpture, literature. The best works will certainly live on when those who created them are dead, and the artists will also gain their own immortality."

"As will their patrons," said Luca, a little boldly.

Cosimo waved a self-deprecating arm: "We sponsor beautiful art for its own sake, not for our own glory. Beauty is at the heart of Humanism: it reflects inner virtue and value."

Well, yes, thought Luca and no doubt Cosimo de' Medici passionately believes what he's saying, but the sponsorship of art is also an expression of wealth and power. Lets you know who's boss. He didn't articulate the thought.

Cosimo de' Medici placed the scroll on the desk. "Please sit," he said, and as Luca did so, added, "but I didn't call you here today to discuss the precepts of Humanism, fascinating as they are. Unfortunately the day-to-day business of life gets in the way of such high-minded philosophy." He leaned closer to Luca. "Well, Notary Ferrante seems to have completely disappeared. No-one has seen anything of him for a day and a half. As you're aware, we have every reason to believe he was implicated in the plot against us all. But we know he can't have been acting alone: he was, as it were, merely the puppet. We must find the puppet-master."

"Do you fear the Notary's been murdered, sir?"

"The puppet-master cutting the strings? It is a distinct possibility. But we need to be sure. Personally, I have the feeling that Ferrante, slippery as he is, has somehow contrived to escape. I've no proof, of course.

"And that's where you come in. I've plenty of eyes and ears in this city, to report on who said what to whom and when. What I need is a brain, too, to pull together all these threads and make a decent cloth. And as a young and, may I say it, unknown and inconspicuous fellow, you can ask questions too, and maybe receive answers others might not."

"I see, Sir. I'd be happy to help of course. But the dome ..."

"Ah, the dome, always the dome ..."

"But it is important, Sir. A work of art which will live forever – as will those associated with it."

"Yes, yes, but as I suggested yesterday, we've been putting up the dome for the best part of five years and it'll be many more before we're finished. After the next month or so, anyway, Brunelleschi's going to have far less time to spend on the dome. He is to be a *Priore* of the *Signoria* for the months of May and June."

A *Priore*! One of the nine members of the republican government of Florence. They were elected from members of the city guilds and theoretically anyone from a butcher to a lawyer could be one of the *Priori*, but in practice only men with connections and influence attained these positions. It was a singular honour for Brunelleschi and although the architect would no doubt grumble loudly about the role taking up too much of his time, he would be secretly pleased with the recognition of his status. And there were probably political machinations of which Luca knew nothing.

"As is the custom," Cosimo continued, "Filippo will theoretically be confined to the *Palazzo della Signoria*, though no doubt he will be allowed to escape from time to time to inspect vital parts of his beloved dome. Battista's perfectly competent and he can get on with the next stone chain without him being there every day."

"Yes, but..."

Cosimo laughed again: "And, of course, we'll have the invaluable aid of the third *Provveditore*, Lorenzo Ghiberti."

Luca again said nothing, but he knew that, like Brunelleschi, Cosimo de' Medici had a poor opinion of Ghiberti's architectural prowess, much as he admired him as a sculptor and bronze-maker. Perhaps Brunelleschi's new elevated status would enable him to remove his rival, at last, from his Supervisor's job.

"You can undertake my task in your spare time and still act as messenger between Battista at the *duomo* and Filippo in the *Palazzo della Signoria*. But to our business: how much do you earn as, how was it you described yourself? Assistant Building Supervisor? Some forty or fifty florins a year, is it?"

So Luca had to confess that for the past year, his earnings as Assistant Building Supervisor had been precisely nothing: he relied on his uncle for his board and lodging and on Donatello's generous 'money satchel' for his modest day-to-day expenses.

Cosimo was shocked; "How can you possibly live on nothing? Even the lowliest labourer needs something to feed himself and his family."

He picked up a brass bell on the desk and rang it. A servant appeared within moments and was asked to summon the Secretary.

"Nothing! How can this be?" Cosimo continued.

Luca explained that he wanted for little, with a roof over his head, an aunt who cooked his meals, washed and mended his clothes and a generous friend for whom giving away money was of no consequence. As he finished, Cosimo's Secretary arrived.

"Allonzo, I want you to prepare two purses for this young man," Cosimo told him. "One of five gold florins and the other an equivalent amount in silver." Turning to Luca, he said: "The silver is for your immediate expenses in our project: money will open doors and loosen tongues. The five florins are a part payment for last year's earnings: keep them safe. I shall make sure that the *Opera del Duomo* regularises your position straight away. What was Battista thinking of?"

Cosimo spoke to the Secretary again: "And we'll set up an account for *Messer* Luca here at the Medici bank, with an initial Discretionary Deposit of forty-five florins. See to it please." And as the Secretary was about to depart, he had another thought: "Oh and yet another purse of silver, perhaps five florins' worth again. Then *Messer* Luca here can replenish Donatello's horn of plenty!"

33

Federico, the bull-necked man, reported to Niccolò Peruzzi that Giovanni Ferrante had disappeared from the face of the earth: "I grilled the housekeeper again and shook up the old man a bit, but I'd swear neither had a clue where he'd gone. And I searched the house from top to bottom. Nuffing. Even broke into his desk: just some burnt-down sticks of sealing wax and a few bits of ribbon."

"Hasn't he got any other family in Florence?"

"Brother. Went to see him. Put the frighteners on, shook him up a bit, too, but he didn't have a clue either. No sign of him at the cathedral, nor anywhere."

"What is the bastard up to? Where's he gone?"

"Said 'e was going to Greve, didn't he? Got relatives there, according to his Dad. Works in the church of Santa Croce, like you said."

"I somehow think that's the last place the slippery bastard is going to be. He's been planning this for some time…"

But the discussion was interrupted by a soft knock on the door and the entry of a servant who said that a lawyer was downstairs asking to see him. The man's name was familiar: his firm had practised in Florence for generations, although the Peruzzi had never done business with them. Niccolò was curious and asked for him to be shown up.

The lawyer was not alone: he had a burly clerk with him, carrying an oaken box. After the formalities of greeting, the lawyer signalled to the clerk to place the box on the table and, producing a key from the folds of his black sleeveless gown and unlocked it with a flourish. He's more like one of those oriental street conjurors than a lawyer, thought Niccolò, but he couldn't resist looking inside, where he saw five dull brown pouches packed in snugly. The lawyer now produced a paper from his gown, which he carefully unfolded. "Sir," he said, "I have here a document which discharges the debts owed to you by *Ser* Pietro Ferrante. And here..." he pointed to the box, "...are five hundred florins. Sign the document, Sir, and the debt is repaid."

"Where on earth did the old fool get five hundred florins?" asked Niccolò, as Federico and the lawyer's burly servant eyed each other up suspiciously. "Don't tell me he won at backgammon!"

"It doesn't come from him, but from his son."

"Giovanni Ferrante! So, you've seen him! When was this? Today?"

"No, two days ago, in the early afternoon."

That was before I saw him, Niccolò calculated, disappointed. He was here that evening to report that he'd poisoned Donatello. "Did he say where he was going?" he asked the lawyer.

"No he didn't. He instructed me to bring this money to you next week, but when I heard that he'd disappeared I wanted to get this matter settled as soon as possible."

What a fool, thought Niccolò, if Ferrante really has absconded, the lawyer should have kept the money and no-one would have been any the wiser. Niccolò was in two minds over his own course of action. Half of him, in his anger and frustration over Giovanni Ferrante's disappearance, wanted to have his father thrown into *Le Stinche* for debt. That would show that bastard that he couldn't cross Niccolò Peruzzi. On the other hand, the old man wouldn't stay there long, now that funds were available to pay off the debt and any fine that accrued. Added to that, Giovanni's father didn't owe him much above four hundred and fifty florins, so there was a tidy profit in it too. Perhaps it would be better to take the money and deal with the father later, when he'd disposed of his son.

"Wait here," he told the lawyer and went into the anteroom where he unlocked a desk drawer and riffled though a pile of papers. Within a few minutes he returned with a dozen or so sheets of various sizes and colours. "Here are the old devil's promissory notes and receipts from the men I bought them from. Give me that paper and I'll sign it."

While the lawyer checked the notes against his own list, Niccolò eased his bulk into a chair beside the table and snapped his fingers. "Ink! Pen!" Federico hurried to the shelves by the wall fountain and brought an inkwell and quills. As he was reading through the lawyer's document, Niccolò asked: "Are you sure Ferrante gave you no clue as to where he was going?"

"Absolutely none," said the lawyer firmly, "but I'll tell you a most peculiar thing. You've heard about the goose that laid the golden eggs?

This man is becoming increasingly irritating, thought Niccolò. I'd quite like Federico to 'shake him up a bit' too. But he just nodded.

"But have you heard about the chicken that laid the golden pouches? Ten of them to be precise, each with one hundred gold florins inside" The lawyer looked at the other three men in the room triumphantly.

"What in God's name are you talking about?" said Niccolò, "Get on with it and just tell us what this is all about."

The lawyer seemed somewhat put out that his dramatic revelations were being so contemptuously dismissed, but rapidly told them how Giovanni Ferrante had come into his office with a large basket. "I'd already prepared the paper you're just about to sign and after Ferrante had read it, he took the cover off his shopping basket to reveal ... a whole dead chicken!"

"Your drama won't last long in the streets if it reveals nothing more exciting than a dead chicken in a basket," Niccolò scoffed.

"Ah, yes," said the lawyer triumphantly, "but have you ever seen a dead chicken with ten pouches of gold coins nestling underneath it, just like a clutch of eggs?"

Dexterously he removed the paper Niccolò had just signed, folded it and put it back in his pocket. Then he took the pouches from his strongbox, one by one:"Here you are. He gave me these five from underneath the chicken and took the rest away with him." He snapped the box shut and handed it to his clerk. "Still, whatever their provenance, these golden eggs have had the desired effect."

Niccolò was amazed: Somehow Ferrante had contrived to amass one thousand florins and had disappeared with five hundred of them. What was the slippery son of a vixen up to?

"Our business is concluded, Sir, with thanks," said the lawyer, "and I'll bid you good day." He bowed low, like a player at the end of his performance, and headed for the door, his clerk behind him carrying the empty box.

"I'll kill that bastard Ferrante," said Niccolò, finding that his emotions were limiting his vocabulary. He picked up one of the pouches, weighing it in his hand: "He won't have much time for his golden eggs when I catch up with him. But where is he and what's he going to do with the five hundred florins? " Niccolò paused. "Or rather five hundred and fifty florins," he said, remembering the fifty florins he'd given Ferrante after he'd reported that, supposedly, he'd poisoned Donatello. "The bastard," he said again.

34

Everyone in Donatello's workshop stopped what he was doing and watched in amazement as Luca poured a purseful of silver into the open canvas satchel hanging from the hook on the ceiling beam. Nobody had ever seen anyone, except for Donatello himself, putting money in: the sculptor's friends and apprentices were expected to take money out as they needed it.

When Luca first entered, Donatello had been chipping away at Habbakuk, muttering under his breath. Now he stood with mallet and chisel poised in mid air, as the coins chinkled on the canvas.

"My dear Luca, what on earth are you doing!"

"I just got paid," said Luca, mindful of Cosimo's insistence on secrecy about his new project, "and it's only right to repay a small part of all you've loaned me over the past year."

"Dear Luca, so kind, but totally unnecessary: money is of such little importance." He pointed his chisel at Habbakuk. "This is what matters – and I'm having the devil's own job getting his hand right." He ran the tip of his chisel along the prophet's forearm, down to the unfinished hand that was just beginning to emerge from the marble. "Come on Pumpkin Head," he grumbled at the statue, "tell me what you're thinking."

Habakkuk's strained face looked down on Luca with a piercing gaze and his mouth was slightly open as if, indeed, he was just about to speak. You could see the prophet was a troubled man and, from talking about it with Donatello, Luca understood that this was because Habbakuk had asked God why He allowed all the violence and injustice in the world to go on, without taking action to stop it. A tough question to which, it seemed, the prophet had received no answer. Luca thought about Rocco Rossi, who in death had become 'Bartolomeo da Siracusa': why had God allowed that to happen and would there ever be justice on this earth for him?

Right now, however, Luca had a more pressing personal problem to resolve. On his walk from the brickworks, once the cat and the chicken had been banished from his mind, he had thought intensely about his relationship with Donatello. The sculptor was becoming more and more possessive and, as well as doubts about his own sexuality, he felt the need to assert his independence. He averted his gaze from Habbakuk and touched Donatello's arm. "My friend," he said in a low voice, "can I have a private word?"

Donatello put down his chisel and mallet and they walked to the back of the room. He took both Luca's hands in his own and looked into Luca's eyes, his gaze more sorrowful than Habakkuk's: "I know what you're going to say. It's been clear for the last couple of days."

"I'm sorry; I want to be your friend, but ..."

"Out of our 'buts' come all the sorrows of our lives."

"It's just ..."

"Please don't explain." The sculptor's voice was cold. "I have a confession of my own. You know during the Cardinal's visit, when I said I'd disappeared for a piss? Well, I lied. Didn't you spot those choristers watching from the transept? One was a boy of such radiant loveliness... I had to see him again, and I have."

"Then you're not too upset?"

"No, now go, before I say something I'll regret."

With a final glance into his friend's face Luca turned and headed towards the workshop door. As he reached it, however, he heard a loud cry and, turning, he saw Donatello sweep all the tools off his work table.

Luca fled with tears in his eyes, which were still there when he reached the baptistry doors a few minutes later and put his hand on St. Luke's bronze head. Feeling drained and listless, he simply hadn't had the strength to go in the cathedral, so instead he sought sanctuary within the baptistry and tried to make sense of his feelings. As he sat gazing at the giant mosaic figure of the Risen Christ, the world somehow seemed unreal, as if an invisible barrier had been erected around him. His mind felt empty, but individual thoughts dripped in unbidden, like water falling from a leaf after a shower of rain.

Donatello loved him, judging by his anguished cry and his angry reaction to Luca's decision. And although Luca knew deep down that he had done the right thing to end his relationship with the sculptor, it didn't diminish his own pain. Then there was the 'radiant' choirboy: he was almost certain Donatello was making him up, but why was a stab of jealousy added to the dull ache of regret? Would he ever meet anyone as caring and considerate as Donatello? Could he ever love a man – or was it a woman he really wanted? The image of *La Bionda* appeared – the tumble of her golden hair, her breasts straining under the tight-laced bodice – and with it a surge of physical desire. Luca felt ashamed: did he really want to exchange Donatello for a whore? He put his head in his hands, feeling very young and very alone. At this moment he wished he was a child again, safe in his warm bed at the watermill, his mother bending over him to kiss him goodnight before leaving quietly, the candle throwing her soft shadow on the wall.

35

How long he sat there, indifferent to his surroundings, Luca didn't know, but he was aroused by the sound of bells, penetrating slowly into his consciousness at first, so he had been unable to count them, but gradually becoming clearer. Rising, he asked a robed sacristan, busy sweeping the stone 'carpets' between the octagonal font and the open doors, what hour had struck. "Why, eleven," said the man, his broom swishing on the sinuous patterns of black, white and red marble.

Luca, feeling slightly better in the sunshine, walked into the piazza where, only two days earlier, he had lain in Donatello's arms after his discovery of 'Bartolomeo's' body. The square was as busy as ever and Luca had to weave his way through the crowds. A boy with a hoop came careering towards him and he had to side-step as he sped past. That eccentric knight, the cooking-pot man, was there again, his cuirass of cast-iron pots clanking as he walked; the hot-pie seller also appeared, and Luca, conscious that he had had no breakfast, bought one: was it only yesterday that Donatello had done the same?

At the stall with the rosy awning, the owner had augmented his usual stock of woollens with vibrant artificial flowers in primary red, yellow and blue, ready for the coming May Day holiday. On a whim Luca bought one of each, costing only a few *dinari*, nothing to a man of his new-found wealth. As he handed over the coins, Luca asked: "What happened to that other stall? You know, the one selling potions and amulets and things?"

The man looked at him. "'You're the boy who discovered the body aren't you? Nasty sight that!"

"You can say that again," said Luca. "I'm trying to forget it."

"Don't blame you. Funny thing about that stall. Never saw it before that morning and never seen it since. I was going to ask the bloke who he was and all that, but they cleared the square before I had the time."

I was right, thought Luca. The stallholder was involved in the murder. The body, covered in the canvas sheet, must have been hidden under the stall earlier in the morning and left to be 'discovered' when the square was cleared.

"What did he look like, that bloke?" he asked.

"Well, he had a big thick neck, shaven head. He wasn't that tall, but well built, you know? Bulging biceps and all that. Sort of man you wouldn't want to argue with."

Luca thanked the stallholder and, clutching his flowers, crossed the piazza and once more entered the cathedral. The loud creaking of the hoist echoed down the nave, augmented by the rumble of wooden rollers and the shouts of men manoeuvring blocks of stone on them. Luca was nervous as, through air thick with dust, he approached his uncle who, as ever, was directing operations. What would he say about the fact that Cosimo de' Medici had found out that he hadn't been paid for a year?

His anxiety increased as Battista signalled him to follow and led him out through the South transept into the square, but he needn't have worried. Battista put a friendly hand on his shoulder. "Lad, lad," he said. "Why didn't you say something about your pay? It completely slipped my mind, what with one thing and another, so we never got your job regularised. I'm truly sorry."

"Uncle, it's of no consequence," said Luca, relieved, "you've looked after me so well in other ways."

"Nevertheless..." Battista shook his head, then added: "Anyway I've sorted it out with that pipsqueak of a pay clerk and you'll get paid regular from now on."

Luca asked: "Is there anything you need me for today?"

"No, all's under control, thank you. Brunelleschi's not here: over at the *Ospedale degli Innocenti* sorting out a problem." He looked at Luca's flowers: "They for me?"

Luca laughed and passed the gaudy flowers to him. "Here you are: give them to Aunt Martha, as a sort of 'thank you'. She deserves it."

Battista looked at the flowers suspiciously, but took them nonetheless, then searched for somewhere to put them down.

"I salute you, uncle," said Luca, taking his leave and setting off down the busy city streets again. This time he was headed for parish church of *San Tommaso*, near the central market. The funeral of Rocco Rossi, latterly known as Bartolomeo da Siracusa, the man who never was, had taken place there that morning and he felt a need to pay his final respects.

36

One of the features of the city that had fascinated Luca when he'd first moved to Florence was the way that all the citizens lived jumbled up with one another: there were no areas within the walls reserved exclusively for wealthy people, nor any 'stews' where only the poor were squeezed together. As he walked he again noticed how the houses of the powerful – some purpose-built *palazzi*, others haphazard accretions on the original house that the family had purchased generations earlier – stood cheek by jowl with retail premises and workshops, with houses and cottages, taverns and wineshops, churches and convents. So businessmen grown rich through wool and silk, as well as wealthy merchants and wealthier bankers, lived in the same streets as clothworkers, stonemasons, armourers, shoemakers, beggars, prostitutes ... the whole panoply of Florentine humanity.

Luca walked past a few of the poorer houses, just two storeys high, with a room on each floor, and then past an insubstantial one-storey cottage, which looked as if it might collapse with the first puff of wind. On one corner, builders were busy converting a noble's old *palazzo* into an apartment house, like the one in *Borgo la Croce* in which Jacopo and Maria had rented rooms.

Donatello had explained to Luca that the disorderly confusion of the city's dwelling places arose from the need for families, in the old days when they had first settled in Florence, to band together for protection from rival factions. Although by now the danger of physical attack had largely disappeared, influential family groups, with their numerous relations and dependents, still clung to the areas first settled by their forebears. There were dozens of these powerbases and everyone was aware of whose law ruled in which streets: the Albizzi, for example, were entrenched just South of the cathedral, while near the *Santa Croce* the Alberti shared their district with wool-cleaning shops and dyeworks. The Strozzi held sway around the monastery of *Santa Trinità* and the Medici, as well as property near the church of S*an Lorenzo*, had their stronghold in the parish of *San Tommaso*, where Luca was now heading.

The pay clerk at the cathedral had told him the time of the entombment and Luca had planned to arrive well after the ceremony was finished and say goodbye to the man he had never known, but for whom irrationally he felt some responsibility. As he arrived, however, the funeral party was still there, standing outside the church door, a dozen or so of them in black or dark-brown clothes, looking out on to the *piazza* as if unsure what to do next.

Luca, conscious of his own inappropriate beige-coloured doublet and hose, wanted to slip away and return later, but the pay clerk spotted him and rushed over. "*Messer* Luca Pasini, or should I say *Assistente Capomaestro*? How kind of you to come. Let me introduce you to Rocco's widow and her family."

So Luca had no choice but to be led into the group of mourners and to meet, first, Rocco's parents: the father, a handsome middle-aged man and his wife, slim, almost gaunt, but still showing signs of an earlier beauty in the high cheekbones visible beneath her veil. The clerk again addressed Luca as *Assistente Capomaestro*, elevating him to a status he didn't think he quite deserved and implying that he was a representative of the *Opera del Duomo* itself. Embarrassed, Luca gave his condolences, apologising for the way he was dressed, trying to smooth down his hair and explaining, lamely, that he was 'just passing by'.

And then a soft voice behind him said: "*Messer* Luca Pasini?" Turning, he saw a young woman enveloped in a hooded black cloak. She held the hood tightly, so that her face was fully covered. "I'm Alessia Rossi," she said, taking his hand in her own, the soft leather caressing his skin, "and I'd like to thank you for everything you've done for us."

"But I've done nothing," said Luca, trying unsuccessfully to see the face behind the folds of the mourning cloak.

"But you have done so much. Ever since Rocco disappeared a week ago our world has been a nightmare. If you hadn't identified him, we would never have known what had happened."

So even if Rocco's parents hadn't mentioned it, their daughter-in-law knew very well that Luca was the man who had discovered her husband's body. No doubt the pay clerk had told her: Luca hoped he had spared her the horrible details.

Alessia Rossi gestured to the funeral group: "And thanks to your connections with *Messer* Cosimo de' Medici all this has been paid for – and a tombstone for Rocco." There was a catch in her voice; she was clearly close to tears. "I can't thank you enough."

Again Luca felt that his part in the matter was much exaggerated: the money came directly from Cosimo de' Medici, with no consultation, of course, with Lucca, a lowly being with no influence whatsoever. But a question suddenly sprang into his mind and he was unable to stop blurting it out. "If your husband disappeared a week ago, why didn't you report it sooner to the authorities?"

He regretted saying it the moment the words were out, but Rocco's widow, who had a calm stillness in her sorrow, said: "The authorities?" she said, removing her hand from his. "We are poor, *Messer* Luca. Don't be misled by today's funeral finery: thanks to *Messer* Cosimo de' Medici's generosity most of our mourning clothes have been hired for the occasion." She drew the hood of her cloak even more tightly around her face and Luca had to lean in to catch her words. "The authorities?" she said disdainfully. "They'd have been no more interested in Rocco's disappearance than they are in investigating his murder. Justice is not for the likes of us."

She turned and walked away from him, joining her late husband's parents and began to talk to them. He blushed, bowed in general to the group and left hurriedly.

For half an hour or more he walked around the bazaar-like neighbourhood, bustling with people in the streets and in the warehouses, storerooms and shops. Luca hardly noticed all the activity, however, for he was thinking about what Rocco Rossi's widow had said. She was right of course: the authorities hadn't shown much interest in pursuing the investigation now that Rossi had been revealed to be a man of little consequence and that Brunelleschi and Donatello had been exonerated. Only Cosimo de' Medici seemed interested in finding out more – and only then to find ways of confounding his enemies rather than seeking justice for Rocco. It made Luca more determined than ever to find out the truth, a feeling reinforced by the soft sadness of Alessia Rossi.

He returned to the market square and to *San Tommaso*, entering the now-deserted church. There was no new tombstone yet on the floor of the nave: no doubt the mason had not had time to carve Rocco's name and restore his identity ready for the Last Judgement. But his resting place was easy to identify by the flowers on the temporary sandstone slab. Nearby monuments celebrated the glory of God, the honour of the city and the achievement of the incumbent in flowery language, but there were also many simpler slabs among the flagstones, some just recording a name and two dates. As in other parish churches in the city there was a surprising mix of elite and non-elite tombs – in death as in life the poor rubbed shoulders with the rich. Falling to his knees, Luca said his final goodbye to Rocco Rossi and vowed to find his killer.

37

Walking back from Rocco's grave, Luca tried to put in order his speculations on the murder. The obvious prime suspect was Giovanni Ferrante, particularly as he'd been missing for a day and a half. It was very unlikely, though not impossible, that he had killed Rocco Rossi himself: devious as he was, physical violence didn't seem to be in his nature. Nonetheless, he was central to the whole plot against Brunelleschi, Donatello and the Medici and was almost certainly the forger of the documents found on 'Bartolomeo da Siracusa'.

Looking back, Luca could see that Ferrante had stage-managed the whole of the demonstration on the cathedral steps, so that the Cardinal would 'discover' the bulging canvas sheet in the baptistry square. But who was Ferrante working for? Whoever concocted the plot was undoubtedly responsible for Rocco's killing.

And then there was the 'non-murder' of Donatello, with the non-poisoned chicken that the house cat had enjoyed so much. Someone had taken that chicken to the *Bargello*, but who? Perhaps the jailer could tell him more. He wasn't the pleasantest of men, but a few more *soldi* would probably loosen his tongue. Luca crossed the cathedral piazza and turned right towards the austere stone fortress of the *Bargello*.

"You're lucky," said the guard when he arrived at the massive studded doorway. "He doesn't start 'til five, but I seen him hanging around earlier today. Hang on, I'll go and get him."

The misshapen jailor was suspicious at first; "What d'you want?" he demanded, poking his foxy, unshaven face into Luca's own and donating his first blast of bad breath. Luca steered him to a quiet corner and used Don Antonio's technique of dangling a pouch of coins under his nose:

"I need some information. Can I buy you a drink?"

The soft clink of the silver had the desired effect. The jailer, Giulio, said: "All right, but not round here. I have to be careful who I'm seen drinking with!"

Despite the unsettling experiences of his previous visit, Luca took Giulio to the tavern where he'd first seen *La Bionda*. The jailer demanded a beer and when it arrived, had a noisy slurp. "Well, now," he said, wiping his mouth on his sleeve. "Show me your money and tell me what you want to know!"

Luca slid the purse across the table and Giulio picked it up, weighing it with a practised hand. He seemed satisfied. Luca said: "That man who brought the chicken for Donatello. What did he look like?"

"Wot did he look like? Well, he looked like Notary Ferrante, that's what he looked like. More than likely 'cos it was him!" The man whispered conspiratorially and Luca had to lean forward to hear his words, braving gusts of fresh beer, stale food and garlic.

"D'you know him then?

"O'course I know him. He's often in the *Bargello*, witnessing the statements of prisoners who've confessed to 'einous crimes."

Well, that was easy, mused Luca, drawing back to try to find some fresher air. Now we know that Giovanni Ferrante delivered the chicken and that it wasn't poisoned. What we don't know is why. "He didn't say why he'd brought it?"

"Just said Donatello was a mate of his and he didn't want him going hungry." The jailer downed the rest of his beer in a noisy swallow and stood up. "If that's all you need to know, I'll be off." He weighed the moneybag expertly in his hand. "I reckon you got your ten soldi worth. Pleasure to do business with you." And with a beery burp, he was away.

Another voice intervened as Luca watched the departing figure. "Are you a friend of Giulio Dogs-breath? He doesn't look your type." Laughing, *La Bionda* squeezed on to the bench just vacated by the jailer, a process which caused her voluptuous breasts to ripple in front of Luca's eyes. As on the previous occasion they were displayed above a tight-laced black velvet bodice, though the dress she wore today was a glowing green. "What's a nice young man like you doing with a low-life like that?"

Luca felt himself reddening as he pulled his gaze up to her face. He smelled her perfume, a musky haunting presence, as, still laughing, she shook her head, rearranging the long blonde billows of her hair. Her glorious full lips and her candid blue eyes, their lashes darkened by artifice, inflamed his desire.

"Er, I don't really know him at all," he stammered.

"Well, I'm glad to hear it. Would you like to buy me a drink?"

"Yes, of course. I, er ..." Luca was redder and hotter than ever, but *La Bionda* took charge, waving to the waiter who obviously knew what she wanted and disappeared to the serving area at the back of the room to get her order.

"So, tell me about yourself," she said. "It's not so often we get a good-looking young man like you in here. Do you live nearby? Have you just got into town?"

Luca heard her words and responded to them, but all his attention was focussed on her looks, those eyes, those lips and those inviting breasts... The sights and sounds of the tavern blurred into a dull background for her shining presence. He was transfixed.

The waiter arrived with a stoneware pitcher and two glazed beakers, placing them on the table. He was smiling and looked as if he was about to make a remark, but *La Bionda* dismissed him imperiously. "Off you go, Tommaso, we'll let you know if we need anything else." She filled the beakers with white wine and handed one to Luca: *"Salute."*

But before Luca could raise his beaker, she had dipped a finger in her own, moistening her lips with the wine, then sucking the end of her finger dry. She looked at Luca with those long-lashed eyes, her smile as bright as sunlight on a stream. "Do you like what you see?"

She leaned forward and pulled one end of the bow which topped the criss-crossed laces of her bodice. She gave a little tug, the bow parted, the laces stretched and it seemed as if those golden breasts would tumble out then and there. Luca watched spellbound as *La Bionda* toyed with the end of the lace and whispered to him: "For two florins you can see all – and who knows what else besides!" Then she sat back, laughing once more and, raising the cup, again wished him health before taking a generous gulp.

Luca took a sip of his own wine, but his heart pounded in his throat and he almost choked. He managed a series of spluttering nods.

"Come on then," she said, sweeping up the pitcher. "I'll take the wine, you bring the beakers." She was up from her seat and halfway across the room before Luca rose too and followed her. He knew every man was watching as she languidly mounted the stairs to the balustrade balcony, her bottom undulating in the green dress. He felt them watching him, too, but he didn't care: all rational thought had ceased, only desire remained.

La Bionda held open one of the doors in the corridor and after he'd entered the room, closed it firmly behind her.

38

The Cardinal sat before a large open window in his private sitting room in the palazzo set aside for his visit to Florence. Don Antonio was at a desk beside him and for a moment or two they both enjoyed the warmth of the sun. "So Ferrante's disappeared," the Cardinal said, helping himself to a piece of candied orange peel from a silver dish. "I told Cosimo to get him arrested before the Wool Guild meeting, but did he listen to me...? No he did not! Now we'll never know who's behind the plot."

The Cardinal took another piece of candied peel. "You must try one of these Antonio. Just the right amount of powdered ginger on them." He proffered the dish of sweetmeats. "By the way, what did you think of the boy who discovered the body? I like the look of him: an honest face and an earnest expression."

"And an unruly mop of hair!"

The Cardinal laughed: "Yes, but we can't hold that against him! It was brave of him to follow up his suspicions like that: I'm sure he doesn't encounter dead bodies on a regular basis; unlike you. And I was impressed by the way he brought Cosimo and me back to earth when we started reminiscing about the old days. That was brave, too, in a different way. Do you think he, too, could become a soldier for Christ?"

Taking a piece of peel, Don Antonio said: "I haven't yet had time to examine him on his religious beliefs, but he looks promising."

"He seemed to me quite unformed, but determined. A boy to watch." The Cardinal eyed the silver bowl, but resisted temptation and placed it firmly back on the table. "But to our own affairs: how long will you take to get to Carlo Malatesta?"

"I don't know. He's somewhere in the Romagna and the nearer I get the easier he'll be to find. The difficult part is knowing how he'll react."

"With the greatest suspicion – and he'd kill you as soon as look at you if he felt the need."

"No different from any other *condottiere* then."

"They're a necessary evil, I suppose: we need mercenary armies to fight our battles and experienced military men to command them, but most *condottieri* are as devious as a devil's grin."

Don Antonio tried to remember all that the Cardinal had told him about the wars that had scarred Northern Italy in recent years, as rival states like Florence, Venice and Milan fought for ascendency. The Church was involved, too, he knew, trying to preserve its rule in the Papal States to the South and East and to create a screen of trustworthy allies further up the peninsula. It was all very complicated, with shifting allegiances among the vying states, mysterious deaths among leading protagonists and treacherous desertions from one side to another by the *condottieri* and their forces.

The Cardinal had explained it all more than once, but Don Antonio had soon become lost in trying to recall who was fighting whom, and where and why. Luigi Mazzini seemed to have no such problems, but he'd told Don Antonio not to worry about the details: "Only three people understand the political situation in Italy," he'd laughed. "One of them is me and the other two have been driven mad."

There were some people who underestimated this portly churchman, with his obvious enjoyment of the finer things in life, but Don Antonio was not among them. He was well aware that the Cardinal's expansive exterior disguised a clever and sophisticated mind; a mind, moreover, dedicated to the service of his beloved Catholic Church. One thing was clear: for the Florentine Republic, and for the Pope and his possessions, the principal enemy at the moment was Filippo Maria Visconti, Duke of Milan, Lord of Cremona, Bergamo, Brescia, Genova and who knew where else besides. A shrewd political operator with vaunting territorial ambitions, he was also a cruel despot. Don Antonio remembered one story the Cardinal had told him.

"Beatrice Lascaris di Tenda, Countess of Biandrate, was the widow of the *condottiere* Facino Cane, a kind and considerate husband who had shared his honours and his riches with her (unusual in *condottieri* wouldn't you say?). After Facino's death the Duke of Milan took her for his wife, despite the fact she was twenty years older than he was. He took her fortune too, four hundred thousand ducats, so it's said, a dowry that funded his ambition.

"But he grew tired of her. The reason is unclear: her childless state, perhaps, or jealousy of her late husband's reputation or, more likely, because her power rivalled his own. He had her accused, falsely, of adultery, spirited her away from Milan with a couple of handmaidens to the castle at Binasco, tortured a young troubadour to make him confess to the adultery and had the whole lot of them executed in the castle courtyard."

All that had happened some seven years ago. Since then there had seemed no end to Visconti's successes and the triple alliance of the Papal States, Florence and Venice had suffered one setback after another in its struggles to contain him. And the alliance was wavering.

"Florence is firm enough," the Cardinal had told Don Antonio, "though they'll baulk at the taxes needed to raise more money for the troops. As for Venice, half of them want to trade with Visconti rather than to fight him, even though he's eyeing up Verona and Vicenza. Our defeat last year at Zagarona was a disaster."

"And Carlo Malatesta was Florence's *condottiere* at that battle?"

"Yes, and he managed to lose, despite having twice as many cavalry as the enemy."

"And Carlo was captured and imprisoned by Visconti?"

"Well, imprisoned might be too strong a word. Confined, maybe. Filippo Maria treated him more like an honoured guest and he was released unharmed. Say what you like about the Duke of Milan, he's a clever politician: Carlo Malatesta changed sides and joined him. Now he's rampaging about the Romagna on Visconti's behalf and our armies seem powerless to stop him."

Despite Malatesta's successes against the Florentine, Venetian and Papal forces, however, the Cardinal had come to believe that the *condottiere* might be the means of undermining Visconti's power. He might be persuaded to return to the triple alliance. As the Cardinal observed: "If a man has turned his coat once, he's more likely to turn it again."

The problem was how to entice Carlo back into the fold: did he want money, territory, titles? Did his conscience ache and could an absolution from the Pope perhaps salve it? The Cardinal wanted to sound out Malatesta, to find out what might persuade him to leave the Duke of Milan and join Florence and the Pope once more. "That's your task," he told Antonio, "a demanding and dangerous one."

"A mission I undertake readily for you and for the Church. But tell me more about the Malatestas. There were three brothers, weren't there?"

"Yes, Carlo himself, Pandolfo and Andrea, all *condottieri*. Andrea's dead now, of course..." The Cardinal went into intricate detail about the Malatesta brothers, their possessions, their campaigns, their victories and defeats. Don Antonio, though eager to learn, found himself drifting off as one fact followed another. But suddenly Luigi Mazzini was asking him a question: "When will you leave?"

"Tonight after dark. All the preparations are in hand."

"Take the greatest of care, Antonio. Any error ..." The Cardinal left his sentence uncompleted, but continued after a moment's contemplation: "I obviously can't risk writing anything down: parchment is so incriminating if it falls into the wrong hands. But I can give you this to establish your *bona fides*." He took from his finger the papal ring, a gift given to all the cardinals on their appointment by the Pope himself. "Keep this safe. Use it wisely when you have to."

Don Antonio put the ring on his own finger and turned it round so the image of Christ Crucified was hidden from view. The Cardinal stood up and Don Antonio knelt before him. With one hand on the priest's head and the other raised in benediction the prelate said: "The Lord bless you and keep you, my son. The Lord make his face to shine upon you and be gracious unto you."

"Amen," said Don Antonio fervently.

39

Luca da Posara, the Cardinal's potential soldier for Christ, lay on the bed naked and ashamed. "I'm sorry. I'm so sorry," he whimpered.

"Don't worry Luca, it happens all the time. You'd be surprised how often – even to the most experienced of men."

"But it was so sudden. I wanted it to last longer, but I couldn't stop myself. I'm so sorry."

La Bionda kissed him gently on the lips, pressing her naked body against him. She moved her arm down and her hand brushed playfully over his flaccid penis. "Not much good to man or beast," she laughed, "nor woman either."

Still embarrassed, and with his ears feeling as red as summertime poppies, Luca held his tongue. The feel of *La Bionda*'s soft skin against his and the heady smell of her perfume revived memories of the excitements of a few moments ago and the wondrous elation he felt as he entered a woman for the very first time; a euphoria, however, which was to be dissipated within seconds as his over-excited body sped uninvited and all-too-rapidly to its climax.

La Bionda nibbled Luca's earlobe and whispered. "Don't worry little Luca." Her hand brushed him again. "Or should we say big Luca? We'll soon have you rampant once more – and longer lasting." She raised herself up on an elbow and regarded him with those light-blue eyes. "Mind you," she said, "it'll cost you. You can't expect two goes for the price of one, y'know."

The sentimental, if embarrassed, reverie into which Luca was beginning to fall was shattered by the vulgarity of her sentiments. It reminded him all-too-clearly that this was a commercial transaction, not a romantic encounter. Suddenly he wondered if he would ever feel aroused again. At present he rather doubted it. Looking at *La Bionda* he noticed that there was a tiredness about her eyes and a certain coarseness of her features, usually disguised by her careful make-up, but visible at close quarters. On the other hand, the firm softness of the flesh that pressed against his own was undeniably alluring and, even as he had half a mind to rise from the bed and leave, she put one long brown leg over his and pinioned him to the mattress. Her lips, still bearing some scant traces of the pink colour that they had originally been painted, but much diminished by their earlier exertions, moved down to caress his nipple, which she then licked lightly with her tongue. It was instantly erect and when she nibbled it gently he moaned softly. Yes, there were signs of new life below.

But *La Bionda* pulled back and again propped herself up on her elbow. "I think it'll be even better if we wait a few minutes," she said, exhibiting a professional knowledge that rather perturbed Luca, even though he was now under no illusions about the nature of their relationship. "So while we wait, why don't you tell me about yourself? Where is Posara and what brings an innocent country boy like you to this wild and wicked city?"

Talking about himself had been the last thing on Luca's mind, but soon, with *La Bionda*'s soft encouraging responses and the feel of her body next to his own, he found he was telling her all about his life in Florence and his pride in working on Brunelleschi's wonderful dome.

"It was you who discovered that grisly body in the piazza, wasn't it?" *La Bionda* said, giving an exaggerated, theatrical shudder and tightening the grip of her leg on his.

"Yes," Luca admitted, "and more than that ..." and before he knew where he was he was telling her about the Sicilian mathematician who never was and his discovery of the real identity of the corpse.

"Oh, we know all that, the Man Who Never Was, the Workman with the Scimitar Birthmark and the Strange Disappearance of the Skinny Notary..." She made each incident sound like a short story, as if it were one of those in the *Decameron*.

"But how...?"

"How do I know?" She kissed him again on the lips. "Well, we working girls soon get to know everything that's going on here. It's a small city after all, Florence, and nothing stays secret for long, especially tales told between the sheets. Mind you, we try to keep our sources confidential, as they say."

"You sound more like a priest than a ..."

"...than a whore," she said, completing his sentence and adding quietly: "I know what I am." She fondled his nipple again: "There's more that tumbles out in these confessionals than in those draughty cupboards in our churches. And who'd you rather talk to, a man in a skirt or a girl who's only too happy to take hers off?"

Luca, whose faith was of a simple rural variety, and who counted the village priest of Posara, Don Giuseppe, as one of his heroes, to say nothing of the gallant Don Antonio and the clever Cardinal, was more than a little shocked by her frankness. He felt as if his youthful innocence were melting away, as quickly as an April frost in the morning sun.

"The biggest mystery, *La Bionda* continued, "is what's happened to that bag of skin and bone, Giovanni Ferrante. Disappeared off the face of the earth, he has."

"D'you know him?" asked Luca. "Oh, is he one of your ..."

La Bionda put her fingers on his lips. "I told you, our sources are confidential. Let's just say none of us girls has seen him for a couple of days ..."

"I think he's the key to this mystery."

"Well, it's a key that seems to have disappeared down a drain hole. Like the man himself: he's scrawny enough to have done so. But I'll tell you a really peculiar story about Ferrante, which happened just before he disappeared. Have you heard about the Chicken that Laid the Golden Eggs?"

"It was a goose, surely?"

"Not this time. That afternoon Giovanni Ferrante was wandering about town with a shopping basket containing a dead chicken, under which lay, like unhatched eggs beneath a broody bird, ten leather pouches, each filled with a hundred florins. That's what I call golden eggs!"

"A thousand florins! Where did the old skinflint get that sort of money? And what did he want it for?"

"Well, he gave half of it to a lawyer to pay off his father's gambling debts – and the other five hundred has disappeared with him."

"Tell me about the chicken," said Luca, his mind suddenly reverting to its insistent theme of 'the cat is alive, so the chicken is fine.'

"What a funny boy you are, Luca. I'm telling you about a fortune in florins and you want to know about a dead chicken!"

"Was the basket covered in a blue check cloth?"

"How on earth should I know? I only know that five hundred florins were used to pay off old man Ferrante's debts and his son has disappeared with the rest."

"Yes, but ..." Luca began, but *La Bionda* cut him short by kissing him fully on the lips. Her hand moved down again, grasping the tip of his penis and pushing down and up again in one quick movement. She paused at the top of her stroke for a second or two, then plunged down and up once more, again stopping at the top, for what seemed to Luca like an interminable age, but was in reality less than a couple of seconds, before plunging down once more. She repeated this process five or six times, then started a series of a dozen or so quick strokes before again holding him erect by the tip. Luca moaned as *La Bionda*'s mouth moved down to nibble his nipple and as she began the whole process again.

Cats and chickens fled from Luca's mind and he once again stood proud and erect, engorged with lust and, like a keen soldier, ready once more to sally unto the breach.

40

It was late afternoon when Luca, a broad grin on his face, again walked through the centre of the city, on his way to report his latest findings to Cosimo de' Medici. A scatter of pigeons took off in front of him as he rounded the corner of the *Via dell' Oriuolo* where it opened into the broad space in front of the towering South wall of the cathedral, gleaming green and white in the afternoon sun. How well he felt, how fit, with every muscle and fibre in his body seemingly glowing with health.

He was a man, a real man, at last, and he wanted to embrace every passing stranger, male or female, in sheer exuberance. He grinned at two laundrywomen passing by, laden with bundles of dirty washing. At first they looked affronted but, infected by his high spirits, clucked to themselves, then smiled too before continuing on their way.

As well as the celebration of his graduation from boy to man, there was another reason for Luca's good humour. When the afterglow of his love-making had dimmed, his mind had again turned to the subject of Giovanni Ferrante. "Tell me," he'd asked *La Bionda* as he pulled on his doublet, "who was the lawyer that Ferrante gave the five hundred florins to, to pay off his father's debts. And who owned the debts in the first place?"

"You don't want to know, Luca. Such men are dangerous. Keep well away."

But as Luca gave her four florins from his purse he noticed how greedily she looked at the rest of the coins and boldly, on the spur of the moment, he asked: "I wonder if another five florins might liberate the secrets of the confessional?" *La Bionda* leaned forward, the sheet dropping from her voluptuous breasts, and took all the money. She looked around as if frightened of being overheard, then said softly: "Niccolò Peruzzi. He's the man who owned Ferrante's father's debt."

"Who?"

She pulled Luca towards her and whispered in his ear: "Niccolò Peruzzi. But have a care Luca. He's a vicious bastard. Tell no-one I told you, for the love of God and his Saints."

Passing the baptistry, Luca again stopped to give St Luke a rub on his head and hurried on to the Medici house in *San Tommaso*. The Secretary greeted him warmly: "You look very well, *Messer* Luca, but rather hot. Have you been indulging in vigorous exercise?"

Luca waved a deprecating arm as the Secretary continued. "My master will be pleased to see you. He has more news of *Ser* Giovanni Ferrante. The banker *Messer* Federico Morelli has just left. It seems..." But the old man broke-off, apparently thinking better of continuing. "It will be more fitting if I take you straightaway to *Messer* Cosimo. He'll explain."

"The banker Morelli?" Luca began to ask, but the Secretary walked silently down the corridor and showed him again into the library, where Cosimo sat in his favourite oak chair with its red leather cushion.

"Ah, Luca," said Cosimo, motioning him to sit in a folding curule chair opposite him. "Why, you look very animated and rather flushed. Are you well?"

"Perfectly well," said Luca, "in fact weller, I mean better, than I've ever been." Cosimo looked at him rather strangely, but only said: "Allonzo, get one of the servants to bring *Messer* Luca here a cool cordial. He looks as if he needs it."

As the Secretary left, Cosimo told Luca: "I have just had a most interesting meeting with *Messer* Federico Morelli, one of our lesser bankers, who's been telling me about a loan of one thousand florins he made earlier this week to that dastardly knave Ferrante.

"It seems that Ferrante had set up the loan some time ago and came to collect the money in the afternoon of the day he disappeared. He wanted the money in cash – and you'll never believe what he did with it."

Luca almost blurted out: "Put it in his shopping basket under a dead chicken," but stopped himself in time realising that it would be unwise to steal Cosimo de' Medici's punchline.

"He put it in a shopping basket under a dead chicken!" Cosimo duly obliged. "Ten bags of one hundred florins each: all arranged under a chicken like a clutch of eggs!"

"I can tell you what happened to five of them," said Luca. "They went to pay off Ferrante's father's gambling debts." Cosimo looked a little put out that his protégé had already heard the chicken story, but was more than interested when Luca told him, without revealing his source, the story he had heard on *La Bionda*'s pillow.

"So, who was paid off?"

"Niccolò Peruzzi."

"*Niccolò* Peruzzi?" Cosimo emphasised the first name, frowning. "*Niccolò*? The rest of the family are influential enough, but Niccolò? He's just a nasty good-for-nothing. I thought they'd disowned him."

"Well, it seemed he did own Ferrante's father's debts."

"Did Ferrante pay Peruzzi personally?

"No, I think a lawyer did it on his behalf."

"Which lawyer?"

"I don't know, sir. My source – well, she just wouldn't say."

"She – a woman? Who?"

"I'd rather not say, sir."

"Luca da Posara, let me be very plain with you. As you are on my payroll, you will keep no secrets from me. Out with it. Who was this woman?"

So Luca was forced to reveal her name. "*La Bionda*?" said Cosimo. "Does she have no other name?"

"I-I don't know, sir."

Realisation dawned on Cosimo's face. "A whore! She's a whore! You've been spending my money on whores."

Luca bowed his head, which now felt as hot as bread fresh from the oven. But he looked up as he heard Cosimo chuckle. "Still no matter," the banker said. "It is the result that counts. Now at least we have a name: Niccolò Peruzzi. There may be others, of course. But he certainly had a hold on Ferrante and could well be one of those in the plot against us."

Luca, whose mouth was dry, felt he had to say. "But she – *La Bionda* that is – she made me promise to tell no-one. She seemed very frightened of this Niccolò Peruzzi, whoever he is."

"She has some cause, he has an evil reputation. But don't worry; we'll soon get to grips with *Messer* Niccolò."

Just then a servant knocked and came in with the cool cordial Cosimo had ordered. Luca drank it gratefully. Cosimo chuckled again:

"Well, Master detective, now you and your ardour are cooled, shall we review the situation? As you and the Cardinal would say: '*One*, Niccolò Peruzzi had a hold over Ferrante because of his father's debts and therefore could be one of the conspirators against us. *Two*, Ferrante raised one thousand florins before he disappeared and has taken five hundred of them with him, wherever he's gone."

"But why did your banker friend Morelli lend him all that money in the first place?" Luca interrupted.

"Oh, he told him he had a wonderful investment opportunity with a *lanaiolo*, who was set to make a killing with a new dyeing process. Morelli was already impressed because Ferrante had previously told him he had insider information that the price of alum was about to rise rapidly because of increasing demand. Morelli bought alum and made a killing."

I'm sure he wasn't the only one, thought Luca. Hadn't someone told him the Medici controlled the alum trade?

"Let's continue our review of the situation," said Cosimo. Where were we? Oh yes: *Three:* If Peruzzi controlled Ferrante he was likely behind the killing of that man with no name ..."

"Rocco Rossi," said Luca quietly.

"Yes, yes. And behind the plot to discredit us all. It'll take a few days to gather my allies together; the Peruzzi are a powerful family. But we still need to find Ferrante. He's the sort of man who'd break under a little forceful questioning."

Luca said: "Oh, and I found out from the jailer at the *Bargello*, that it was Ferrante who took the poisoned chicken to Donatello – only it wasn't poisoned."

"What does that mean?"

"Well, sir, I've been thinking about that. Perhaps this Niccolò Peruzzi ordered Ferrante to poison Donatello, but he only pretended to do so."

"Sounds a bit complicated to me," Cosimo sighed and added, "but, point *Four*, we still haven't the faintest idea where Ferrante is. You can go a long way on five hundred florins."

41

That afternoon, the man whom both Cosimo de' Medici and Niccolò Peruzzi wanted urgently to lay their hands on, the one to question him vigorously, the other no doubt to throttle him slowly, was enjoying a plate of asparagus in a tavern in Pisa.

Enjoying was perhaps not quite the right word for although the vegetables were fresh, some of them tasted rather strange. Giovanni Ferrante called the waiter over and asked how they were cooked. "Well," said the boy, "they're all supposed to be cooked in olive oil, but we just ran out. So some are cooked in butter."

"And how I am supposed to tell which is which?"

"Well, you could sniff 'em, I suppose."

Such impertinence! If Giovanni had only been twenty years younger, he'd have thrown the plate in the boy's face, drawn his sword and chased him round the room. Not that he'd ever worn a sword, but in the exhilaration of his escape, he seemed to be reinventing himself as an adventurer, ready to undertake any deed of derring-do.

More rational considerations rapidly emerged, not least the need not to draw any attention to himself. So he smiled thinly – and sniffed. Yes. It was possible to distinguish between those cooked in oil (as they should have been, with a few green onions and some nutmeg) and those cooked in butter which, judging by the smell, was a little rancid. He pushed those to one side and ate the others.

Giovanni had secured a place on a freighter which was due to sail for England by the late evening tide and he was taking an early supper before returning on board. Sipping on his wine, a cool white from one of the villages of the Cinque Terre, he contemplated the events of the last few days.

After he'd slipped out of his house, evading both the bull-necked man and the watch, he'd spent a restless night in the inn, not helped by bites from bed bugs and the prodding of the money belt, which he would not take off. He'd worried too about what to do with the phial of poison, still sealed, lying in the pocket of his cloak: he had to find a way of getting rid of it.

Giovanni had left the inn early in the morning, walking down to the Arno from the *Porta al Prato* and booking a passage on one of the many barges that left daily for the fifty-mile journey to Pisa. He was dressed in a faded mustard-coloured *cioppa* and a matching *cappuzzo*, its long woollen scarf wrapped around his neck, half obscuring his face. As well as the money pouch concealed under the day gown, Giovanni also had a leather purse, secured by a brass stud, slung from his belt and in it were documents, the results of much labour by candlelight with parchment, paper, ribbon, wax and seals, which identified the bearer as Bartolomeo de' Verdi, civil administrator. How proud Giovanni was of the *laissez passer* from the Florentine government with its elaborate seals from the *Signoria* and of the letter of commendation from the *Gonfaloniere* himself.

He considered the 'Bartolomeo' to be a masterstroke, a final private joke against his enemies. Just as he'd created Bartolomeo, the Sicilian mathematician, he'd now invented another Bartolomeo, the civil servant whose documents showed that he had been born in Genova to a father with a common surname, which in itself brought a certain anonymity.

There had been no problem at all with his papers: they merited no more than a cursory glance from the petty officials who controlled movement along the river highway and although the barge trip was expensive, it was far safer than the hazardous journey along the dirt road from Florence, where unemployed mercenary bands lay in wait to rob travellers and to murder those who resisted. With five hundred florins or so under one's *cioppa*, the huddled obscurity of the barge was far preferable. The journey was a slow one, though, and the conditions cramped and smelly, especially when a fellow passenger relieved himself over the side, but after a day, a night and the best part of a second day, the barge and Giovanni – or rather Bartolomeo – arrived, unremarked, in Pisa. He'd even been able at night, while taking a piss himself, to jettison the phial of poison into the Arno's murky waters.

If he had one concern, apart from being discovered, which seemed less and less likely, it was for his father and wrath of Niccolò

Peruzzi. Would that nasty piece of work have the old man imprisoned for debt or even do him harm? Giovanni worried, but he thought it probable that Niccolò's greed would out-trump his anger and that he would take the money and sign the paper discharging his father's debt. One could not legislate for all possibilities, however, and his father would have to take his chances.

So, finishing his wine, settling his bill and resisting the temptation to scold the waiter, Bartolomeo de' Verdi set off, like Brutus of Troy, for a new life in Albion, hoping to set sail 'with a fair wind for the promised land.'

42

A few hours later that day, in the chapel of a convent near the Florence city walls, a man knelt alone, staring at a picture above the altar, lost in prayer: *"Ave Maria, gratia plena, Dominus tecum. Benedicta tu in mulieribus ..."*

The convent was richly endowed and as a consequence could afford to light the altarpiece with many candles, perhaps three dozen of them in all. The gilt frame glistened and within it the haloes of Jesus and his Mother, and of half-a-dozen angels, glittered and twinkled. Mary and Christ sat on a splendid throne, patterned in red and gold and Our Lord, in a dark pink gown, was in the process of placing a crown on Mary's head. The Virgin was in simple white, her hands demurely on her lap. *"Sancta Maria, Mater Dei, ora pro nobis peccatoribus, nunc et in hora mortis nostrae. Amen"*

Of course there was nothing in the Bible about Mary being crowned when she arrived in heaven, but Don Antonio had long felt a special allegiance to the Virgin, his glorious queen, truly blessed among women. As well as praising her, he prayed for a safe journey and a successful return. He repeated his Ave Maria, then rose reluctantly from the altar rail.

Had you never seen Don Antonio before, you would never have taken him for a churchman. He looked far from priest-like: he was booted and spurred and wore a deep-red tunic and hose, all covered in a maroon cloak. His face wore a serious, even severe, expression and his demeanour, even as he crossed himself before the altar, seemed more martial than ecclesiastical: like St George, he was ready for action.

The Mother Superior, who had been waiting at the back of the chapel, came forward with his sheathed sword, which he had taken off and handed to her before praying. When they reached the cloister together, the *cavaliere* replaced the sword on his belt, covering it with his cloak. The Mother Superior picked up a lantern and led him through the garden, in which he caught a fleeting scent of Evening Stock, to a low gate in the city's encircling wall. She unlocked it and as Antonio squeezed through, blessed him and quietly closed the gate again.

After the calm of the afternoon, the wind had picked up and now it blew angry clouds across the moon, still in its first quarter. There was again a hint of rain in the air. For a few moments Antonio felt disorientated, almost blind. He heard a horse nicker, then saw the light of a shaded lantern swaying in some trees thirty or so paces ahead of him.

There were two horses under the grove of umbrella pines, whose angular branches were revealed when the cloud suddenly cleared the moon, and two grooms, one with the shaded lantern beckoning him forward. No word passed between them as the other groom bent, interleaving his fingers to provide a step for the *cavaliere* to mount to the saddle, with its elevated pommel and a cantle which hugged his hips. The second horse, tied to the first by a long leading rein, had a light-brown bag strapped across its back and two others, longer and thinner, strung fore-and-aft.

Don Antonio, or rather *Cavaliere* Antonio Falcone as he now called himself, spurred his horse and, to a murmured "Godspeed" and a softer "Amen," moved out from under the trees as clouds again obscured the moon.

43

During the following week there were no developments in what *La Bionda* would undoubtedly have described as The Continuing Case of the Missing Notary. Ferrante's whereabouts remained a complete mystery.

Niccolò Peruzzi, too, had disappeared from his palazzo. Cosimo de' Medici's agents had made discreet enquiries and it seemed that he had left to inspect his country properties. When he was to return, no-one knew.

Luca had little time for any investigations of his own, for Battista kept him busy and he seemed to be mounting the steps to the top of the dome more than a dozen times a day – and despite worries about the consequences, he usually managed not to count them. Brunelleschi collared him more than once, fussing about putting in place the next stone ring in the dome. "I want you to understand completely what it's all about," the architect told him, "so you and Battista know exactly what you're doing when I'm imprisoned in the *Palazzo della Signoria*."

Among the 'secrets of the dome', apart from the double-shell construction and the ingenious arrangement of the millions of bricks, were the stone 'restraining rings' that girdled the cupola, embedded in the inner shell. "They're like giant hoops around a barrel," Brunelleschi explained, "and they do more or less the same job. You see, as we build upwards and inwards, the problem is not just that the dome will fall to the ground, but also that it will splay outwards. These rings are designed to stop that happening."

In all there were to be four stone rings, one each at the top and the bottom of the dome and the other two evenly spaced between them. Now, as the structure curved inexorably inwards, it was time to put the second stone restraining ring in place.

"We call them rings," said Brunelleschi, showing his drawings to Luca, "but because the true shape of the dome is octagonal rather than circular, we can't just wrap a simple chain around it. Our restraining rings also have to be octagonal in shape."

"Yes, I see that," said Luca, "they need to be strong and rigid, so they keep their shape under pressure." He picked up one of Brunelleschi's drawings, tracing his finger along the outline of one of eight stone ribs. "But at the same time they mustn't deform these ribs, which are the corners of the dome."

"Clever boy! Absolutely right. If only some of those numbskulls in the *Opera del Duomo* could grasp things as well as you."

The first stone ring, built on top of the tambour, was already in position, of course. In each of its eight sections there were two parallel sandstone beams, their blocks connected end-to-end with lead-glazed iron splices, and at right-angles to the beams and notched into them, were overlapping stone cross-ties. This stone ring was now largely covered by the outer shell, though the ends of the cross-ties could still be seen protruding outwards from its base.

Luca's uncle Battista had already begun hoisting up the sandstone blocks for the second ring and the masons were busy fitting them into position. Among them, Luca's brother-in-law Jacopo, who had at last turned up for work, though as far as Brunelleschi and Battista were concerned it was debatable whether they would have been better off without him. For on his return Jacopo seemed more disruptive than ever.

He was still drinking more than his share of the watered wine Brunelleschi provided for the dome workers to accompany their noontime meal but, perversely, he now refused to eat the food prepared in the kitchen specially set up so that the mason-sculptors, wall-makers and labourers could eat in the dome itself, without a time-wasting descent to the ground. Maria told her brother: "I don't know what's got into him. He seems to think someone's trying to poison him." Jacopo insisted that Maria prepare his food herself and bring it to him, a major problem since she was terrified of heights and couldn't climb into the dome. She had, however, found a boy who was willing, for a *soldo* or two, to take up to Jacopo the small wooden box containing his meal.

Jacopo was still grumbling continually about his wages and urging others to do the same, even to the point of suggesting that they formed an illegal union and threaten to withdraw their labour if their demands were not met.

"It's got to stop," Brunelleschi told Luca. "If it goes on like this I'll sack the lot of them and start again. I asked you last week to have a word with him. Have you done so?"

Luca confessed that he hadn't. "I'll talk with him today," he promised.

Jacopo was surprised when Luca suggested they go out for a drink. "Oh, my high-and-mighty *Assistente Capomaestro* brother-in-law deigns to drink with me, does he?" But he agreed readily enough and later that day, he and Luca left the precinct together.

"Where d'you want to go?" Jacopo asked and Luca could smell the wine on his breath and thought his voice was already a little slurred.

"I don't mind? What do you think?"

To Luca's consternation, Jacopo led him to the tavern where he had had his encounter with *La Bionda*, but they were through the door before he could make any objection and, anyway, he wasn't quite sure how he was going to explain to his brother-in-law why he'd rather not go in. Although the room was very crowded there seemed, mercifully, to be nobody there who recognised him, with no sign either of *La Bionda* or of the friendly waiter Tomasso. Quite a few people seemed to know Jacopo, though, including the morose man who was there again silently regarding his pitcher of wine, who looked up and gave a sad smile. Luca was also concerned to see that two or three of the heavily painted women also seemed to be familiar with his brother-in-law. "Buy us a drink, Jacopo," shouted one of them, showing far too much of her cleavage.

"Not tonight, darling." Jacopo smirked, "Got my little brother-in-law in tow. Don't want to pervert his tender morals."

It's a bit late for that, thought Luca, but held his tongue. When Jacopo had bought a pitcher of red wine, they found a corner where they could sit. Jacopo took a big slurp while Luca sipped his.

"So, you recovered from your grisly encounter last week?" Jacopo asked, before taking another swig. Luca said yes, he had, thanks for asking, but he was concerned that no-one seemed very interested in seeking justice for Rocco Rossi or his wife and children.

"Don't you worry about them," said Jacopo, "I hear banker Medici's looking out for them, so they'll not starve."

"But they won't know who killed their father and husband or see them punished for the crime."

Jacopo looked at his brother strangely. "Punished, eh? You think it would help if someone was hanged for the crime? Or tortured with the *strappado*? Can you imagine what that must be like?" He took another mouthful of wine. "Still, it was a pity you had to find the body. Terrible sight, I'm told."

Luca was surprised: he couldn't ever recall having a sympathetic word from his brother-in-law in the past, but before he could reply Jacopo rapidly changed the subject: "Anyway, what do you want to talk to me about?"

"Well," Luca replied hesitantly, "Uncle Battista, um, and *Messer* Filippo are very concerned about your behaviour at the dome ..."

"My behaviour! Who do they think they are? Schoolteachers?" Jacopo slammed down his beaker, spilling wine on the table. "And why do they send a snotty little schoolboy to tell me?"

"Getting cross with me won't change things," said Luca bravely. "I'm only the messenger." And before his brother-in-law could fulminate further, he added rapidly: "The way you're going you'll lose your job. Brunelleschi will fire the lot of you if you try to form an illegal guild and demand more money. Then where'd you and Maria be?"

His brother-in-law looked at him truculently for a moment, then said: "There's plenty more money around in Florence if you know where to look. And Brunelleschi and his precious Cosimo de' Medici aren't the only game in town."

"But what about the dome? It's the most marvellous construction in the world. Aren't you proud to be a part of it?"

"I'm proud of my skill – and all I'm asking is fair pay for my work. Just because you're erecting a masterpiece doesn't mean you should use slave labour."

"Slave labour! The *Provveditore* makes sure you're paid well for what you do."

"Well, we get the going rate, that's true. But Brunelleschi's mate Medici makes in an hour what it takes me a year of hard graft to earn. It's about time people like him learned the true value of labour."

They argued back and forth for some time, their looks across the table meeting like sword blades and with Jacopo becoming more belligerent with every mouthful of wine. Soon the pitcher was empty and Jacopo picked it up to wave for more. Luca, however, got to his feet and, downing his own beaker, said: "Not for me. It's getting late and it'll soon be curfew. Aunt Martha'll have my supper on."

"Aunt Martha'll have my supper on!" Jacopo mimicked. "What a baby boy you still are Luca. You've swapped your mother's apron strings for your Aunt Martha's. You want to get out more, have a bit of fun while you're young. Get yourself a woman ..."

If only you knew, thought Luca, glancing up at the balustraded balcony. "That's as maybe," he said, "but now I'm off."

"Well, I'm not," said Jacopo, handing his pitcher to a hovering waiter and looking around the motley crew in the tavern. "There's good fun and fine talk to be had here." He rose unsteadily, waving his empty beaker. "Eat, drink and be merry, for tomorrow we die." He staggered away to the centre of the mêlée without a backward glance at his brother-in-law who, with a despairing shrug, turned and walked out, breathing deep the gathering gloom.

44

It took Don Antonio more than a week to find Malatesta and his army. He lost count of the days, but then one morning he saw the smoke from their numerous campfires smudging the cloudless azure sky. After an hour or so, as he followed the banks of the Montone river, a group of four armed horsemen emerged from a copse ahead and cantered towards him. Don Antonio reined in his horses and waited patiently for their arrival.

The leader of the group, a dark-haired man with a well trimmed beard and moustache, mounted on a fine white horse caparisoned in red trappings, asked his business in polite but authoritarian tones, and on being told that Don Antonio wished to enlist in Malatesta's forces, undertook to take him to the *condottiere*. He rode beside Don Antonio while the other three horsemen fell in behind, next to the packhorse. They set off at a gentle trot and once through the wood, emerged into a large meadow, perhaps three hundred paces square.

Don Antonio was struck at first by the noise: the pounding of the hammers of the armourers, the clash of steel as men-at-arms practised their sword-fighting, the barked commands of sergeants and the thunderous thuds of horses' hooves as mounted lancers rehearsed their manoeuvres. The sights were impressive, too: a dozen knights, some in full armour were tilting at a quintain, laughing at the efforts of their comrades. One fine older man, grey-bearded and wearing a wide-brimmed brown leather hat with a splay of white feathers on its crown, was cantering around on a chestnut horse, waving his long spear. I am not sure whether I would be more frightened being on his side than opposing him, thought Don Antonio. There were foot soldiers, too, some wearing cuirasses, others simply in skirted tunics and hose of a variety of colours, a stunning mauve, maroon and mustard among them. They fought each other with short swords and varying degrees of enthusiasm, fending off the blows with rounded shields.

All around this martial meadow were tents of various sizes, with pointed roofs. The smaller ones, which were clearly for the men to sleep in, were arranged in orderly lines, while other larger tents served as warehouses for the quartermasters or mess halls for the troops. Don Antonio's party stopped in front of one of the bigger tents, surrounded with banners on long poles, the largest of which depicted a sinuous midnight-blue serpent with a man in its jaws, the Duke of Milan's coat of arms. Two men-at-arms with spears stood guard outside the entrance. Don Antonio was asked to dismount and his horses were taken away by his escort as he was marched in by one of the guards, past a young officer at a trestle table by the entrance, who was studying what appeared to be lists of troops. Beyond him, at the rear of the tent, Carlo Malatesta was sitting at a larger table, looking at a map.

In his late fifties, the *condottiere*'s face was sallow, although the creamy light coming through the canvas added some colour to it. His dark hair, cut *en brosse*, was speckled with silver. A dark-red sash was thrown over one shoulder of his burnished cuirass, which was worked into an idealistic representation of the male torso, giving the impression, no doubt intentional, of a Roman general, perhaps even Caesar himself. Don Antonio came to attention in the centre of the tent and gave, as seemed appropriate, a Roman salute, his right fist against his chest.

"So, you want to enlist in my forces," said the *condottiere*, dismissing with a gesture the guard who had brought in Don Antonio. "But where's your sergeant, your page, your men at arms?"

"At present, there is just myself, My Lord, and my skill with sword and lance." Don Antonio bowed low.

"Hmm. Why do you think I need a solitary free lance?" But the *condottiere* was obviously impressed by the bearing and stature of the man before him, for he added: "Come over here and let me have a good look at you." It was just the opportunity Don Antonio was looking for and as he approached the table where Malatesta sat, he twisted the Pope's ring round on his finger so that the image of Christ Crucified was revealed. He covered it quickly with his other hand and approached the table like a supplicant before Mass. Stopping at the very edge he suddenly revealed the ring and heard the *condottiere* gasp.

"I also have access to other power that might interest My Lord," the solder-priest murmured, but before he could say more Malatesta held up his hand and said in a loud voice to his staff officer, still hunched over his lists:

"Mario, if you would be so good, please convey my compliments to Capitano Lugorso and ask him to make an inspection of the outer pickets. You are to go with him, too, and report back to me." As the man left Malatesta motioned to Don Antonio to take a chair. "What's this all about?" he asked. Sitting, Don Antonio began to explain delicately and at some length the Cardinal's proposition.

"But what's in it for me," the *condottiere* asked. "It seems to me that My Lord the Duke of Milan has every chance of success and when he triumphs, I'll take my share of the spoils."

"If the Duke of Milan is to be trusted," Playing with the Papal ring on his finger, Don Antonio continued in a softer voice: "And what shall it benefit a man if he inherit the earth..."

Malatesta looked at him sharply: "You're talking of my immortal soul?"

"His Holiness has the power to..." But before the priest could say more, Malatesta interrupted him. "Let me see that ring," he said, holding out his hand. Reluctantly Don Antonio handed it over to him, but after examining it Malatesta suddenly leapt up, knocking over his chair and drawing his sword. "Treachery," he yelled. "Treachery!" and he pointed the tip of his sword at Don Antonio's throat. Don Antonio stayed in his seat, too surprised to move.

In an instant the two guards rushed in and menaced Don Antonio with their spears. "Arrest that man," said the *condottiere*, waving his sword. "He comes to spread foul treason against my Lord of Milan." More guards arrived and surrounded Don Antonio, who had now risen to his feet but made no attempt to draw his sword. One guard savagely pushing the point of his spear in the priest's face, drawing blood. "Don't kill him yet," said Malatesta. "I need to know more of this plot. Take him to my own tent and bind him well. I'll question him later, then we'll dispose of him as all traitors deserve."

Don Antonio put his hand to his cheek to stem the trickle of blood as the guards prodded him out of the tent. As he emerged into the sunlight he passed a very fat young patrician attended by a fierce-looking, bull-necked man with a shaven head, awaiting an audience with the *condottiere*. But he recognised neither of them and had other, more pressing, matters on his mind.

45

May Day in Florence. The whole city, it seemed, was up early and heading for the countryside. Aunt Martha and Uncle Battista were preparing to join them, the latter grumbling good-naturedly that every other day in Florence seemed to be a public holiday and asking when he was ever going to get that dratted dome finished. Somehow he'd procured a horse and cart and now the carthorse steamed and stamped outside their house in the warm morning air.

Aunt Martha and the servant girl Luisa bustled over baskets of food, enough to feed a regiment. Pride of place went to two glistening loaves of 'meats in aspic': pieces of chopped pork, rabbit and chicken in a clear jelly that had been clarified with egg whites and given a warm golden colour with saffron. There were trout in aspic, too, flavoured with bay leaves and lavender, and small fruit patties filled with apples, dried figs, raisins and walnuts, sprinkled with sugar. Luca was amused to note that Giovanni Ferrante's basket, with its blue check cloth, had been pressed into service to carry them.

Luca helped Luisa to carry the food down to the cart. The girl's freshly-washed auburn hair fell to her shoulders and she had fastened a carmine artificial flower into it. He noticed the swell of her breasts under her russet smock and white *camicia*. Her face and lips appeared brighter than usual and he presumed that they'd been subtly painted; her eyes, outlined in black, seemed larger, too. Luisa gave him one of her slow smiles and as he followed her down the stairs Luca quite forgot to count.

As he and Luisa packed the baskets of food in the cart, Luca smelled the girl's herbal scent, a hint of rosemary if he wasn't mistaken, and he was just about to speak to her when Aunt Martha bustled through the door, followed by Battista. "Come on Luisa," she said, walking round to the back of the cart. "Help me up." When the girl had done so, she held out her hand and pulled her up to sit beside her. Luca took his place on the bench seat at the front and shuffled sideways as Battista eased up his bulk and took the reins.

The streets were crowded with other brightly dressed citizens, some on foot, some on horseback, but most, like Luca and his family, in lumbering carts. There was a hubbub of goodwill and a feeling of anticipation of pleasures to come. The tide of people and animals flowed slowly towards the city gate of *Porta al Prato* and, after a delay because of the constriction, out on to the highway from the city.

Soon they were in the *contado*, the countryside surrounding Florence, and, as the sun warmed their backs, they took in the sights of this glorious May morning. The vivid colours of wild flowers, yellows and purples predominant, splashed the fields, multi-shaded in green. Crimson poppies bobbed in the verges and on a hillock clumps of broom were covered with sprays of flowers as bright as a canary's chest. After a few miles they turned off the highway, down a bumpy track and into a riverside meadow, fringed by pollarded willows. There were many other families there already, friends and neighbours of Battista's who had arranged to celebrate the day together. In a corner a fire had been lit and a piglet turned on a spit above it. Some women were singing and clapping out a rhythm, accompanied by a man on a flute.

While the women laid out the food on linen table cloths, Luca and Battista went for a stroll along the riverbank, mainly spent in companionable silence, watching a family of Mallard ducklings scuttling about in the reeds. There were eight of them and when their mother called, seven tiny chicks rapidly joined the flotilla, but there was an eighth who always seemed to lag behind and had suddenly to scuttle to catch them up, to the accompaniment of his mother's angry quacks.

Then their own mother duck was calling: "Come on you two," Aunt Martha's voice sang across the water meadow. "Food's ready."

As they walked back Battista asked: "Have you had that word with Jacopo yet?"

"Yes, I have but I'm not sure it did much good. He's full of some pent-up anger, but I am not sure why."

"It seems we're going to need more drastic action. But let's talk about it tomorrow. Today's a day for celebration."

Soon Luca was tucking into a slice of the meats in aspic and Battista was pouring him a generous measure of red wine. He gradually succumbed to the delights of the food and the drink and to conversation and laughter with friends and neighbours. His eyes also followed Luisa as she moved around offering slices of the roast pork to all the company, and when the time came for dancing after the meal he sought her out and whirled her energetically around the meadow, to the accompaniment of lute, recorder and flute. He had to admit his dancing was not of the best, since he was more intent on counting the steps than listening to the music and the rhythm, but what he lacked in grace he made up for in enthusiasm. And he was stirred by the sight of the young girl before him, in the springtime of her youth, limbs supple, skin soft and eyes sparkling.

But Aunt Martha seemingly disapproved of his intimacy with a mere servant, for after their dance she kept Luisa near her and found a dozen tasks for the girl to do. So Luca sought out the shade of a hawthorn tree, lying beneath its spikey branches, gazing up through the myriad of white flowers with their dark red stamens, listening to the midges and the bees, slipping into sleep in the Springtime sun.

46

That afternoon, on his return to Florence, Luca walked alone through the flower-decked streets of the city, full now of young men in their finest clothes carrying *maii*, branches of blossom hung with sugared nuts and wrapped in blue ribbons, hurrying to their girlfriends' houses to hang these tributes on their doors.

Earlier in the day, his snooze under the hawthorn tree hadn't lasted long: soon he'd been recruited to join his family and friends in gathering armfuls of flowers to decorate their carts – and the horses – before setting off on the journey home. At the city gate hundreds of such carts waited to re-enter, a wonderful sight augmented by the noise of cheerful voices and the almost overwhelming scents of the flowers.

In the afternoon it was the custom for mothers and fathers to remain at home while the young men set off with their *maii* offerings and Aunt Martha had persuaded Luca to go out too, making sure that Luisa had many tasks to confine her to the house. Wandering *maii*-less, Luca's thoughts turned to Alessia Rossi and to his pledge to bring her husband's killer to justice. He felt guilty that he'd surrendered to the addictive pleasures of the May Day celebrations and when he found himself passing by Giovanni Ferrante's house he determined to make amends. He knocked boldly on the door and it was opened in a few moments by a tall woman, wielding a broom.

"Is *Ser* Pietro Ferrante at home?"

The woman looked him up and down and said: "That all depends on who's calling."

"My name is Luca Pasini," he said, in a voice deeper than usual. "I am *Assistente Capomaestro* of the *Opera del Duomo*, a colleague of *Ser* Pietro's son, *Ser* Giovanni. I must talk with him."

The woman assimilated this information for a moment or two, as if searching for a reason not to admit him. Finding none, she asked him to come in and showed him into the parlour, where in a few minutes he was joined by Giovanni Ferrante's father.

Luca was hard-pressed to see any resemblance between father and son. *Ser* Pietro, while not fat, was rounded where his son was angular and his countenance was more suited to joviality than disapproval; his lips were turned up in a smile, not down in a sneer. Yet there was an air of vulnerability about him and he seemed eager for Luca's company.

"How kind of you to call, *Messer* Luca. Do you have news of my son?"

"It was a question I was about to ask you, Sir."

"I am afraid I know nothing. I'm worried about him."

"I am sure he'll be fine, Sir," said Luca, now confident that Giovanni had organised his own disappearance.

"And is all well at the cathedral? In the administrative department, I mean, rather than on the construction site?" Aha, thought Luca, he's worried that Giovanni might have embezzled some of the *Opera del Duomo*'s funds. It was well known that the most common crime among lawyers was stealing their clients' money.

"All is well there, Sir. Your son left the administration neat and tidy, with the accounts in good order." Luca was by no means sure that this was the case, but it seemed wisest at this juncture to reassure the old man, and he added boldly: "We can see where everything is and that nothing is missing." He feared he might have gone too far in answering *Ser* Pietro's unspoken question, but the old man gave a small sigh and seemed pleased with what he heard. "Have you no idea at all where *Ser* Giovanni might have gone?" Luca went on to ask, pressing his advantage, and when Ferrante's father shook his head, he tried a more oblique approach, adding. "Did he ever mention somewhere, in Italy or elsewhere, that he might like to visit?"

The old man appeared to ponder the question and Luca added vaguely: "France...? Spain....?"

"Oh, I don't think so," said the old lawyer, then laughed, "although he did say once he'd like to visit England – to teach them to cook!"

"To cook?

"Yes, didn't you know that my son was a wonderful cook? It was his greatest pleasure, perhaps his only pleasure. I do miss his cooking..."

"I didn't know..."

"...and now, Fidelia cooks all my meals for me. Not the same thing at all!" The old man looked rather downcast.

"Fidelia?"

"My son's housekeeper. She moved in when Giovanni left. Said I needed someone to look after me, keep me from harm. The net result is I'm confined to the house, haven't been out for a decent game of backgammon for a week or more."

Just then the parlour door opened and the tall housekeeper came in: she'd obviously been listening outside. Unabashed she said: "Now, now Pietro, don't go upsetting yourself. You know it's for your own good. Have a care for your heart."

She calls the old man plain Pietro! Not *Ser* Pietro or even *Messer* Pietro. Someone's taking advantage of the situation, Luca thought.

"Now you're here, perhaps you'd fetch some wine for us," *Ser* Pietro asked her and turned to Luca again: "*Messer* Luca, you'll join me in a glass of fine Tuscan wine to celebrate this glorious May Day afternoon?" He added under his breath: "Not that I've seen much of it."

Fidelia said: "I'm sure the young man has more pressing calls on his time."

Luca took the coward's way out. After all, the relationship between Giovanni Ferrante's father and his housekeeper was none of his business and he was unlikely to glean any more information from the old man. So he admitted, yes, he did have another appointment and much as he would like to talk with the distinguished lawyer, he really must be going. The tall housekeeper bustled him out of the room and out of the house door. "*Buona festa*, have a good holiday," he cried over his shoulder as he was ushered out into the street.

The young men, having given up their *maii*, now hung about in groups, talking and laughing with each other, with some good-natured pushing and shoving. On other corners, or on another side of the street, groups of girls had accumulated, also dressed in their best, with fresh flowers in their hair. The girls walked up and down, linking arms with their friends, eyeing the boys, laughing and giggling. The boys, while pretending not to notice, eyed the girls, too.

Luca walked through this comedy of manners at a loss of what to do next. Walking around the South side of the cathedral towards the *Canto dei Bischeri* and the *Via dell' Oriuolo*, he suddenly caught sight of Jacopo, deep in conversation with none other than *La Bionda*. Not wishing to re-open his arguments with his brother-in-law, nor to speak to *La Bionda* in his company, Luca made a swift about-turn and headed back around the other side of the cathedral. Jacopo and *La Bionda*! How well did they know each other? Their conversation seemed very intimate and Jacopo had had his hand on her arm! Of course Luca knew she was a whore, but somehow the idea of Jacopo and *La Bionda* together was disgusting, not just for Maria's sake but for his own. He was well aware that he had followed other men to her bed, plenty of them no doubt, but Jacopo ... it was repellent.

Nursing these thoughts, Luca wandered unhappily and purposelessly through the city, oblivious to the celebrating crowds, heading vaguely West towards the Dominican basilica of Santa Maria Novella. Reaching the square, he remembered that this was the quarter in which the Rossi family lived. Rocco, his wife and their two young children had lodged with his parents in a street just off the piazza, and the cathedral pay clerk had told him that Alessia and the children were still there. He sought out the street and looking along it from the piazza he saw a warren of apartments in an old nobleman's palazzo that had seen far better days and half-a-dozen tumbledown one- and two-storey houses. Outside the nearest of these, not twenty paces from where Luca stood among the passing crowds, two women sat in raffia-backed chairs, peeling fava beans into a blackened cast-iron saucepan. A little girl sat with a wooden rattle on a cushion at the younger woman's feet while a small boy pulled at her skirt, demanding attention. The older woman scolded him with a gesture.

Alessia no longer wore a hood, although she was still in mourning clothes: her jet-black hair, shiny in the sunlight, was cut short, so that her long neck was exposed. Her hands, busy with the menial task of taking the pale green beans from their darker pods, were so delicate and beautiful that they might have been painted by Giotto himself.

For a few moments Luca stood transfixed as the late afternoon sunlight illuminated the group. Then he turned and lost himself in the jostling crowds, knowing he was in love.

47

Don Antonio's May Day was rather more confined than Luca's. He lay on his stomach on the hard ground inside Carlo Malatesta's tent, his hands tied behind his back and his feet bound together. There was a pain in his ribs where the guards had kicked him a few times and the cut on his cheek, though the bleeding had stopped, was attracting flies, which kept resettling despite his attempts to shake them off.

He was amazed at the speed with which Malatesta's attitude towards him had changed, from the quiet examination of the Papal ring and a seemingly sympathetic hearing of the Cardinal's proposals to the sudden cries of treason and the arrest, the manhandling and imprisonment. The Cardinal had talked about the fickleness of *condottieri*, but Malatesta's rapid mood change had taken him completely by surprise.

The guards had prodded him into the *condottiere*'s tent, forcing him to the ground with their pointed lances. One of them had sat on his head, causing much amusement to his comrades by farting as he did so, while two of the others roped his hands and feet. They'd taken his sword and dagger, or course, which were now lying on a table besides Malatesta's camp bed, and his pouch of money. No doubt that would have already disappeared, divided among them. Happily they'd missed the dozen florins sewn into the hem of his tunic and his faithful lancet, secreted in the sole of his boot.

How long he'd been there he could only guess, but he'd listened to the revelry as the troops took their mid-day meal and drunken cries as they celebrated May Day well into the afternoon. The shadows were lengthening fast when he heard approaching footsteps and then Malatesta's slurred voice. "I hope our trait'rous chicken's well trussed."

"Yes, My Lord."

Don Antonio rolled on to his side, flexing his fingers and toes to get some blood circulating into them, as Malatesta staggered into the tent. He was carrying a plate with a couple of chicken drumsticks on it and an earthernware pitcher, which he put down on the table and rapidly knelt at Don Antonio's head, bringing his lips close.

"When I bash my fist against my palm, I want you to cry out, as if in pain," he whispered in a perfectly sober voice, astonishing Don Antonio yet again. But when the *condottiere* stood up and punched his own hand, the soldier-priest duly let out a loud "Aargh."

"You trait'rous swine," Malatesta bellowed, apparently drunk again, "I'll unravel this treach'rous plot against my lord of Milan." He hit his hand with his fist once more and Don Antonio yelled. Malatesta called out for the guard, who pushed his head through the tent flap. "Go and get me some pincers. We'll see how this scoundrel likes having his fingernails removed, one by one. Oh, and have you eaten?

"No, my Lord." The guard looked surprised by the *condottiere*'s concern.

"Then grab a morsel on your way back. And some wine, too. It is May Day, after all. But return within the half hour." Malatesta kicked Don Antonio in the ribs, for real this time and the priest did not have to fake his cry of pain.

When the guard had gone Malatesta knelt once more and started to loosen the rope round Don Antonio's hands. "Sorry about that last kick," he said, "but we had to make it look realistic."

"What's going on?"

As Malatesta moved to loosen the ties around Don Antonio's feet, he explained that while he was certainly interested in the Cardinal's proposals, his current overlord, the Duke of Milan was a deeply suspicious man and saw plots against himself everywhere, even when none existed. Malatesta knew the Duke had spies in his camp, and suspected that Mario, the young officer who had been present when Don Antonio arrived, was one of them. He'd sent him off so they could talk, but he'd be suspicious of any visitor and his mission. "He was all ears when my next visitors told me that Florence was ripe for insurrection. And hearing of your arrest, he'll be convinced that I am wholly committed to Visconti and his plans."

Malatesta had not fully undone Don Antonio's bonds, so he helped the soldier-priest to sit up, hands still loosely tied behind his back. Then, as delicately as an indulgent mother with her child, he fed Don Antonio with one of the chicken drumsticks. "So tell me more about the Cardinal's scheme – and absolution by the Holy Father," he said.

Between grateful bites Don Antonio went through the Cardinal's suggestion in some detail. Malatesta fed him another drumstick and poured a beaker of wine for him, holding it to his mouth as he took thirsty gulps. From time to time the *condottiere* punched his hand and Don Antonio cried out, for the benefit of any passersby, and once Malatesta kicked the ground with his boot, inducing a well acted grunt of pain.

Malatesta also undid the cords that held in place one of the rear canvas panels of the tent. "Wait until dusk, he said, then go. You'll find your horse a dozen paces down the hill, on the edge of the woods. I suspect the pickets will be less efficient than usual, but in case you're challenged, the word of the night is 'Obelisk' and you ride for Visconti. Oh, and you'll need this." He produced the Cardinal's Papal ring and thrust it into a pocket of Don Antonio's doublet. As he did so they heard the guard returning. Malatesta pushed him roughly to the ground and rushed to the tent flap, wine pitcher in hand.

"Put those somewhere he can see 'em," Don Antonio heard him tell the guard, his speech again slurred. "Anticipation of pain is often as great a tongue-loosener as the reality. I'm off for more wine. I'll deal with him when I return."

The guard came in with a menacing pair of iron pincers and placed them as instructed on the table in front of Don Antonio, whose eyes widened in horror. The guard gave him a kick in the ribs for good measure before resuming his post outside the tent.

When dusk came an hour or so later, Don Antonio pulled apart the ropes holding his hands and his feet, rubbing his wrists and ankles. He rose gingerly and collected his sword and dagger. The latter scraped on the tabletop and he stood still for a good minute, concerned that the noise had carried, but when he heard the guard sighing and shuffling outside he moved rapidly to the rear of the tent, pulled aside the canvas panel and escaped into the evening air.

He found his horse, which gave a little whinny of recognition, mounted it with a gasp as he again felt the pain in his ribs, then trotted quietly though the woods. He heard the pickets, but saw no-one, and within an hour he was again tracing his path along the riverbank, this time heading for home.

48

"England?" said Cosimo de' Medici when Luca reported to him next day. "Why on earth would anyone want to go to England if they didn't have to?"

"I'm not sure that Ferrante really wanted to go there," said Luca. "It was just something his father mentioned."

"*Penitus toto divisos orbe Britannos*," said Cosimo. Oh, no, thought Luca, another dead Roman poet, I suppose.

"Virgil considered that the Britons were completely separated from the rest of the world. Not true now, of course, we do a lot of trade with the English these days, but there's no denying they're a race apart. And as for the Scots..."

"Ser Giovanni could well have been joking. He told his father he wanted to teach the English to cook."

Cosimo laughed, "A worthy ambition. My agents in Lombard Street tell me the *cucina inglese* leaves much to be desired."

"But don't you think it was just a joke? We've no evidence that he really meant it."

"But it's not impossible. It may be true, however improbable it seems. I'll have my London agents make enquiries."

They were sitting in the library of the Medici house, Cosimo again in the oak chair with its red leather cushion and Luca in the curule chair opposite him.

"You've done well with your investigations," the banker said. "Not only do we now have the possibility of tracing Ferrante, but we also have a more important name, Peruzzi, implicated in the plot against us."

"Have you been able to locate Niccolò Peruzzi?" Luca asked. "I am worried about my, er, source."

Cosimo laughed again. "Ah, yes, the infamous *La Bionda*. Your concern is touching." Then becoming serious, he added: "But no, we haven't found him. He went to inspect his family's estate near

Reggello earlier in the week, but he left there several days ago and nobody has seen him since. Rest assured we'll be on to him as soon as he returns." Cosimo stood, to signify the audience was at an end. Luca rose too and, after saluting the banker formally, headed for the door. Thank goodness there were no more Latin quotations today, he thought as he began to leave.

"*Aeque pars ligni curvi ac recti valet igni,*" said Cosimo. "Crooked logs make straight fires: we may have little to go on, but we must work with what we've got."

Luca shut the door behind him with a sigh and set off for the cathedral. As he walked, he once again refreshed his vision of Alessia Rossi, bathed in the sunlight, with her soft face and delicate hands. He'd done so a dozen times since waking that morning. She was so beautiful, so much in need of protection.

Work was progressing rapidly on the second restraining stone circle and as soon as Luca arrived, Battista put him to work on the piles of iron bars which were stacked in the South Transept. These were the vital fastenings to hold the sandstone blocks securely together and they came in various shapes and sizes. It was Luca's job to sort them, count them and have them placed in hessian baskets, each to be marked with a Roman numeral I to VIII corresponding to a section of the octagonal dome. As he worked Luca could hear the thud of mason's hammers high above him and the clash of metal chisels on stone. The hoist creaked and the oxen grunted as yet another block was carried skywards.

During the morning Battista came over for a word. "That dratted brother-in-law of yours is back at work, but he's as unmanageable as ever. He's even talking of swinging on a rope and grabbing pigeons' eggs from their nests in the dome. I'll swear he's not quite sober, even in the mornings. You said you'd had a word with him?"

"I did," said Luca, "but it didn't do any good. He told me to mind my own business. He said you and Filippo Brunelleschi were treating him like a schoolboy."

"That's because he behaves like one, and worse. Well, I'll give him until the end of the week. If he doesn't mend his ways by then, I'll have to take action, whether or not he's married to my niece."

"What sort of action?" asked Luca, but Battista was already moving back towards the Crossing, so Luca returned to his sorting and counting. He began thinking about Donatello. He wanted to see him again and renew their friendship, but he was nervous: they hadn't met since Luca fled from his workshop. When was it? Nine, ten days ago. A lot had happened to him emotionally since then, not least his escapade with *La Bionda* and his flirtation with Luisa (if you could call it that: Aunt Martha made sure that nothing came of it). But above all there was Alessia Rossi: he'd fallen in love with her, like Dante with Beatrice, at first sight. (Well, second sight if you counted the day of Rocco's entombment. But that didn't count surely, since she was in such deep and all-concealing mourning?) His mind was awash with thoughts that flowed and eddied like waves in a rock pool as the tide comes in.

He resolved, however, to see Donatello during the noontime break and he set off for the workshop soon after noon, worrying about what would he say and how he would begin. Inspiration came just outside the workshop when he heard the cry "Fresh meat pies. Pies, hot pies..." and saw the fat vendor with his tray. Luca bought two and hurried inside.

As he entered he heard the chink of metal on stone, as a chisel gouged another furrow, and muttered imprecations for Habakkuk to speak. Donatello and the prophet were alone in the workshop and as he entered Luca saw that Habakkuk's anguished piercing gaze was still unwavering, but his open mouth, as ever, was silent. Donatello was standing on a low stool, working on the shoulder clasp that held the prophet's toga-like robe. Luca stood by the lower folds, which had now been further defined so that, although dishevelled, they flowed sinuously and invited the eye to move around the sculpture. "Am I forgiven?" Luca said quietly, offering up a warm pie.

Donatello jumped down, putting his mallet and gouge on his work table, and grabbed the pie, biting off a large mouthful. "I purpow ho," he said.

Luca laughed: "You always seem to be speaking to me with your mouth full!"

When he had finished swallowing, the sculptor gave a little smile and repeated "I suppose so." He put his hand on Luca's arm. "I've been thinking about it all week and I've come to the conclusion that if we cannot be lovers we can at least be friends." And then, with a grin, he took another bite out of the pie: "Oh meeded rat."

"You needed that?" Luca said, interpreting.

"Yes, I certainly did. I can't remember the last time I had anything to eat." Donatello eyed the second pie. "Is that for me, or for you?"

"Oh, they're both for you. I don't think I could eat another thing after all the food we had yesterday."

And so their friendship was re-established and confirmed by a libation of red wine from Donatello's pitcher. While Donatello ate, Luca brought him up to date with the news of the past few days and told him of the clue that Ferrante might be in England. "But we're still no nearer finding out who killed Rocco Rossi and bringing justice for his young widow and fatherless children."

Donatello pulled his face into an expression of concern, but Luca felt that his friend was no longer interested in the case, now that he and Brunelleschi had been cleared of suspicion. As he ate his way through the second pie his eyes were drawn once more to the marble figure who loomed over them. Luca sighed: "I'll let you get on," he said, rising.

Donatello gave him a big hug and they kissed each other on both cheeks, but before Luca was halfway across the workshop, the sculptor had turned back to the prophet. "Now then, Zuccone," Luca heard him say, "that's enough for the top half today. Time to pay attention to those scrawny feet of yours."

49

It was dusk when Luca let himself in to the storage area on the ground floor of his uncle's house. Just as he was about to mount the internal steps he heard a rustling noise from the far, dim corner where Battista had his workbench. At first he thought it was a rat, they were common enough, but then a soft voice called from the darkness: "Luca."

Walking over in the half-light he found the servant girl Luisa sitting on the bench swinging her legs. "Luca, here you are at last. I've been waiting for you." She grabbed his arms and pulled him towards her, stretching up to kiss him on the lips. Then, slipping from the bench, she wrapped her arms around him and thrust her body against his. Luca's instant arousal was augmented by the feel of her breasts against his chest and for a moment he returned the pressure before pulling back.

He said foolishly: "Shouldn't you have been at home by now?" The girl lived with her parents nearby and returned there every evening.

"I've been waiting for you," she repeated. "Don't you want me, Luca?" She moved to kiss him again and Luca saw that her cheeks were rouged and her large eyes again outlined in black.

"No, yes, I, er…" Luca didn't know what to say, but he took both her wrists and holding them firmly to her side pushed her back to the workbench, knocking over in the process a box of iron nails, which fell with a clatter to the floor. The girl tried to thrust her hips towards him once more.

"You wanted me yesterday, Luca. Why not today?"

"Luisa, this is not possible. Aunt Martha… your position here…" (To say nothing, which Luca didn't, of his new 'pure' Dantesque love for Alessia Rossi, which was scarcely a day old.)

"Aunt Martha!" the girl said derisively. "I thought you were a man."

"It's...just...not...possible," Luca said slowly and firmly. "I'm sorry; you're a beautiful girl, but..."

Luisa broke free from his grip, slapped him hard on the face and fled out of the door. Nursing his cheek Luca bent to pick up the nails and replace them in the box. He waited another five minutes before mounting the stairs (one, two, three...) and greeting his aunt and uncle. Neither seemed to notice any residual glow on his cheeks, nor to have heard the clatter of the falling box of nails. Battista was standing at the window looking out into the street, beaker in hand, while his aunt stirred the squat iron pot suspended over the fireplace. His uncle poured Luca a beaker of wine before they all sat down to enjoy supper together.

Luca went to bed early again that night, but he slept fitfully, at one point dreaming his teeth had fallen out, at another that he was flying across a landscape, but, like Icarus, he was having difficulty keeping aloft and constantly in danger of hitting a tree or crashing into the hillside. In his semi-lucid moments Alessia, Luisa and *La Bionda* chased each other round and round in his mind as if in a vortex. He rose early in the morning, tired and anxious, taking his slop pail down the stairs (don't count!) with some trepidation about meeting Luisa. Aunt Martha was poking the embers of the fire, talking to the servant girl, who was holding the other slop pail. Luca handed her his own, which she grabbed furiously before stomping out of the room.

"I don't know what's got into her this morning, said Aunt Martha. "Like a bear with a sore head." She peered up at Luca. "You don't look that perky either, Luca. Had a bad night?" His aunt stood, a little creakily, the better to look into his face.

Luca, thinking that he could escape from the house while Luisa was busy at the cesspit, gave her no time for a closer inspection, but turned and hurried towards the door. "Got to rush," he said. "Work to do..."

"Well, really," said his aunt as he disappeared down the stairs. "The youth of today. No manners. Just don't know how to behave."

"Mind you," said Battista who had just come into the room, "you didn't always behave yourself when you were young!" and he gave her a playful pat on her bottom.

At the cathedral even counting iron rods and numbered baskets (...IV, V, VI...) brought little comfort to Luca, who was feeling increasingly sexually frustrated, not least because he had turned down Luisa's advances. His new-found love for Alessia was of a pure and abstract kind and what he was experiencing now was simple lust. To satiate physical desire was not to be unfaithful to *il codice cavalleresco*, the knight's chivalric code, was it? He resolved to visit *La Bionda* at the noonday break. After all, she might have some further important information for him...

50

The tavern was already filling up when Luca entered shortly after noon, but the fresh-faced waiter Tommaso recognized him and came over smiling.

"*Buongiorno!* You eating?"

"I was looking for *La Bionda*. Is she here?"

"Well, she is and she isn't, if you get my meaning." Luca must have looked puzzled, for Tommaso continued, looking up at the balustrated balcony. "She's here, but she's 'otherwise engaged'. Shouldn't be long though. Want to eat while you're waiting?"

Suddenly Luca was sickened by the whole procedure and his part in it. He turned and fled, hearing Tommaso call out to his departing back: "Dish of the day is beans. Fresh fava beans in meat broth."

Luca strode though the streets with no idea where he was going. His mind was a maelstrom, but the main emotion was self-loathing. He was consorting with whores, flirting with servant girls and at the same time pretending to be a *parfait gentil* knight with a pure love for a woman in distress. Life had been much simpler when he had been Donatello's lover.

As he paced along, head down, he bumped almost literally into Maria. Or rather, he pushed roughly past his sister and was only halted by hearing her crying out his name.

"Luca! Luca, are you all right?"

Luca turned and the sights and sounds of the market of Sant' Ambrogio, of which he had been oblivious, came flooding back.

Maria still looked beautiful, though there were signs, even though she was still only 18, that her youthful radiance was fading. Today she looked washed out and her brown eyes with their long dark lashes stood out from her pale face.

"Maria, how lovely to see you, it's been too long ..." It must have been the best part of a fortnight since he last saw her, that embarrassing afternoon when he'd gone to tell her, erroneously, of

Jacopo's death. They embraced each other warmly, then Maria, searching Luca's face, said: "Something's bothering you. What is it?"

Luca remembered those hours years ago in Posara when they'd lain on the grass by the millstream and he'd told her of his ambitions and his dreams, but somehow he felt unable to confide in her that he'd been buying a prostitute and seducing a servant girl, or even of his secret, undisclosed love for Alessia, so he merely said: "Oh, it's nothing, just worrying about technical problems on the dome." To change the subject, he added: "And you, what have you been up to?"

Maria pointed to the raffia basket she was carrying over her shoulder. "I've been taking Jacopo's mid-day meal to the cathedral."

"You'll spoil that man. Why he can't eat in the communal kitchen like everyone else, I don't know."

"Oh Luca," she said, "you don't understand how he's suffering. Someone's trying to poison him, he's convinced of it."

"Who does he suspect?"

"He won't tell me."

They were passing a *trattoria*, one of those street-side establishments that sold simple inexpensive meals, and Luca's sensitive nose caught the aroma of beef stew coming from one of the cauldrons. "Have you eaten?" he asked his sister, who shook her head.

"Let's grab a bite to eat," said Luca, wanting to learn more about Jacopo and his troubles. He chose the stew, called *peposo* and made with beef, red wine, peppercorns and bread, while Maria took some *ribollita*, another local speciality with beans, vegetables and bread, served lukewarm. As he paid, Luca, thinking how much Jacopo must be spending on alcoholic drink and, it seemed, whores, suddenly asked Maria: "Are you all right for money?"

"Oh, yes, Jacopo makes sure I always have enough. He likes to keep a check of my spending, of course, but he always gives me money when I need it for housekeeping and the like." Maria sighed: "We've enough money, that's not ..." She left the sentence unfinished.

It was usual with *trattoria* food to eat 'on the go', but this establishment had provided a few chairs and a table by the wall of the street and Luca and Maria sat down with their food. He noticed that there were lines of tiredness around her eyes and that her hair, normally shining, was dull as lead. As she lifted the spoon to her mouth she winced and the movement of her arm was stiff. "What's wrong with your arm?" he asked.

"Oh, it's nothing," his sister said brightly. "I banged it on the corner of the bedside chest. Silly thing to do, but it's just a bruise."

"So tell me more about Jacopo and his troubles. Why does he think he might be poisoned?"

"I don't know. He doesn't want me to worry about his affairs. But I do. And he's getting more and more troubled, probably because he's sleeping so badly." (That's surprising, thought Luca, with all that wine he's getting through, I'm amazed he's not knocked out for the night.) "He has dreadful nightmares," Maria continued, "He beats his hands on the mattress, then wakes up, clutching his face, crying 'No, no!'"

"What's all that about?"

"He won't tell me that either."

Finishing off his *peposo*, Luca realized that his sister had given him a lot to think about.

51

Seated again at his dining table, Niccolò Peruzzi took another gulp from his goblet and gave a satisfied belch. His cook had excelled herself in producing a delicious trout, well spiced and cooked in pastry, far superior to the indifferent fare he'd had to put up with during his five-day journey back to Florence. He felt replete, content.

The expedition to the Romagna, despite the dusty days on the road, had been very rewarding, with Carlo Malatesta eager for information about the families and factions who would support the Duke of Milan were he to besiege Florence. The *condottiere* said he would pass on this information to the Duke, and when the time came Niccolò would no doubt play a major part in mobilising those elements, so that the city would be attacked from without and within. Malatesta had assured him that following Filippo Maria Visconti's success he would be well rewarded with lands and a title. Niccolò wondered of which city state he might be Lord.

His reverie was interrupted by a knock on the door and the entry of Federico, the bull-necked man, who he had sent out earlier in the morning to check what had been happening in Florence in their absence. His countenance suggested that Niccolò's contentment would not be long-lasting. "Well?" he asked.

"Well, I think there's trouble brewing with that Jacopo Alderici."

"Trouble? How?"

Well, he's drinking bucketfuls and making out he knows a lot more about that so-called Bartolomeo's murder than he's lettin' on."

"Hmm – and he knows enough to implicate us all."

"You included, Sir. Perhaps it was a mistake for you to be there when we knocked that bloke off and messed him up."

"Maybe it was, but I wanted to see it for myself." Niccolò smiled at the memory of Rocky Rossi's murder before continuing. "All right, we'll have to deal with *Messer* Jacopo Alderici, before his tongue betrays us all. Unless you think his fear of what we'd do to him will keep his mouth shut."

"Well, he's scared alright. Even reckons we're trying to poison him." Federico told Niccolò how Jacopo refused to eat the food provided by Brunelleschi's kitchen in the dome, insisting that his wife prepared his midday meal, but then he said: "But booze seems to dissolve his fears."

"And there's another thing. Jacopo's brat of a brother-in-law's been sniffing around asking questions. Don't know who he's working for, but he's been quizzing the *Bargello* jailer and drinking with Jacopo, so God knows what beans are being spilled."

Niccolò sighed: "D'you know the whelp?"

"No, but he should be easy enough to find."

"Looks like we'll have to stop his mouth, too."

"Want me to see to it?"

"Straightaway. While I think of what to do about our troublesome mason."

52

Don Antonio had also arrived back in Florence early that morning, nursing his tired horse among the crowds streaming towards the *Porta al Prato*. Ahead of him a fat young patrician on a chestnut mare had seemed familiar. But as they entered the gateway, the sound of their horses' hooves echoing from the high arch, his back was soon hidden by the four mounted horsemen who followed him.

Don Antonio's maroon cloak was dusty, his boots dustier, so he'd taken an hour or so in the communal baths and had his face shaved by a barber in the *mercato nuovo* (who also gave him an unguent for his bruised ribs) before changing into his cassock and biretta and presenting himself to the Cardinal.

"So the *condottiere* is for turning," said the prelate, "and, praise be to God, he values his immortal soul above worldly pomp."

"So it would seem Your Eminence," said the priest, "but I think he's as twisty as the serpent on the Duke of Milan's flag. Who knows which way he'll turn?"

The Cardinal sighed. "True enough. We leave for Rome in a week or so. Let's see what His Holiness considers our best course of action. Which reminds me, do you have my ring?"

"My apologies, your Eminence, I nearly forgot," said Don Antonio, bringing out the ring from the recesses of his cassock.

"I'm surprised no-one noticed I wasn't wearing it," said the Cardinal, replacing the gift from the successor of St Peter on his finger. Don Antonio knelt to kiss it and the older man bestowed his blessing.

"And what is the news in Florence, Sir?" asked the priest as he rose.

"Not much. The notary Ferrante is still missing and he's got at least five hundred florins in his pocket, so he could be anywhere."

"The whole city knows about the chicken and the golden eggs. The barber told me all about it in the market this morning."

Yes, and thanks to Luca da Posara we know that Niccolò Peruzzi is implicated in the murder in the baptistry square and the plot to implicate Brunelleschi, Donatello and the Medici.

"Niccolò Peruzzi?"

"The black sheep of a none-too-white family. Old nobility, hankering after what they see as the good old days before this new-fangled democracy."

He added: "That's about all the news. Oh, Brunelleschi's installed in the Palazzo Della Signoria as a *Priore* for two months – and despite his absence the dratted dome continues to rise."

"Your Eminence doesn't approve?"

"I approve of church-building for the glory of God, but these Florentine Humanists seem to think the dome rises by their efforts alone. I sometimes wish our Lord would send them a sign of His omnipotence, so puffed up are they with their own pride."

"Which comes before a fall," said Don Antonio thoughtfully.

53

As Luca climbed the steps to the top of the cupola the next morning, his inner counting voice mercifully silent, he met Donatello scurrying down.

"What are you doing here? We don't often see you up in the dome."

"Good day, Luca, how lovely to see you, too! But you're right. These places always make me feel a bit uneasy, hemmed in. I don't like it. But Battista wanted my help: he's found a hairline crack in one of the sandstone blocks in the restraining ring and he's worried that it might split in two. He asked for my expert opinion."

"Oh. And…"

"Well, I think it's just superficial. No need to replace the block."

"Battista will be pleased."

"Yes, he is … but now, much as I love you, I simply have to get out of here. It's far too oppressive for me." The sculptor hurried on downwards and Luca watched as his dark-brown doublet and hose, with matching brimless cap, disappeared into the gloom.

The noise at the workface at the top of the uncompleted dome was compounded by the hammering of carpenters constructing another scaffolding platform in one of the dome's eight sections. Battista was there, ensuring that everything was being carried out properly, but seeing his nephew he walked over and together they sought out a corner which was slightly quieter. Battista pointed out the crack in the sandstone block.

"Your mate Donatello tells me it doesn't go through the whole block, but I'm still a bit concerned. Have a good look yourself, then I want you to go to the *Palazzo della Signoria* and tell Filippo all about it. He may want to slip out and see it for himself. You know what he's like."

"And what about the rest of the work, Uncle? All proceeding according to plan?"

"Yes, we're doing well with the second restraining ring, despite your brother-in-law stirring up the other masons. Tell Filippo that I reckon it could be complete in another six to eight weeks."

After inspecting the suspect sandstone block Luca set off for the *Piazza della Signoria*. As he wove his way through the busy street he thought of Alessia Rossi, her beautiful sunlit face and her delicate hands. Within a few pleasant minutes he was in the great square, contemplating the great building that dominated its Eastern side.

The *Palazzo della Signoria*, residence of the ruling Priors and seat of justice, was the symbol of secular power in the city. Luca never failed to be impressed by its solid beauty and was now able to enjoy the building even more with the knowledge of architecture and its terminology he had gained in the year or so he had been in Florence.

The rusticated stonework, he'd been told, was some sixty *bracchia* high, crowned by a projecting crenellated battlement supported on corbelled arches, some of which could be used as embrasures for pouring boiling oil or water and hot sand over invaders. The façade was pierced with two rows of Gothic windows, each with two lights surmounted by a trefoil arch. As he looked at the building, Luca delighted in running the technical words through his mind.

Crossing the immense paved piazza he again admired Arnolfo's tower, reaching up another sixty *bracchia* above the palace roof to a crenellated gallery in which the bells of the city were kept. To his right was the magnificent *Loggia*, its three arches supported on clustered pilasters with Corinthian capitals, where only last week Brunelleschi and the other newly elected Priors had been sworn in.

Entering the *Palazzo della Signoria*, Luca asked to see the architect and after a short wait a green-liveried servant came down to escort him to the suite of rooms set aside for Filippo during his two-month tenure of office. The main *salotto* was not large, but it was extravagantly appointed, with fine furniture and wall hangings. When Luca was shown in he saw Brunelleschi sitting at a table looking at a book propped up on an oaken reading stand. He stood as Luca came in, straightening the ermine cuffs of the crimson coat that was the uniform of the Priors.

Luca was intrigued by the contrast between the dishevelled, distracted architect of last week and the elegant, urbane Prior before him. Brunelleschi's ermine-lined gown was immaculate; he was clean-shaven, well groomed, commanding. Luca had to repress an urge to kneel and kiss his hand.

Filippo had obviously taken to this political life, but he immediately reverted to his old ways by grumbling: "So here I am, held captive in my gilded prison while there's so much important work to be done outside." What nonsense, thought Luca. Although Priors were expected to remain in the palazzo, it was easy enough to go out and many of them didn't even sleep there overnight. But Brunelleschi wouldn't be Brunelleschi without a grumble or two. "So, what's happening in the real world?" the architect asked.

"Battista estimates that the second stone ring will be complete in six to eight weeks," Luca reported.

"And then we'll be at the point the Wardens of the *Opera del Duomo*, in their wisdom, have decreed that all work is to be stopped while we review the situation and decide how to proceed." If Luca had expected a diatribe against 'the idiots in the *Opera*', he was disappointed, because Brunelleschi continued: "For once, I'm inclined to agree with them, we're reaching a critical time and we must make sure nothing goes wrong."

Brunelleschi paused, then added. "Speaking of which, is your brother-in-law continuing to stir up trouble?"

Luca had to admit that Jacopo was still sowing dissent among his fellow masons and reported that Battista had threatened to take action if Jacopo didn't mend his ways by the end of the week, although he hadn't specified what this action might be.

"I'm minded to get rid of the lot of them and start all over with new masons and wall-builders. This project is too important to be messed about by trouble-making workmen."

Luca didn't know what to say and after a silent moment, Brunelleschi added in a more kindly tone: "Not that any of this is any of your fault, Luca. It's something that Battista and I will just have to sort out."

"There's one more thing I ought to tell you about *Provveditore*," said Luca, finding his tongue. "It may be nothing, but ..."

"Out with it!"

"Battista has discovered a hairline crack in one of the sandstone blocks and he's worried it might break right through. Donatello's had a look at it and says it's just superficial, but Battista's not sure. Neither am I."

Brunelleschi sighed. "I suppose I'd better see for myself. I am sure I can contrive to escape for a short period, but I'll need to change out of this uniform into something more suitable for a dusty building site. Go and tell Battista that I'll have a look at that block and help him sort out Jacopo and the masons – and that I'll be with him within the hour."

A few moments later Luca was out on the red-brick paving of the piazza, swerving to avoid a visitor to the city who, without looking, had taken a step backward to admire the lines of the arches of the loggia. A lone horseman on a chestnut mare, his white cloak gathered about him, trotted past a group of tonsured friars deliberating under the dais in front of the palazzo, while towards the centre of the square a prestidigator, performing tricks with a silver *lira*, had attracted a crowd. Groups of men were scattered about, chatting animatedly. Luca passed one such gathering, four men in long day-gowns, one black, one white, one red and one dark-green, and failed to notice that after he had gone on a few dozen paces the latter broke off and followed him.

As Luca turned down an alleyway, a short-cut towards the cathedral he had used a dozen times before, he heard footsteps hurrying behind him and then a voice crying "*Messer* Luca Pasini?" Turning, he saw a bull-necked man in a green cloak, who repeated as he approached: "Are you Luca Pasini?" Even as Luca was replying in the affirmative, the man punched him hard in the stomach and as he bent double in pain, chopped at the side of his neck with the edge of his hand. Luca collapsed like a sack from which grain has been poured out, falling face down on to the pavement. Bending over the body and putting his knee in the boy's back, the bull-necked man took a garrote from the pocket of his doublet and pulled it around Luca's neck.

54

Half an hour or so earlier Don Antonio had been examining the zigzag patterns of bricks at the top of the uncompleted dome, nodding with enthusiasm, though with limited comprehension, as Battista d'Antonio explained the engineering principles behind the way that they were laid.

He'd collared Battista in the Crossing, explaining that the Cardinal had been amazed during his visit a couple of weeks ago that the massive vault could be constructed without a wooden centring to take the weight as it was being built. "He understands it's something to do with the way the bricks are laid," he'd told the *Provveditore* and, stretching the truth just a little, added: "He's intrigued and would like to know more. God, as His Eminence says, is in the details."

Looking up into the vast space above them, Don Antonio continued, "I am sure the Cardinal would have liked to have seen for himself, but he suspected the ascent might have been a little too much for him." There was a pause while both men considered the vision of the portly Cardinal puffing his way up the stairwells of the octagon and tambour and then negotiating the final steps in the gloom between the inner and outer shells of the dome itself.

"Give me a moment or two to get things organised here," Battista had told him, "and then I'll take you up. I want to see how the work's progressing anyway."

Within ten minutes they'd climbed almost to the top, Battista surprisingly agile for a big man, and now they stood on a wooden scaffolding platform, looking at the latest courses of brickwork. "It's perfectly safe," Battista assured Don Antonio, "but don't go too near the edge." The master mason proudly showed off the herringbone bricks, indicating with sweeps of his arm how the forces were distributed to prevent the weight pulling the structure earthwards.

A voice called from the wooden platform just above them, where a couple of masons were working: "*Capomaestro*, could you come and look at these iron fastenings in Section III? We want to make sure they're exactly in the right place."

"Please go," said Don Antonio, "I've already taken up too much of your valuable time. I can find my own way down." As Battista set foot on the ladder between the platforms, Don Antonio took a last look over the edge of the planking, then turned and started his descent.

He was nearly at the bottom of the octagon when he heard footsteps coming up. Pulling back into an alcove, Don Antonio saw a boy emerging from the shadows, carrying a wooden box, its long canvas strap over his shoulder. "Where are you going?" he asked as the boy drew level, a rather superfluous question since the only answer was 'up', but the boy answered him politely.

"I'm taking *Messer* Jacopo Alderici his mid-day meal, Monsignore. He's one of the masons and I'm taking him the food prepared by his wife." He held up the light wooden box by its strap and waved it.

"Then Godspeed," said Don Antonio as the boy disappeared upwards and he continued his descent.

Leaving the cathedral, he set off towards the *palazzo* set aside for the Cardinal during his visit and within a few dozen paces he saw Luca da Posara, in his dun-coloured doublet and hose, his hair as unruly as ever, turn into an alleyway ahead of him, followed by a bull-necked man in a dark-green *cioppa*, whose face and figure were also vaguely familiar. Reaching the turning himself, Don Antonio saw Luca face down on the ground, with the bull-necked man kneeling over him and wrapping a garrote round his neck.

He had no time to do anything but take a few quick paces and give the man a hefty kick in the backside before he could administer the fatal twist with his garrote. The man sprawled in the gutter, his brimless cap dislodged by the impact of Don Antonio's boot, revealing his shaven head. But as the priest rushed to grab him he was able to squirm away and flee down the passageway.

Luca moaned and Don Antonio bent to look after him rather than pursuing the would-be assassin. He turned Luca over and propped him up in a doorway. "Where does it hurt?" he asked.

"Here," said Luca rubbing the side of his neck, "and here," holding his stomach, "although I think I was just winded." He tried to get up, but it was a struggle and Don Antonio said: "Just rest for a moment, and then I'll get you home."

"I can't go home," said Luca, "I've got to get to the cathedral and tell Battista that Brunelleschi's on his way – and I suppose *Messer* Cosimo ought to know what has happened." Trying to rise again, he winced at the pain in his neck muscles.

"I can do all that," said the priest, fishing in the deep pockets of his cassock and producing a small bottle in brown fluted glass. "But first, let's put a bit of this on that neck of yours. It's an unguent I bought from the barber in the market place and it's worked wonders for my ribs." He undid the top few buttons of Luca's doublet, unstopped the bottle and rubbed some of the liniment into his neck.

"That feels better already," said Luca and once more began to rise to his feet. Don Antonio helped him up, noting that he was now much less pale. He never ceased to be amazed at the resilience of youth.

"I'll tell you what we'll do. I'll walk with you to the Cathedral and you can report to Battista. Then leave *Messer* Cosimo to me. I'll tell him, and the Cardinal, what has happened."

As they walked, Luca taking deep breaths but seeming quite steady on his feet, Don Antonio asked: "Did you recognise the man who assaulted you?"

"I've never seen him before in my life."

"If you had you'd have recognized him straightaway. He has a very distinctive appearance: bull-neck, shaven head ..."

Luca stopped walking. "Say that again."

"What? Bull-neck, shaven head?"

"That's it! That's just the way the stallholder in the piazza described the man who ran the amulet stall. Bull-necked, shaven-headed. It must have been him." Luca told Don Antonio about how he'd worked out that the body he'd discovered in the Baptistry square had been hidden beneath the stall selling amulets and potions. When the square was cleared the body, under its canvas sheet, had been left behind for the Cardinal to 'discover'.

Don Antonio <u>had</u> recognized the man, although he didn't know who he was: he remembered him standing outside Carlo Malatesta's tent with that fat young patrician, waiting for an audience with the *condottiere*. He didn't pass this information on to Luca.

55

Battista d'Antonio gasped when Don Antonio and Luca told him what had just happened. Over his nephew's protests and with the priest's support, his uncle had ordered him to go home. "Martha'll look after you. Get some rest, for goodness' sake. You've had enough excitements in the past few weeks to last a lifetime."

"I'll take him back," said Don Antonio, grabbing Luca by the elbow and propelling him down the nave. When they reached Battista's house, Don Antonio wanted to come up, but Luca insisted he was quite capable of mounting the stairs on his own. The priest again fumbled in his cassock pocket and fished out the brown bottle. "Here, rub some more of this on your neck before you go to bed. And get a good night's rest."

Luca thanked him, bade him goodbye, let himself in and climbed the stone steps to the first floor (...ten, eleven, twelve) and on entering received his second surprise of the day, this time a more pleasurable one. For there, sitting at the dining table, larger than life, tucking into a hunk of bread and a thick slice of creamy pecorino cheese while his aunt poured him a beakerful of red wine, was his elder brother Marco.

Luca stood dumfounded in the doorway and it was Marco who spoke first. "Hello, little brother, you're looking as fragile as ever," he said, smiling, getting up and holding out his brawny arms to be hugged. Luca submitted to the embrace, which he thought must be like being squeezed by a bear, and winced slightly as he felt a pain around his neck and as the spikey stubble on Marco's cheeks rub against his own smooth skin.

As Luca pulled away he studied his brother. Used as he was to the latest trends in clothing worn by the fashion-conscious Florentines, Marco seemed quite the country boy, in his short yellow overgown, tied at the waist, blue hose and his knitted hat, pointed and ribbed, which matched the colour of his hose. Marco had a broad, honest face, tanned from many hours working in the open air. Twenty-two years old, he was as strapping as ever: he'd pushed up the sleeves of his gown and the flexor muscles in his forearm bulged, the result, no doubt of picking up all those *quintale* sacks of grain and flour. Luca noticed with some amusement, and perhaps relief, that Luisa the servant girl, who had been stirring a pot suspended over the fire was staring at them, too. Marco's wife would have had something to say about that had she been there.

"So," said Luca, "to repeat, what on earth are you doing here?"

"Well, I'd like to say I just came to see you," Marco said. "And Aunt Martha and Uncle Battista, too," he added quickly "But we've got a problem with some of the mill machinery and, believe it or not, I need your advice – er, and Uncle Battista's – about how to design some new parts, and get them made here in Florence."

It seems a long way to come just for that, Luca thought and he wondered what rumours might have reached his brother's ears, prompting his journey, which was a hundred miles or so. Perhaps his family had heard of his ghastly discovery in the piazza, or (heaven forfend) his relationship with Donatello or, perhaps about Maria and Jacopo's deteriorating marriage. As if reflecting his thoughts, Marco said: "and how's my little sister and that husband of hers?"

It turned out that Marco's plea for help with designing new equipment for the mill was true enough: it involved maximising the flow to the mill wheels and it was going to require some intricate iron castings which might be better made in one of the cannon foundries of Florence.

But, yes, Marco had heard some disturbing stories about Maria and Jacopo, that he was neglecting her, even abusing her, and it was as much as his mother's worries about this as his father's concern about improving the mill's efficiency that had prompted his journey. "Who brought these stories to Posara?" Luca asked. He hadn't written to Don Giuseppe for some time (he felt guilty about it) and he would never have talked about Maria and Jacopo if he had written to the village priest, so how had his mother heard of her only daughter's marital difficulties?

But Marco was vague: "Oh some old biddy at Fivizzano market, I think," he said with a dismissive wave. "But are they true? Is he mistreating her? I'll kill him if he is."

Aunt Martha looked dismayed: "I'm sure it's not as bad as that," she said, her hand to her mouth, "and anyway, you shouldn't be discussing family affairs in front of..." She rolled her eyes in Luisa's direction. Marco, although he must have been three times the bulk of his aunt, looked suitably chastened. Aunt Martha turned to Luca "But what are you doing home from work at so early an hour?"

So Luca had to explain again how he'd been attacked on his way from the *Palazzo della Signoria* to the cathedral and how Don Antonio had rescued him. He talked about the blow to his shoulder, which was beginning to ache again, but didn't mention the garrote.

56

"Bull-necked, shaven-headed, accompanying a fat young patrician? That ring any bells for you, Cosimo?"

The Cardinal, Don Antonio and Cosimo de' Medici were once more ensconced in Cosimo's library. Luigi Mazzini had again expropriated the oak chair with the red leather cushion while Cosimo had to make do with the folding curule seat opposite.

Don Antonio stood near the window. He'd just told the older men of the attack on Luca da Posara and of his realisation that he'd seen the bull-necked man before: he'd been waiting with his patrician master for an audience with Carlo Malatesta when the guards had hustled Don Antonio at spearpoint from the *condottiere*'s tent. "I didn't have time to examine them closely," he said. "I had other things on my mind." He gave a self-deprecating smile. "But I am sure it was him. And then I remembered something Malatesta told me later in the day. He said something like 'my next visitors told me that Florence was ripe for insurrection.' That must have been the message those two had brought."

"This is a serious matter," said Cosimo. "Treachery and treason. It seems that the recent plot was not only against us, but the whole republic. With Visconti soon to be at our walls, it seems that there are some who would undermine them from within."

The Cardinal quoted Cicero: "An enemy at the gates is less formidable, for he is known and carries his banner openly."

"Yes," said Cosimo, not to be outdone and completing the quotation: "The traitor infects the body politic so that it can no longer resist. A murderer is less to fear. The traitor is the plague."

"*O tempora o mores*," said Don Antonio, almost to himself.

"Yes, yes," said the Cardinal, somewhat dismissively.

But while one part of Cosimo's brain had been recalling his Cicero, another it seemed, had been unconsciously deliberating on other matters. "I wonder," he said. "...a fat young patrician, could it be, could it just be, Niccolò Peruzzi."

"But," the Cardinal responded, "echoing what Cosimo had told him: "As you said, the rest of the Peruzzi are powerful enough, but Niccolò's nothing but a debauched nasty piece of work."

Cosimo said: "I know, but he seems to be involved at every turn. Perhaps he has delusions of grandeur or wishes to re-establish his standing in the family."

Perhaps, but let's proceed logically, from the facts we actually know, and not let two and two make five. Unless, of course," the Cardinal added mischievously, "you Humanists can make it so through sheer willpower."

"Enough, Luigi, not now." Cosimo paused, then added: "Oh, by the way, I think I can add another name to our list for those who plotted against us. My spies tell me that Luca da Posara's brother-in-law, a troublemaker who drinks too much, has taken to implying in his cups that he knows far more about this affair than he's letting on. Luca's told me nothing of this, either because he regards Jacopo as family or because he simply doesn't know about it."

"Jacopo?"

"Jacopo Alderici, one of the Master masons on the dome."

Don Antonio joined the conversation: "Jacopo Alderici? I know the name."

"Battista tells me he's a thorn in the flesh of Brunelleschi and the dome project."

The Cardinal held up his hand. "But there are too many tenuous links. Peruzzi may have had a hold on Giovanni Ferrante, but was he the mastermind behind the plot? There must be others involved, surely? And is the bull-necked man who attacked Luca da Posara the same one who Don Antonio here saw at the Malatesta camp? Does he work for Niccolò Peruzzi? "

"Well, the last question is easily resolved. I'll get my agents to investigate that right away."

"The sooner the better. Isn't he likely to strike again?"

Cosimo pondered for a moment. "You're quite right. I think we ought to bring *Messer* Bull-necked Shaven-head here for a little questioning."

"Why not let the law deal with him?"

"The law's too slow. We have no time. Besides if other families are involved in the plot and the potential insurrection he could be beyond the reach of the law. No, speed and surprise are our two best allies."

The Cardinal pondered "If, as you say, other influential families are involved, how will you proceed against them?"

"*Divide et impera*. Like Caesar in Gaul, we must divide to rule. If we cannot take them all at once, we must do so one at a time. Our first task is to excise Niccolò Peruzzi from the body politic. And I have an inkling on how that might be done."

57

When Luca came downstairs early next morning his brother Marco had already left the house, "to see the sights of the city," Aunt Martha said. Luca walked with Battista to the cathedral, keeping a sharp lookout for bull-necked men and glad of his uncle's bulk at his side. When they arrived they found, as usual, a couple of hundred day-labourers gathered in the space to the South of the building, crowding noisily around a low platform on which an overseer, protected in a wooden cage, handed out permits to the fifty or so who were to be employed that day.

Entering through the South door and walking up the shady coolness of the nave they found the ox-keeper harnessing one of the beasts to the capstan pole of the hoist. Apart from the clamour of the day-labourers, which filtered indistinctly through the walls, it was unusually quiet in the Crossing without the creaks and groans of the hoist and the hammerings of carpenters and masons. A few 'coos' came from pigeons high above and the occasional flap of wings as one ousted another from a favourite roosting spot.

"Can you just pop up top," Battista asked his nephew, "and have a look at those fastenings in Section III? He added: "I ought to go myself but, to be quite honest with you, all this to-ing and fro-ing, upping and downing is quite wearing me out. And you've got younger legs than me. Filippo and I told them all just what to do yesterday, but I want to make sure everything's just right. You might like to look at all the ironwork in the other sections, too, just to be on the safe side."

"Of course, uncle," said Luca, who felt remarkably fit despite yesterday's excitements. He didn't know what was in Don Antonio's embrocation, but he'd hardly had a twinge from his neck in the night. He'd rubbed in a few more drops when he got up, more as a precaution than anything else. He was turning towards the doorway in the Octagon that led to the steps to the cupola, when Battista added: "When you've done, and if all's well, you can go straight to the *Palazzo della Signoria* and report to Filippo. Oh, and tell him I've managed to find a replacement for that cracked sandstone block. Two masons will work on it today, shaping and dressing, and I hope to get it up top later this afternoon."

At the top of the workings Luca worked his way gingerly around the scaffolding planking, inspecting the ironwork ties and cross beams that had so far been put in place (there were many more to come), paying particular attention to those in Section III, which seemed to him to have been fitted perfectly. He reached the spot where the cracked block had been removed and leaning through the gap, contemplated the city below him. Giotto's bell tower rose elegantly to his right and by straining outwards he could just see the niche that was awaiting Donatello's Habbakuk. Beyond was Arnolfo's slim tower above the *Palazzo della Signoria*, with the bells of the city in the castellated gallery at its summit. Beyond were the gentle slopes of the hills on the other side of the Arno and he thought he could just make out the green and white stripes of the façade of *San Miniato al Monte* through the trees. What a beautiful city – and made all the more so by the fact that Alessia Rossi lived in it...

After a few moments taking pleasure in the view and thinking of his new-found love, Luca started his decent. But he was battling against a rising tide of *scalpellatori, muratori* and the other workmen coming up the steps, which meant frequent stops to let the others pass, so that, what with a '*Buongiorno*' here and a '*Salve*' there, he'd quite lost count when he reached to bottom.

His uncle accosted him as soon as he emerged. "Ah, Luca, here you are. Before you go to the *Signoria* I need your help. We've more ironwork to get up top, but it's all in one pile and it's got into a bit of a mess. I wonder if you could sort it out for me and put it into appropriate baskets for the hoist."

It took Luca some time to bring order to the chaos, and during the process he was interrupted by his brother Marco, who wanted to discuss the new parts for the mill machinery. Marco had already prepared drawings and, after they studied them together Luca was able to make some suggestions for subtle refinements which would make the mill operate even more efficiently.

So it was well after eleven before he set off to report to Brunelleschi. On his way he was careful not to take any short-cuts through alleyways, keeping to the main streets and occasionally glancing behind him to make sure he wasn't followed. He made it safely to the *Palazzo della Signoria*, however, and again sought an audience with the architect.

Brunelleschi was worried about Luca's wellbeing. He'd heard he'd been attacked, he said, and hoped that he'd suffered no ill effects. When Luca told him he was well, he patted him on the back and smiled broadly. He was gratified, too, with Luca's progress report, and in particular that the damaged sandstone block was to be replaced, but their interview was cut short by the arrival of the green-liveried servant, who said that it was now time for Brunelleschi to attend a meeting of the *Signoria*. Within a few more minutes Luca was back in the sunshine of the *piazza*, just as the bells of the city were striking noon.

58

Jacopo Alderici had had a good morning, not only laying stonework, which he loved, but also stirring up more resentment in his colleagues over their pay and conditions on the dome worksite. His masters would be pleased: hopefully it might get them off his back. The other workers had left for Brunelleschi's kitchen lower down the dome, but Jacopo remained at the workface, examining the stone block he had just fitted in place, running his hand over the dressed sandstone, feeling the smoothness of the finish. Above him the Spring sky was a luminous light blue and, although there was a faint breeze, Jacopo felt the heat, having drunk far too much wine the previous night.

To admire the new row of masonry blocks as a whole, he stepped back carefully, almost to the very edge of the wooden scaffolding, beyond which there a dizzying drop to the cathedral floor more than a hundred *braccia* below.

Jacopo heard footsteps on the stairs that led up darkly between the two overlapping shells of the dome and saw a figure emerge and edge towards him, a hand on to the stonework for support. As the outline became clearer he gave a start of recognition.

"You!"

"Yes, me."

"What are you doing here?"

"I brought you this, you bastard."

Jacopo ducked instinctively as a small wooden box swung towards his head. It struck his temple and he staggered back, arms flailing. He grabbed the box, but lost his balance. For one moment, his eyes wide in terror, he was poised on the edge of the scaffolding. Then he fell, screaming, into the void.

59

Luca was more than three-quarters of the way along the near-deserted nave when he heard the scream and saw the body fall. There was a dull thud as it hit the floor and then two sharper cracks as a flimsy wooden box bounced and smashed on the paving slabs. Slices of salami, blood red and fatty white, spilled and scattered and a dirty *panino* rolled erratically towards him. Then, a dozen paces ahead, he saw Jacopo's crumpled body, with his head and one of his legs bent at unnatural angles. A small but growing pool of purple blood surrounded the head.

Two priests in black cassocks were first on the scene, kneeling by the body, crossing themselves and murmuring low prayers. Half a dozen workmen soon joined them, obscuring Luca's view of the body. He remained where he was, seemingly frozen, unable to move.

It was a few more moments before he saw someone he knew: Don Antonio arriving from the North Transept. Having glanced over the shoulders of the crowd, he came over and took Luca by the arm. "I'm so sorry," he said, "I'm afraid he's quite dead." Animated at last, Luca moved forward to try to see for himself, but Don Antonio restrained him.

Battista appeared, red-faced and puffing, Donatello came hurrying in from a side chapel and at the back of the crowd Luca suddenly saw his brother Marco, still wearing his dark-blue knitted hat. What was he doing here?

Looking over Luca's shoulder, Don Antonio suddenly stiffened. Turning, Luca saw Maria standing at the side of the aisle, as pale and still as a pond by moonlight. It was difficult to tell if she was coming or going, but then she made as if to move forward towards the crowd around the corpse. Suddenly Donatello was in front of her, placing his hands on her shoulders, talking to her softly. As Luca and Don Antonio went over to join them, Maria held up her raffia basket: "Luca, Luca. I'm just taking Jacopo his mid-day meal." She tried to break free from Donatello's embrace, but Marco had also come up and blocked her way forward. She dropped the basket and burst into a flood of tears.

Donatello put an arm around her: "Come on Maria," he said gently. We have to get you out of here." Maria's sobs grew louder and she gave a despairing glance at Luca, but allowed herself to be led away by Donatello, with Marco accompanying them.

"Where will we go?" her brother asked. "She can't go back to her lodgings – and there's no room at Battista's."

"We'll take her to Cosimo de' Medici's. She'll be safe there and the women of the household will know how to look after her. Come on."

As Luca watched them go, his eyesight suddenly became peculiarly distorted, his field of vision filled with three pictures of the same thing, each in a triangular frame, as if somehow Brunelleschi's perspective experiment had come to life, but with two mirrors reflecting reality, not just one. And colours were not only more intense but blurred: Maria's three skirts were iridescent blobs of green, while Donatello's doublets glowed dark brown. Luca screwed tight his eyes to try to clear his sight, but to no avail.

Sounds, too, were distorted, so that the words of the three Don Antonios seemed to be both booming and distant: "Come on Luca. We must get you home, too." Unprotesting, he let the priest guide him down the nave. They stopped for a moment as the trio of priests bent to pick up Maria's three raffia baskets.

Luca's vision returned to normal during the walk to his uncle's house, but he felt too weak to resist when Aunt Martha insisted that he be put straight to bed, a command reinforced by Don Antonio. When his aunt brought him up a beaker of almond-milk soup a little later she found him asleep, tossing fitfully, muttering from time to time. She stroked his hot temple and tried to smooth his hair, but was careful not to wake him.

Luca had a disturbed night: in his mind's eye those triangular images returned and in the prisms faces loomed and receded again and again, their voices muffled and repetitive. Here was red-faced Battista: "I could murder him for the way he's carrying on. I could murder him, murder him, murder him..."

Then Cosimo with his long nose and protruding ears swam into view: Ah, that Donatello! It's true he has the sweetest disposition most of the time. But he can easily lose his temper, his temper, his temper..."

Brunelleschi followed, hair dishevelled, eyes tired with overwork: "If he doesn't change his ways I'll have to take action, action, action..."

The bull-necked man was there, too, brandishing a garrote, calling "Are you Luca da Posara, Luca, Luca?" Had he been in the nave too? Luca couldn't recall.

And here was Marco's bulky head whirling towards him in triplicate: "Is he mistreating her? I'll kill him if he is. I'll kill him if he is... I'll kill him if he is..."

And then three Marias, each materializing in the cathedral nave, holding up their raffia baskets: "I'm just taking Jacopo his mid-day meal, his mid-day meal, his mid-day meal..."

Luca awoke with a start, sitting bolt upright, all his senses alert. Somewhere a clock struck midnight, not mid-day, but Luca knew he had to examine Maria's basket straightaway. He had a vague recollection that Don Antonio had put it down somewhere in the ground floor storeroom before helping him up the stairs.

He was out of bed in a instant, his feet cold on the wooden floorboards, feeling his way to the doorjamb and out into the passageway (mind the slop-pail!), where he could hear Marco's emphatic snoring from the room next door. Down the first flight of stairs, too distracted to count them, to the landing, with its door to the silent bedroom of his uncle and aunt, across the landing and down more stairs to the big first floor room, where the faint glow from the embers of the fire, diligently raked to the back of the chimney piece, gave him enough light to seek out the stub of a candle in its brass holder. Finding a spill above the chimney breast, he lit it from the embers and put it to the candle's wick before continuing his descent.

Luca's shadow loomed large behind him, sooty black, grossly elongated. He turned and held the candle high. Yes, there it was, in the middle of the room. He picked up the raffia basket, put it on the bench, scene of his recent encounter with Luisa, and carefully placed the candlestick on a shelf next to the box of nails. The candle spluttered and nearly died, but Luca protected it with his hand and it flickered bravely to life again. He looked inside the raffia basket. There was a woman's purse, obviously Maria's, a headscarf in green wool and a maroon brimless hat that he couldn't remember Maria, or Jacopo, ever wearing. But it was what was not in the basket that worried Luca. The candle flame guttered and died and he mounted the cold steps on his hands and feet in the dark.

60

"Did he fall or was he pushed?"

"I don't know Pippo, I honestly don't know. But I don't think he was the sort of man who would have fallen, even though he wasn't entirely sober most of the day. He was a careful workman, give him that."

Filippo Brunelleschi and Battista d'Antonio were sitting in the architect's rooms in the *Palazzo della Signoria*.

"Of course, they'll say I pushed him – or you, come to that!" Brunelleschi said.

"Well, I presume you were here all day yesterday and can easily prove it. And I don't think anyone's going to accuse me."

"How's Luca taking it?

"Very badly. He was delirious last night and he's still in his bed today. I went up to see him this morning and he was just lying there. Didn't want to get up and didn't want to say anything. Strange. I didn't think he was that close to his brother-in-law."

"Luca's had an exciting few weeks, what with seeing enough dead bodies to last anyone a lifetime and being attacked with a garrote. I wouldn't begrudge him a day or two in bed."

"Well, it's true we could do without him for a day or two. Everything's under control at the dome. After they'd cleared everything up yesterday…" Battista gave a small shudder at the recollection. "After they'd taken him away and scrubbed the stones, I was at able to get the hoist working again and put that replacement sandstone block in place. There's a lot more blocks to go in, but the men seem to know what they're doing now, so it all looks reasonably straightforward. Luca's sorted out all the iron ties and braces, so they'll be ready when we are."

"What about Jacopo's section? How will you manage that?"

"Well, I've had my eye on that assistant mason in Section III for some time. He seems very competent and keen, mutters much less than the others. So, with your permission, I thought he could take over Jacopo's section."

"Of course, Battista. You know much more about the day-to-day running of the project than I do, so I bow to your superior judgment." Brunelleschi did just that, giving a little mock bow in his seat. "So, given there are no hiccoughs, you think the second ring will be finished in a month or so?"

"Yes."

"And that's when we'll have to stop. The *Opera del Duomo* is adamant."

"Not a bad idea in all truth," said Battista.

"No, but it looks like most of job of working out what we're going to do next is going to fall on you and me."

"What about our esteemed colleague Lorenzo Ghiberti? He's still the third *Provveditore della cupola*."

Brunelleschi grinned. "Not for much longer, I'll be bound." But when Battista asked him why, he just put his finger on the side of his nose and tapped it. "You'll just have to wait and see."

They continued their talk about the dome for some time before Brunelleschi said. "Well, old friend, time for you to be going, I fear. I have an appointment with San Bartolomeo!"

"What?" said Battista, and then as realization dawned, "Oh Yes, that special mass. When is it again?

"The day after tomorrow. And I've some special effects to design to capture the saint's attention."

After Battista had left Brunelleschi pulled a few sheets of paper towards him and worked on a series of elaborate drawings and diagrams that he had begun earlier. These weren't plans for further work on the dome, nor on Filippo's *Ospedale degli Innocenti,* nor even for his proposed alterations and extensions to the *San Lorenzo* church of the Medici. For while engineering and architecture were Brunelleschi's passions, theatre, or rather the production of theatrical effects, was his hobby.

From time to time special religious performances re-enacting Biblical stores were given in city churches and Filippo took the greatest of pleasure in making elaborate scenery and complex machines for these productions. It was a release from the pressures of constructing real buildings that were always subject to the inexorable forces of nature.

Creating illusions of reality gave him a true feeling of freedom. He'd invented machines that made men rise from the grave and angels fly through the air among spectacular displays of lights and fireworks. This year he'd built sets for a representation of *Paradiso* in the old church of *San Felice in Piazza* across the Arno, which included a device that, by an ingenious arrangement of cranks and gears, shafts and tubes, enabled an operator to expose all at once a vast array of burning candles, bringing paradise to earth.

It was the Cardinal's suggestion that they should invoke the aid of old San Bartolomeo in ensuring that the dome of the cathedral did not come tumbling to the ground, and the idea had been endorsed by Cosimo de' Medici, perhaps to reassure his ecclesiastical cousin that Humanists were religious people who acknowledged God's power in ordering human destiny. San Bartolomeo was ideal for the job since, thought Brunelleschi, he might be regarded as the patron Saint of 'weightlessness', a good man to have on your side when you were trying to keep thousands of tons of masonry and brickwork in the air above your city's most prestigious building.

Two 'weighty' miracles were associated with the saint, specifically in his incarnation in Lipari, a small town on an island off the Sicilian coast. When, centuries earlier, Bartolomeo's body had been washed ashore, the local bishop ordered the men of the town to bring it to the cathedral. But they found it too heavy to lift. So the bishop sent a group of children instead and they raised the body with ease and carried it though the town.

With the saint safely installed in the cathedral, every year on his feast day the people of Lipari carried a silver statue of Bartolomeo through the town in solemn procession. On one occasion, however, the statue became so heavy that the men carrying it were forced to put it down to regain their strength. This happened three times. When the men lowered the statue the third time, a stone wall further along the procession route suddenly collapsed: if the townspeople had been passing at that moment many of them would have been killed.

Of the two miracles, Brunelleschi considered the one with the children was the most appropriate: mysteriously collapsing stonework was not perhaps the message that he wanted to convey.

Yes, children it was, and although it was often devilishly hard to get them to do what they were supposed to do, when they were supposed to do it, there was always the 'aaaah' factor to consider: the audience loved angelic little ones, particularly if he dressed them in white.

So, he'd have half a dozen brawny men carrying in the saint's body, lying on a simple catafalque – wooden planking covered with a golden cloth. Not much lighting: perhaps half a dozen candles in pillar holders. The men would suddenly stagger under the weight, put the saint down and *exeunt*.

Enter left six toddlers in white tunics ('aaaah') who arrange themselves around the bier, which slowly rises from the ground. When it reaches head height, they put their tiny hands up to steady the saint and the whole group exits right as black curtains are drawn back to reveal serried ranks of candles. He could use the same contraptions he created for *Paradiso*. It was a pity he hadn't access to a heavenly choir as well. He'd have a word with the sacristan to see if they could provide half-a-dozen singers, to add music to the visual spectacle.

Filippo sketched out the scene on a sheet of paper. Black drapes behind and at front top, the former to camouflage the black-painted wires from which the saint and his planking support were suspended and the latter to hide the machinery which would lift him up and transport him off stage.

Then Brunelleschi's devious mind conceived another idea. We don't know whether Jacopo Alderici fell accidently or was pushed, he thought. Suppose at the end of my scene I was also to create a facsimile of his death. Would that smoke out the killer, if there were one?

He pulled out another sheet of paper and began drawing.

61

After the servants had cleared the dining table and left the room the Cardinal and Cosimo de' Medici pulled their chairs closer together. They'd dined, just the two of them, on San Vincenzo's Day Eels, a little late for the saint's feast day, it had to be said, but as delicious in May as in January. The slices of grilled eel, with their sauce of orange, lemon and pomegranate juice, were another of the Cardinal's favourite dishes. He said: "You spoil me, Cousin."

"Not at all, Luigi. After all, *bis vivit qui bene vivit.*"

"Then I am living not just twice, but many times over, you look after me so well. I fear with Seneca, though, that the abundance of food hampers intelligence."

"Nonsense, Luigi, you're the cleverest man in Italy, apart of course from your views on Humanism."

The Cardinal laughed. "Let's not start that argument again, though that death in the cathedral shows that the unexpected can always occur in human affairs."

"A tragic accident, no more, no less."

"Unless he was pushed."

"I'm inclined to think he fell. Battista mentioned he had a drink problem."

"His widow is staying here I believe. How is she bearing up?"

"With remarkable fortitude and although she says little she has a stillness about her that one cannot but admire." Cosimo sat back, contemplating Maria's pale beauty, the dark eyes, the black bonnet of hair, and the Cardinal, as perspicacious as ever, seemed to read his thoughts.

"A lovely girl, to be sure, but is it wise to keep her in your house?"

"She's safe here. My wife and her women will look after her." Cosimo hoped he didn't sound too defensive.

"And what of her brother, the conscientious young Luca."

"The strange thing, so I hear from Battista, is that he's taken Jacopo's death very much to heart. He's been in bed for two days, hardly saying a word."

"Was he close to his brother-in-law?"

"No, but he is to his sister. You'd have thought he might have come over to see her by now. And me, for that matter, not least because I have some news for him of the bull-necked man who tried to kill him."

"You've found him?"

"Yes, or rather my agents found him. In the cathedral piazza, actually, on the day that Jacopo Alderici fell to his death."

"And does he work for Niccolò Peruzzi?"

"Well, yes he does. Or rather he did.

"He did! Is he dead? You haven't had him killed?"

"No, no, he's very much alive. He works for me now."

"And did he tell you of Peruzzi's embassy to the Malatesta camp."

"He did and although he was not allowed into the meeting with the *condottiere* himself, he confirmed that Peruzzi's mission was to assure the Duke of Milan of substantial support within the city. Treacherous swine!"

"Steady Cosimo, think before you do anything rash."

"I will, but as well as undermining my city, he has also attacked me personally. In this matter I am at one with the kings of Scotland: *Nemo me impune lacessit*. No-one provokes the Medici with impunity."

62

Aunt Martha came into Luca's bedroom early next morning with her arms full of folded clothes. "Luca, you've got to get yourself out of bed."

Unshaven, with scratchy eyelids and his hair more tousled than ever, Luca responded listlessly: "I don't want to get up."

His aunt put the clothes on a chair and pulled back the cover. "This behavior has got to stop, Luca," she said, speaking to him as if he were a recalcitrant child. "Three days is more than enough. Get yourself up and get yourself down to the public baths. The stench in here is likely to curdle milk."

Luca sat up reluctantly, unused to his aunt being so forceful. She pointed to the chair: "These are mourning clothes, sent courtesy of *Messer* Cosimo de' Medici for you to wear at *San Bartolomeo*'s service today."

"What service?" asked Luca, then remembering added, "Oh, that service, getting the saint's help with the dome. Is that today?"

"It certainly is, at 11 o'clock, and *Messer* Cosimo wants to see you at his house beforehand, so you've got to get a move on. And when you've bathed, have a shave and see if the barber can do something with that hair of yours at the same time."

Luca felt weak and wobbly after being in bed so long. Was it really three days? Friday afternoon to, what was today, oh yes, Monday. Monday morning. More like two-and-a half days, but Aunt Martha was quite right, it was long enough. He pulled on his old dun-coloured doublet and hose, slipped into his shoes and went downstairs (twelve, eleven, ten…")

His aunt insisted he drink a bowl of warm almond-milk soup, into which he dunked pieces of day-old bread: it tasted good and he found he was very hungry. Aunt Martha was soon back in her usual solicitous mode: "Well, that's certainly put a bit of colour in your cheeks, you poor boy, but you still stink like a horse's stable after the *Palio*. Get yourself off to the baths. You got money?"

Luca went over to his aunt and kissed her on the top of her head, then headed out, wondering as he did so how on earth she knew about the smells of steamy stables after Florence's famous horserace.

The bath certainly did revive him, and the shave and the haircut. The barber, by the use of some lotion with a sickly-sweet smell, even succeeded in sticking down the unruly tuft.

"That's better," said Aunt Martha when he reappeared a couple of hours later, "but you've still got to keep moving. And I've got to change, too. Wives are to come to the service, though no doubt we'll have to stand at the back. Maria'll be there, too. I'll be glad to see her."

"Where's she been for the last few days?

"They took her to the Medici house after..." His aunt tailed off, then with a shake of the head added: "Not much room here and they've taken good care of her by all accounts. When Marco goes perhaps she'll come over to stay. But they say she's safer there, whatever that means." Yes, thought Luca, I wonder just what the Medici mean by that.

"And where's Marco? Is he coming today?"

"No, he's not invited. It's just for folk involved in the dome. But I must say he's in a funny mood. Refuses to wear mourning. He's gone off to the cannon foundry this morning."

"Oh, that'll be to make castings for the new mill machinery. Funny time to go there, though."

Half an hour later Luca was walking through the crowded, sunlit streets towards the Medici house in the *San Tommaso* parish. Although his new clothes fitted him very well and the dark-brown doublet and hose were of a higher quality than he was used to, Luca felt self-conscious in the full-length black gown and the black *cappuzzo* hat, its scarf folded over his shoulder. He also felt rather hot. People deferred to his mourning clothes: a small nod of the head or a sympathetic smile, and one older woman even crossed herself as he passed.

He passed a girl sitting outside her doorway shelling beans and realized with a start that he'd hardly thought of Alessia Rossi recently, little wonder, given the dreadful conclusions he'd come to during his feverish days in bed. She was the one pure thing in his life; everything else was deception and delusion. And now he faced a seemingly insoluble dilemma: should he keep the truth he'd discovered to himself or should he reveal it, whatever the consequence? Still confused and agitated, he reached the Medici house.

He was shown into Cosimo's library, where he found the banker sitting once more in his favourite chair, in his red 'official' gown and matching brimless cap. Beneath these he was, as ever, modestly dressed, in a blue doublet and dark-green hose.

"Luca, how are you?" said Cosimo, rising and taking Luca's hand. "I'd heard you'd been very unwell."

"I'm much better now, thank you, sir."

"My heartfelt condolences I was sorry to hear of your brother-in-law's death. *Quoniam tamquam faenum velociter arescent.* Like grass, all of us will wither."

Well, that's cheered me up no end, thought Luca, but he only said: "Thank you again. And my sister Maria, how is she?"

"She's borne her loss with true dignity. You'll want to see her of course."

"I'd like to, but..."

Cosimo misread his reluctance. "Oh, I see what you mean. It's about time we set off for the church. Oh, well, you can come back afterwards and you'll have more time to talk to her properly then." He rose: "Come on, you can walk with me to *San Bartolomeo* and I'll tell you what's been happening in your absence."

63

When they arrived at the church of *San Bartolomeo* in the *Santa Croce* quarter Cosimo de' Medici dismissed the two burly servants who had escorted them through the city and he and Luca joined the queue pushing through the West door. Inside tall lancet windows with pointed arches illuminated the interior, a barn-like space. The East window and the altar, however, were hidden by a black curtain hanging from a ceiling beam. There was a further arrangement of black drapes framing the nave just below the altar steps. Two large candles in pillar stands burned on either side while another six were lined up in front of the black curtain at the rear.

It was customary, of course, for the congregation to stand during church services, but Luca saw that today a dozen or so chairs had been lined up in front of the curtains, with four or five rows of benches behind them, filling perhaps a third of the nave. The Cardinal, again resplendent in scarlet, was already seated and, seeing Cosimo, waved to him to come forward.

It took some time for the harassed sacristan to ensure that everyone found his proper place: the most dignified dignitaries on the chairs; the cathedral masons, members of the *Opera del Duomo* and various other officials on the benches; and the lesser mortals like Luca standing at the back. And behind them, the women, although when Cosimo's wife appeared a chair was hastily produced for her and, next to it, one for Maria, who was enveloped in a dark mourning gown with its hood pulled closely about her face. Luca stood directly in front of his sister but the sacristan moved him and the other men a little to the side to create an aisle though which the ladies could view the spectacle.

Luca turned and took his sister's black-gloved hand: "Maria, how are you? I'm so sorry."

He felt an answering squeeze and heard though the folds of the hood her soft voice. "I am well enough but Oh, Luca, I've missed you."

But further conversation was precluded by the Cardinal standing up at the front of the church and clearing his throat. As the prelate stepped into a shaft of sunlight streaming in through one of the lancet windows Luca had a feeling of having experienced all this before and he remembered the first time he had seen the Cardinal, on his visit to inspect the dome. When was it? It seemed like a lifetime ago, before the discovery of the battered body of 'Bartolomeo da Siracusa' in the baptistry square and all the harrowing subsequent events, including Jacopo's death, but in truth it was less than three weeks. And here was Luigi, Cardinal Mazzini once more doing his trick of moving into a shaft of sunlight before he spoke:

"Dearly beloved, we are gathered here to appeal to Almighty God, through the intercession of his beloved servant Bartolomeo, to look with His favour on our efforts to construct in this city a great cupola, an embodiment of the vault of heaven itself, to reflect His Glory and to remind us of our insignificance in the vast firmament He has created…"

The Cardinal continued for several minutes, saying how it was sinful for men to believe that such tasks could be completed solely by their own efforts and that without the Grace of God nothing could or would be achieved. He went on to talk about *San Bartolomeo* and the miracles he had performed, stepping a few paces to his left as he did so and reading from a paper in his hand. "After the body of the blessed saint had been washed ashore on the island of Lipari…"

These words were clearly a cue: an unseen choir began singing a motet in praise of God as six men appeared from behind the drapes on the audience's left, bearing at shoulder height a plaster saint on a stretcher covered with a gold cloth. The Cardinal continued reading: "…the bishop sent strong men to bring the Saint to his cathedral. But they suddenly found it far too heavy for them to carry…" The men duly staggered with their load. "…and were forced to lower it to the ground." The brawny pall-bearers did just that and trooped off behind the curtains to the right.

The Cardinal turned to the audience: "So the bishop sent little children in their stead…" He paused as six small boys, with white tunics tied with golden cords, tripped in from the left. The church certainly does know how to put on a show, thought Luca, as there was a collective 'aaah', which turned to laughter when one child, obviously seeing someone he knew in the audience, gave a cheery wave.

The children positioned themselves around the grounded saint, three on either side, kneeling and holding the poles that supported the bier. The choir grew louder and the Cardinal raised his voice above them: "...and the children had no difficulty in raising up the blessed Bartolomeo."

As he spoke there was a creaking noise and then, somewhat jerkily at first, Bartolomeo rose from the ground. Soon the little ones, who had risen to their feet as the saint ascended, had to stretch high to steady the poles on either side. Then the bier began to move to the right. As the hidden singing reached a crescendo and as Bartolomeo and his escort of children moved away, the side drapes were pulled back revealing metal holders in which burned a profusion of bright candles.

The music stopped, children and saint disappeared, when suddenly, from beneath the right hand side of the upper curtain what looked like a human form appeared, dressed in a brown doublet and hose. It hung poised for a moment, then plunged to the floor.

In the shocked silence that followed, Maria give a high-pitched wail, followed by a series of gasping sobs, between which Luca heard her say in a thin voice:" Jacopo, O Jacopo, I didn't mean it..."

64

Luca sat once more in the curule chair in Cosimo de' Medici's library, while the banker stood looking out of the long windows that looked out on to the terrace.

"I don't know what on earth possessed Filippo to pull a trick like that," said Cosimo, sighing in exasperation, "but this time he went too far."

It's true, thought Luca, Brunelleschi can never leave well alone: he always wants to concoct some devious scheme or other.

"He says he was only trying to smoke out whoever killed your brother-in-law," Cosimo continued. "I've never seen him more contrite, nor apologise so profusely." Well, that's a first: Luca had never heard Brunelleschi apologise for anything before.

"When did you first suspect that Maria was responsible for Jacopo's death?" Cosimo asked, moving from the window to sit in his favourite chair.

"It was around midnight on the day he died," said Luca, "I'd been delirious for hours, I think, and various theories about his death had floated through my brain." Luca was glad to talk, pleased that, at last, everything could be revealed. "There were so many people who seemed to want him dead, or at least they'd gain from his death, and in my fevered state I suspected all of them."

"All of them? Who do you mean?"

"Well, for instance, Brunelleschi himself and my uncle Battista clearly had a motive for killing Jacopo. And I remembered my uncle saying 'I could murder him for the way he's carrying on.'"

"Just a figure of speech, nothing more, surely?"

"Oh, I'm quite sure of that now. But he was up in the dome at the time Jacopo fell. And *Messer* Filippo said he would take 'drastic action' if Jacopo didn't mend his ways."

"But he was confined to the *Palazzo della Signoria*..."

"Yes, of course. There was, however, the possibility that other people, knowing of his anger at Jacopo's behaviour, might have taken 'drastic action' on his behalf. Like Donatello, for instance."

Cosimo looked amazed: "Donatello? Surely not!"

"You yourself have said that while he usually has the sweetest of dispositions, he can easily lose his temper. He's also fiercely loyal to Filippo Brunelleschi and he's passionate about the dome. So he might have taken matters into his own hands – and he, too, was in the cathedral."

"But he didn't do it!"

"I know that now, but the possibility was there in my fevered imaginings. And then there was the Church."

"The Church? What can you possibly mean?"

"Well, His Eminence the Cardinal has suggested on a number of occasions that we Florentines..." Luca realized that he already considered himself a native of the city. "He said that we Florentines," he continued, "seemed to believe we could finish the dome by our own efforts alone, unaided by God. I wondered, I just wondered, if he thought we should be taught a lesson..."

Cosimo looked incredulous: "I can't see Luigi clambering to the top of the dome and throwing your brother-in-law off to teach us all a lesson. Can you?"

"Oh no, sir, of course not. But perhaps someone close to him, hearing his words, thought that this might be a way..." Luca tailed off.

"Someone close to him? You mean the muscular Don Antonio?"

"Well, as I tossed and turned it seemed feasible. It was a bit strange when he went to the top of the dome and started asking all those questions."

Cosimo said: "Your mind <u>was</u> in a fevered state. Were you sure at this point that Jacopo <u>was</u> murdered? Couldn't it have been an accident?"

"He just wasn't the type to throw himself off the scaffolding, although he had been drinking too much and muttering about plots to kill him. I suppose he could have dwelt on those thoughts and thrown himself off in despair, but I doubt it. On the other hand, I thought, what if the threats <u>were</u> real?"

"Explain more," said Cosimo.

Luca said: "Well that bull-necked man who tried to kill me..."

"Federico."

"Yes, Federico. Well, as you told me this morning, he was working for Niccolò Peruzzi – and Peruzzi was behind the plot to kill Rocco Rossi, disguise him as Bartolomeo da Siracusa and disgrace Filippo Brunelleschi."

"I've every reason to believe that Federico actually killed Rossi," said Cosimo, "and that Jacopo was there. Jacopo was beginning to talk too much, so when my agents picked Federico up outside the cathedral three days ago, he could have been on his way to murder Jacopo."

"But he didn't get there..."

"No."

"And then," said Luca, "another, horrible possibility entered my mind. My brother Marco had heard rumours that Jacopo was mistreating our sister. He said he'd kill him if he had been. He's got a temper on him, too. And he was at the cathedral that day."

Cosimo spoke again: "But in the end you suspected none of them. Why was that? Why do you think you sister killed her husband?"

"It all hinged on that raffia basket Maria was carrying. She said she was taking Jacopo his midday meal, but the wooden box containing his meal wasn't there. In fact it, or one very like it, had already fallen from the scaffolding with Jacopo."

"So what did that mean?"

"Well, it either meant someone else had taken another box up to Jacopo, or Maria had already taken it up herself."

"But you told me she was afraid of heights and that she sent a boy up with the box."

"I don't think she did that day. I think she summoned up the courage to go herself. She came earlier than usual, before the boy who took the box had arrived. We can find him and ask him if we need to."

Cosimo shifted uneasily in his seat: "I don't think that'll be necessary."

"I also think she must have disguised herself," Luca continued. "I found a maroon brimless hat, which I'd never seen before, in the basket. I reckon she pushed all her hair into that, so she'd look more like a boy."

"What about her skirt?"

"Well, all this is speculation, but she might have taken it off and put it in the basket, hidden that in some alcove and set off up the steps in her doublet and hose. It's just a theory. We could find out the truth if we ask her."

Cosimo said, quite sternly: "I don't think that'll be necessary either."

"On those dark stairways a 'boy' carrying a wooden meal box wouldn't attract any attention."

"And what happened afterwards?"

"I think after Jacopo fell she rushed down the steps, put on her skirt, took off the cap and shook out her hair and set off down the nave. She stopped and looked back at the crowd around the body – and that's when I saw her."

"So you think she lied to you when she said she was in the process of taking Jacopo his meal. She'd already done so."

"Well, that's the conclusion I came to that night. Can you wonder that I didn't want to leave my bed for days?"

"It's strange isn't it? While we were all looking for motives that might be political, religious, even artistic, the true answer lay in something domestic. People's opinions and actions depend on their point of view and as far as Maria was concerned, Jacopo's ill-treatment of her built up to a point where she could stand it no longer. From her desperate and embittered viewpoint, what she did was both logical and necessary."

"Yes, sir," said Luca, "I suppose you could say it's all a matter of perspective."

65

That afternoon Niccolò Peruzzi again sat at his dining table, contemplating what recent events meant for his plans and his ambitions. Federico had singularly failed to eliminate that precocious pup Luca da Posara, coming come back with some cock-and-bull story of a Herculean priest who'd knocked him flying and from whom he was lucky to escape.

Still, it had been good news that Jacopo Alderici had been disposed of, in a very appropriate manner too, but Federico had failed to report back after the mason's death. Had he been caught in the act? Arrested perhaps? Or was he simply lying low?

Niccolò took another mouthful of wine from his silver goblet and was reaching for the linen napkin with which to wipe his lips when he heard a door opening behind him. "Is that you, Elisabetta?"

There was no reply and before he could turn round in his chair, he felt the wire of a garrote tight about his fleshy neck. He clutched at it, one hand knocking over the goblet as he did so, but it was held too tightly. The last words he heard were *"Sic semper omne proditores,"* thus perish all traitors, a phrase that, unbeknown to Niccolò, his executioner had learned from his new master.

***

There were whispers about Maria's involvement in Jacopo's death, but with Cosimo's wife, her companions – and Aunt Martha – cautioned to silence, the rumours never took wing and in a few days the young widow's outburst in the *San Bartolomeo*'s church was largely forgotten.

In his meeting with Luca, Cosimo had established that only those nearest to Maria in the church could have picked up her words. At the front, he'd only heard a heart-rending cry and loud sobs: the words themselves were unintelligible. So only some of the women at the rear and perhaps one or two of the men near Luca would have made them out. Cosimo had also suggested that 'I didn't mean it' was an ambiguous statement and could well have referred to an argument between husband and wife earlier in the day, when Maria had said something to Jacopo which she later regretted.

All in all, the dual strategy of silence and obfuscation worked well and soon the general consensus was that Jacopo had fallen accidently and that he had probably been less than sober at the time. Only Luca and Cosimo knew that Maria was responsible and that her actions were premeditated. Whether or not she meant to kill Jacopo or merely remonstrate with him remained an open question.

At Cosimo's insistence, Maria remained in the Medici household, despite Aunt Martha's protestations that she stay at Battista's, now that Marco had returned to Posara. Luca saw his sister a couple of times and noticed how much better she was beginning to look, a positive bloom on her cheeks and fewer tired lines about her eyes. They never talked about Jacopo's death: Luca was chary of introducing the subject and Maria never mentioned it. It was almost as if it had occurred in another life.

***

In the ensuing weeks work continued on the second stone restraining ring of the dome, which was completed, as Battista had predicted, in a month or so, just about the time that Brunelleschi's period as a *Priore* came to an end. Work was then suspended on the orders of the *Opera del Duomo* and Brunelleschi devised fresh ways of lightening the load and clever techniques for spreading the weight as the dome curved towards its summit. As a fellow *Provveditore della cupola*, Lorenzo Ghiberti also made suggestions, which Brunelleschi ostentatiously ignored. In August of one thousand four hundred and twenty-five, Ghiberti was sacked, due in no small part to the intrigues of Filippo during his term of office as a *Priore*. At last Brunelleschi was in sole charge. It was not until the February of the following year, however, that work on the dome began again.

***

Cosimo knocked lightly and entered Maria's boudoir, part of a suite of rooms that had now been set aside for her in the old Medici house. The high Summer sunshine streamed through the windows of Maria's boudoir, picking out the colours on the piece of embroidery on her lap and on the rich greens and golds in her silk gown. Her hair, piled high and garlanded with pearls, shone in the light and the paleness of her face emphasized the deep ruby of her lips. She stood, dropping her embroidery to the floor.

"Are you settling in comfortably, my dear?" Cosimo asked softly.

"Perfectly. I don't know what I can ever do to thank you enough for all you have done for me."

"I'm sure we shall think of something."

"I am sure we will, Cosimo," said Maria, smiling, encircling his waist with her arms and putting up her mouth to be kissed.

***

Bartolomeo de' Verdi, previously known as Giovanni Ferrante, wrapped the scarf of his *cappuzzo* more closely about his face and tried in vain to prevent the wind whipping under the hem of his day gown. The rain had stopped for the moment, but out across the dull-grey waters of the North Sea fresh squalls were approaching, producing angry little waves with off-white crests. It was June, but Giovanni shivered as he turned back towards his lonely room.

He'd been in St Andrews, in the Kingdom of Fife in Scotland, for ten days, having secured a post as Assistant Provost at the collegiate church of St Mary on the Rock, and he'd never felt warm since he arrived. He had fled Northwards from London a month or so ago, when he'd learned that agents of the Medici bank were enquiring after him and putting about his description among the Italian community.

When he'd first arrived in the English capital all had gone well. He'd teamed up with a tavern keeper and invested in his business, although his attempts at bringing some sophistication to the English *cucina* were hampered by the lack of the proper ingredients, notably sour grape juice and olive oil. The English seemed only to use the latter to soften the wax when their ears became blocked! Nonetheless, he was able to introduce some tasty *piatti del giorno* and the tavern began to thrive, until one day there had been a knock on the door as Cosimo's agents sought him out. Luckily he'd been at the market, but the tavern owner foolishly told them to come back in the afternoon.

Of course, Giovanni had tried to get his partner to buy back his share in the tavern, but sensing Giovanni's desperation, the man had refused, so he'd left that day with only a change of clothes and the twenty or so florins that remained of his initial five hundred. Most of those, too, had disappeared as he made his way Northward and he was glad when the Provost of St Mary's, impressed with his papers, took him on as his assistant. The pay was a pittance, but at least he had a roof over his head and his food provided. The food had been a shock, though: the daily unsweetened gruel and the 'delicacy' of offal and oatmeal stuffed into sheep's gut. Giovanni shuddered in remembrance, then shivered again as the wind brought in a fresh shower of drizzle from the sea.

***

His eyes shining, three-year-old Leo Rossi sat on Luca's shoulders, watching the parade, clapping his small hands together as the richly caparisoned horses passed by, each rider holding aloft a great silk banner on a pole, the next always seeming more sumptuous that the last. Twenty *braccia* above them a great cloth 'sky', a canopy suspended from the walls of the houses and decorated with the lily of Florence and the coats of arms of the Guilds, shaded them from the sun. It was the eve of the feast day of *San Giovanni*, the city's greatest festival.

In the intervening weeks Luca had befriended the cathedral pay clerk and through him had renewed his acquaintance with the Rossi household: Rocco's father and mother, their daughter-in-law Alessia and her two children, Leo and his baby sister Francesca. Many an evening, as the days grew longer and hotter, Luca sat with the family and talked of this and that as the shadows lengthened. He was asked to supper and brought treats for the table, a bag of apricots or peaches, perhaps, or a *caraffa* of wine.

No doubt Rocco's mother had noticed Luca's soulful glances at her daughter-in-law and Alessia's shy glances back under her eyelashes, and it was she who had asked Luca to accompany them all to see the procession on *San Giovanni*'s Eve.

The *Podestà*'s silk banner, the most sumptuous of them all, drew level and Leo clapped still louder. Luca felt a soft hand in his, squeezing and caressing. He turned to see Alessia's beautiful face smiling at him, her eyes as bright as her son's.

***

In Donatello's workshop in Florence the sculptor worked alone, until he heard an old man's voice: "Enough, you plaguey sculptor, enough," said Habbakuk. "I am finished." And Donatello, at last, put down his mallet and gouge.

Printed in Great Britain
by Amazon